OFF SEASON

By Randy Kraft

www.Maple57Press.com
Dana Point, California

This novel is a work of fiction.
Any similarity to real persons is coincidence.

Cover art by Tracey Moscaritolo
www.moscaritolo.com
Cover Design by David Smith
www.designdsmith.com

Also by Randy Kraft
RATIONAL WOMEN [Stories]
SIGNS OF LIFE
COLORS OF THE WHEEL

www.randykraftwriter.com

But you must love with a high, serious,
intimate sympathy, with a will, with intelligence,
and you must always seek to know
more thoroughly, better and more.
Vincent van Gogh

IN AUTUMN

The pain of parting is nothing
to the joy of meeting again.
Charles Dickens

Red would be late to dinner, for sure. Two years courtship, thirty years married, and six years since their divorce, Red always arrives late. He was waiting for her only on their first date and on their wedding day. Never since. As if, once she was hooked, she was hooked, and she was hooked at once, for a very long time, until she wasn't.

Expecting to arrive first, Sharon strolled to the restaurant she had reserved for their dinner, roughly thirty-minutes distance from her cottage in Oakland, California, a few blocks south of the Berkeley border. Far enough off the beaten track to escape swarms of students and tourists, close enough to the university to walk the four days a week she's on campus. By day, the streets thrum, the architecture typical of the region and visually interesting. By night, to light her way, she carries a pocket flashlight, pressed into her hand by a white-haired man at the hardware store when she first moved to town.

Might be useful, for more than the light, he said.

I've lived in much larger cities, Sharon replied, with a confidence that belies her uncertainty. *I stay out of the shadows,* she insisted, to reassure him.

Nevertheless, she keeps the tiny flashlight close at hand in a nod to age more than place: stronger of mind, weaker in body.

As she made her way to town, she had a thought that if lives flash before the eyes in the moments before death, a long marriage flickers across the same mental screen on the way to dinner with an ex-husband. She saw in her mind's eye the moments they would have agreed their marriage worked well enough, if they were the sort of people to talk about what works, and on the periphery of that image, persistent disappointments, marring memory like a smudge on an old photograph.

Her brother asked her once, if she could go back in time to a turning point in the marriage, when might that have been?

There is no moment, she answered. *Differences, resentments, they pile up over time, like rocks, until, one day, the weight is just too heavy. You cannot rise up. No going back.*

Irreconcilable was the word, in the end.

She shook off the melancholy. *Good lord,* she scolded herself. *It's just dinner, not a firing squad.*

The walk took longer than anticipated, she so rarely walks in shoes with heels, and when she arrived, she glanced at her watch: three minutes late. She had to laugh at herself. Apparently she cannot be late, even on purpose. However now, she thought, with irritation, she would have to wait at the bar with a glass of wine that will turn warm. Sharon hates to drink alone.

The stone building was as stately as pictured: a page from a distinguished past. She took a deep breath and climbed a wide staircase. At the top, a tall blonde girl stood at a podium, like a sentry. She wore a crisply starched white blouse, long hair pulled so tightly into a bun her eyes popped, and her face thick with make-up, like a starlet.

Hi Professor Mervyn! the girl chirped.

Sharon smiled, although without recognition.

Carly, the girl said, obviously dismayed.

Oh, I'm so sorry. I didn't recognize you. Quite chic compared to the shaggy morning student, Sharon said.

Carly perked up at once. *One must present well at work.*

Well done, Sharon remarked. *Carly, I'm meeting someone. He's likely not arrived, but I reserved a table.*

The gentleman is already here, he's waiting at the bar, she said, pointing across the hallway.

Sharon wondered if Carly might be mistaken, but thanked her, turned, and crossed the hall toward the lounge. When she stopped at the doorway, there he was – unmistakable, even from a distance, and even with his back turned. Half-seated on a stool, he leaned on one long leg, the other bent with foot on the cross piece, like a cowboy at a saloon. Instead of whiskey, however, his typical drink, he gripped the stem of a red wine glass. As surprising as timeliness.

He spun toward the door, as if on alert, as if she might have missed him, then he smiled and stood, well trained from birth to stand in the presence of elders or strangers, and women of all ages. They stood opposite each other, as if in a western movie shootout – Red the mighty rancher, Sharon the stalwart sheriff.

She was struck, as she was from the first, by his size – six feet four inches tall, broad shoulders, long legs like tree trunks, arms dangling nearly to his knees like branches bowed in a storm. Like the stick figures their young sons once drew, she and the two boys diminishing in size order from his disproportionately longer torso.

She described him then as a lean friendly bear with rusty hair, and in those early days, to be in his embrace was as reassuring as thrilling. Now, nearing seventy, no hair on his head to defend his nickname, he is still strikingly fit, even if no longer the athlete he was in his youth, neither the strapping young engineer she met at a party in Boston, so long ago.

Thirty-eight years since they were introduced. Thirty-eight years since she was charmed by the tall attractive man with a perpetually serious expression. Solid and high-minded, like her father, she thought.

Now, so much history behind them, they will shift gears tonight to dine, for no reason, not that she's aware of – he retired, and she, at sixty-four, evolving into the life she aspired to long ago.

As she stepped into the room and made her way to the bar, Red reached for her hands, clasping them between his the way old friends do, also like the overly familiar men she meets on occasion on an arranged date she always regrets.

They hugged, briefly. No acrimony. No pretense. Sharon takes pride in this. They modeled for their sons a dignified separation, despite the inevitable friction, the occasional hostility.

Within her grasp, he felt bonier than he seemed from afar. Muscles softening with age, she assumed, or he may have finally given up warm milk at bedtime, a childhood habit. Beyond typical marriage vows, he asked her to promise to always keep milk and cookies on hand. She agreed. She kept her promise. She kept most of her promises, except the one that mattered most: *until death do us part.*

She said nothing of his less-muscular frame, to avoid sarcasm, and because she had no wish to yield to yet another maddening inequity of age: he thinner, she plumper.

Red pointed to a bottle of red wine on the bar. *Or do you still prefer white?* he asked, grabbing his jacket from the adjacent stool for her to sit.

White, dry, please, Sharon asked the bartender, who showed up suddenly to take her order.

Sancerre? he asked, and she nodded happily.

Still ABC, I see. Anything but chardonnay, Red translated for the bartender, who nodded knowingly as he pulled a bottle from the cooler.

Sharon settled on the stool, folded, and spread her coat across her lap, then reached under the bar counter, searching for a hook to hang her purse.

One of those modest engineering touches that makes sense, Red commented, as if she were a woman he didn't know, but would like to know.

She smiled at his penchant for the rhetorical. *And you're drinking wine? No more brown spirits?*

All his adult life, Red drank bourbon or scotch, like his father – neat, and always premium labels.

He shrugged. *An old dog must learn new tricks.*

Another surprise. Red was never one to express self-effacement.

Quite the place, he said.

One of the three historic landmarks in town. I thought it might appeal to you, she said.

So I read. Julia Morgan, the architect.

Thus, the name.

Yes, but the building, the City Club, was founded as a women's club, yes? he stated, more than asked.

And who better to design the Women's Club than the first female architect licensed in the state, she said.

1929. An inopportune time to open the doors.

She smiled. He had done his homework.

Impossible to predict, she countered.

If you pay attention, there's little truly impossible to predict, he said.

Spoken like an engineer, she said.

Guilty, he said, raising his hands in surrender, a gesture she has seen too often, expressing tolerance, not regret. *Reviews on the place are great,* he added.

Sharon felt the pride she has always felt when she has chosen well, when she has pleased the people whose opinions matter. With anyone else she would have reserved a humbler place with simpler food. She dislikes austerity, but she knew dramatic architecture and formal dining would appeal to Red.

He smiled. *I like the vaulted ceilings,* he said, pointing up, as if she might have missed it. *Terrific chandeliers too. Grand entrance. Sweeping staircase.*

The way things were, in effect, she said.

Exactly. I do admire preservation, as you know.

Sharon nodded. Yes, she knew.

Dine here often? he asked.

They both laughed.

Never been.

Really?

I gravitate to hipper places these days, but I knew you'd appreciate the staging, she said.

I always thought of you as hip, he said, a remark meant to flatter, because they both know she's not.

Sharon had favored the traditional, especially in décor. In this, she and Red were alike. They resided for twenty-five years in a vintage Victorian they remodeled over time and decorated with an urban row-house flair: large plush furniture, floor length drapes, Persian rugs. Not so much opulent as graceful.

An homage to Edith Wharton, she used to say.

Looking back, she imagines dense fabrics and textures might have been meant to absorb what ailed them, the way thick walls and tall ceilings stifle sound.

These days, she's gone eclectic. A mix of old and new. She moved west with one antique mahogany hutch and two squat oak chests. Once settled, she purchased a glass-topped oval dining table set on a teak tripod which she mixed with mid-century modern chairs with square backs and cushy seats. A deep, rounded, flat-back sectional sofa corners her living room. Sea grass rugs dress the dark wood floors. She sleeps on a platform bed with a tall rattan headboard, dressed in densely threaded all-cotton sheets that she loves climbing into at night.

Her sons are amused, but the style suits her.

The bartender delivered her wine and Sharon took the first sip before she saw the disappointment on Red's face. He held his glass aloft, waiting to toast, to punctuate the moment, but she needed wine to still her nerves. She cannot imagine why. She knows this man inside out. Nothing he might say or do will truly surprise her. Nonetheless, she has been jittery all day, and when her friend, Hank, stopped by, she noticed at once. Hank notices everything.

They met soon after she relocated. An imposing brown woman, christened Henrietta, she's the sort of friend who stops by without calling. The friend who advised the best places to shop and dine, and places to avoid. She is also the one to comment if something is amiss.

You seem a bit anxious, Hank said.

Sharon was browsing earrings at that moment, bypassing danglers, choosing silver studs shaped like a rose – a starter pair from her 60th birthday piercing.

Why do you say that? Sharon replied, unaware until that moment she was.

Well, you untied and retied the wrap on that skirt twice, with no real difference, and three sweaters are spread on the bed. All quite attractive, by the way. If I didn't know better, I would think you had a date.

Well, I suppose, I do, just not someone important, promising, I mean, Sharon stammered.

Hank peered down her nose with an amused expression, and a smile spread across her cheekbones like butter melting on wheat toast.

What? Sharon asked.

You're rather tight-lipped about him. At times you make a comparison to a character in a book or a film, but you see him and speak to him regularly, with hardly a mention.

We see each other with the boys. Co-parents.

That's it? Hank asked, with obvious skepticism.

That's it. Past tense, Sharon insisted.

No one you've slept with for years is ever totally past tense, Hank pronounced.

Fine, but it's the first time in years, since we split, in fact, we're getting together without the boys or without purpose related to the boys.

So maybe you want him to see how snuggly you fit in your skin. No seams, no snags.

Yes. And...

And? Hank queried.

I guess I want to look good. Cannot say why.

You must have looked good to him from day one. And you always look good to me, Hank said.

Thank you, Mam, Sharon replied, with a curtsy.

Why is he called Red anyway? Hank asked.

Named after his dad. Albert Mervyn, Junior. His mother was adamantly opposed to another Albert, the most obdurate that sweet woman ever was, so she demanded a nickname, and he was born with auburn peach fuzz. By the way, his brothers are strawberry blonde and British ginger.

Sounds like something out of Rockwell.

Sharon chuckled. *Oh, in more ways than hair color. Classic middle-American middle-class family. By the time Red was forty, he was going gray and going bald, so he shaved his head into the buzz cut of his athlete days to minimize transition. Only a trace of color left, in his eyebrows, for a time, until they went gray.*

So, even now, after all the years, you want him to see you in a different light?

Makes no sense, I know. He just never got it.

Ah, a man who cannot see what he cannot see.

Exactly. Sharon suddenly broke out in laughter. *In the first year we were married, we lived in a tiny boxy apartment, and while Red was away at a conference, I wallpapered the bedroom in a gorgeous English print. Deep green vines cascaded over the walls like a fairy tale castle. I was so proud of my handiwork, hardly a bubble. Took him two days to notice.*

That recollection was still on her mind at the bar, like an annoying tune that turns into an earworm.

When did you get in? she asked Red.

Late morning. I explored all day.

When was the last time you were on this side of the Bay? she asked.

Never, he said, emphatically. *Always the city.*

Surprising. Where are you staying?

A bed and breakfast in town. The Rose.

Sharon startled. *That's where I stayed while I was scoping things out.*

She had a sudden sensation his footprints had been imprinted on her turf, like an invader.

I grabbed lunch and then walked around the university. Alice Waters meets Jerry Rubin. I'm sure I heard echoes of tree huggers. I hoped to run into you.

It's quite a big campus, you know, and I had office hours most of the afternoon. Good flight?

The bartender set down an earthenware bowl filled with a mix of olives and Red grabbed a handful, popping one into his mouth while cradling the others in his hand, as if he might juggle.

Fine. Interesting, he mumbled, as he spit a pit into his other hand to drop into the smaller empty bowl served with the larger, and at the same time, popped a second olive into his mouth, his hands and mouth levered like a precision instrument. Like the smart-city technology he worked on the last years on the job and still tinkers with in a tiny workshop he carved out in the back of his townhouse, so her sons have reported.

Sharon often thinks of him as a form of artificial intelligence, ignorant of anything not programmed.

What was so interesting? she asked.

An elderly woman on the plane kept asking me the same question. Over and over. Her daughter, mirror image, was sitting by the window, mother in the middle, me on the aisle, of course, and the daughter thought I was bothered, which I wasn't. I insisted I didn't mind, but she made the mom switch seats anyway.

In the early years of their marriage, whenever they flew, Red claimed the aisle, needing to spread out those long legs, and Sharon, by default, sat in the cramped middle seat. After a time, she took to booking the opposite aisle seat. When they traveled as a family, each of their sons sat with a parent, in the middle seat, until they too sprouted tall and leggy, and then whined about being crowded, so she sat them in window seats.

Everyone in their position, Red would proclaim proudly, as if connections on a circuit board.

I read a piece once about an older woman at a beauty salon, Sharon said. *I think it was the New York Times magazine...*

Do you still read the Times? Or the Tribune?

The digital highlights, yes, mostly the Chronicle.

Do you also read the East Bay Times? I picked one up. Newsy enough, he commented.

A good local. As I was saying, this woman at the salon, every time she bent her head back to have her hair washed, would sit back up and ask what time it was, then bend her head back, then sit up again and ask again. The young man washing her hair thought it was just odd, but then, when she seemed disoriented, they called paramedics. Turns out, every time she bent her head back, she shifted into the exact position to compress blood flow to her short-term memory center. She never remembered asking the same question or the answer. Not so much age, or dementia, but anatomy.

I bet you think of that every time you have your hair done, Red said, and, in punctuation, he pressed a palm over his dome – a lasting habit of tidying hair no longer there.

In truth, Sharon was uncomfortable with her neck pressed against a hard metal sink at the salon, and she had taken to washing her hair before her appointments, but she would not admit to that.

By the way, I like your new hairdo, he said.

Thanks. Small concession to age, she said.

She had recently added brown lowlights, what

she'd sworn she'd never do, but she wasn't ready to go all the way to gray, and a cropped cut, just to the neck, softening a squared chin and calling attention to her big blue eyes, so the hairdresser said.

An air of distinction. Most flattering, he added.

And you look well, very well. A slightly age-worn version of your younger self, she said.

You think?

She could tell he was pleased by the flattery.

And no gray hair for me, he said, smiling at his self-reflective humor.

Sharon has seen that sort of smile before, and she realized he too wanted her to see him in his best light. She took a sip of wine and examined him more closely. He's nothing if not consistent. The same aftershave, subtle and woodsy. The same rimless glasses he's worn all his life, bifocal now, which partially veil pale blue eyes. The same way of dressing: a starched blue shirt, open at the collar, tucked into charcoal gray khaki trousers with creases down the front.

He had claimed, even as a young man, it was difficult to think in a tie, but kept one in his office in case of a spontaneous client meeting. He called it a mental straight jacket and Sharon thought at the time emotional repression is the straight jacket. On the rare special occasion, coerced into wearing a good suit or tuxedo, he was appeased only when she assured him he looked like Warren Beatty at the Oscars.

Two years ago, at their last big event, Red wore an expensive suit to attend their younger son Brady's graduate school commencement in Manhattan, nearly three years to the day of older son Jamie's graduation in Philadelphia. Both worked a while before advanced study – messing around, Red said, by backpacking in Asia and Europe, to Sharon's delight – then setting sights on careers: Brady an urban planner and Jamie a management consultant.

At that commencement dinner, surrounded by family and a few close friends, Red pronounced, as if a personal achievement, his sons were at last launched.

Sharon laughed at his naiveté. *For the moment,* she declared. *This generation shifts like the seasons. On the path to the paths not taken.*

Not like Red, who set his radar to engineering in high school, never wavering, or Sharon, who aspired to be a professor, like her father, who died a year after he retired from a lifelong position at Tufts University, as if no further point to living.

Red had migrated from Chicago to Boston to earn his advanced degree at MIT. When they were introduced, Sharon was working as an associate editor for a small press while finalizing her master's, with the goal of a doctorate. After marriage, while he fulfilled a two-year apprenticeship, she juggled working with her studies. After Jamie was born, he moved them back to Chicago to establish a partnership with a classmate, and because the early years were tight financially, her PhD was put on the back burner. She taught high school English instead. And then Brady was born.

She rationalized local teaching hours were more compatible with parenting, convinced of the nobility of her concession, and never shifted gears into reverse.

Five years ago, she migrated west to earn a PhD in Victorian literature, despite trepidation she would be sixty-four before her dissertation would be finalized.

When she expressed that fear to Hank, she said, as casually and profoundly as Sharon would come to expect of her, *you'll turn sixty-four either way, before too long, with, or without, the degree. Your choice.*

Been ages since we broke bread, he said loudly, to recapture her attention. *I mean, just you and me.*

Indeed, she replied, biting into an olive to still the rumbling in her stomach. *And you said you're here on business. What business?*

Oh, this and that, he answered.

Having listened to his rants on exasperating clients and projects fouled by bureaucrats, she had assumed he was relieved to leave all that behind when he retired last year. He said recently, when midwestern winter settles in, he abandons the golf course and tennis court and curls up in his reading chair to catch up with the histories and biographies he's yet to read or binge-watch the dark police procedurals she cannot abide. She was never good at hiding her disdain for violence masquerading as theatre.

In turn, she freely enjoys PBS documentaries on writers or history, or indulges a fondness for shows on extraordinary homes or amazing chefs.

She was about to inquire about members of his family when Carly arrived to escort them to their table. Red left a generous tip on the bar, and they followed her, as she led the way, wine glasses and nearly full bottle balanced precariously on a tray she held aloft.

When they arrived at a quiet corner table, she smiled, as if keeping the secret of their rendezvous.

A crisp white tablecloth was snowy white and silver service sparkled under crystal chandeliers.

Not cozy, but expansive, Sharon said, spreading her arms wide. A word to describe herself these days, she thought with pride: expansive.

Good spot for a visit, Red said.

To Sharon, the quiet corner table was painfully reminiscent of their last meal when still married. The night she told him they had come to the end.

The end of what? he asked.

The end of our marriage, she answered.

Red stared at her that night in stunned silence, and she stared back, stalwart. They had been banging against a brick wall for years.

At last, he recognized the look in her eyes, an expression he'd seen on the faces of project managers or planners: disappointment bordering on despair. Her look, however, was laced with the rage of helplessness.

I won't stay where I'm not wanted, he retorted that night, before gulping down most of his bourbon and striding out of the restaurant.

In my next life, I'd like to study the brain, Red said, snapping Sharon back to the present.

Maybe wiring just wears down, like an old lamp.

I'd find a way to diddle with the circuits, he said.

A memory engineer, she said.

Red laughed, loudly, and more jarring than the remark warranted. An anxious quirk she recognized at once. But why would he be nervous?

She wondered what she might have considered sooner: something must be amiss.

Memory is selective, he went on. *For example, at this moment, the sounds and smells, the clothes we're wearing, like the blue of your sweater, what would you call that, federal blue? Matches your eyes, by the way. So, this is all being recorded in our memory centers, and we'll recall the details the next day and the next with less accuracy. The specifics increasingly fuzzy.*

True.

What I'll remember first and foremost is how lovely you look. You've found gold in California, for sure. Your new home, your pursuits, all serving you well.

He tipped his wine glass toward her. *Here's to memory.* They clinked. *On the other hand, I do wonder, even if you lose some detail, the contiguous distractions and such, there's a better appreciation of priorities. Not what chore needs doing or what project to complete. I would hate not knowing where I am or who people are, but not sweating the small stuff sounds good.*

Practicing mindfulness in your old age? she asked, with a chuckle.

Ha! I'll leave that to Buddhists and Millennials. Besides, once an engineer, always an engineer. For us, it's all about the small stuff.

The small stuff, not the significant, she thought, like a wife taken for granted, second to work and sport and late hours in a garage workshop.

Maybe the woman on the plane who kept asking the same question had a need to know. Forgetting is not the same as not knowing, she commented.

You always get right to the heart of things. Must be all the poetry. 'Beauty is truth, truth beauty'... forget the rest.

Sharon was struck dumb. The engineer quoting Keats? Flummoxed by the citation, and the praise, she was about to question him, to get to the bottom of his intentions, when her stomach rumbled assertively.

She picked up the menu. *Shall we order? I hope you'll find something to your taste. I'll want greens and fish, but I'm sure the meat is grass fed.*

She pointed this out for his benefit because he was still a meat and potatoes man.

A waiter appeared at the table as if lying in wait. His long white apron, like the tablecloth and napkins, starched and spotless.

To her amazement, Red ordered for them both, which he never had, not that she could recall.

Two green salads to start, both lightly dressed, with the goat cheese on the side, and for dinner, we'll have striped bass, with the fries extra crispy please, and a double helping of sautéed spinach. Lots of lemon on the side. Another glass of Sancerre for my wife, with the meal.

That should do us for now, yes? he asked her.

Shocked he remembered her tastes so well, she was also stunned by the discordant reference to wife.

Remember the daily catch in South Beach? Red asked, abruptly changing subject. *Melt in your mouth!*

I loved that town. Like another country.

But not always hot or sunny, he said.

Sometimes as hazy as here, she replied.

We managed to stay warm, he said.

She stiffened at the uncharacteristic nostalgia and wondered again why he has come.

So. First visit to Berkeley, and you want to talk about memory? What's up? she asked.

Why does something have to be up?

Because we haven't been out to dinner for an age and you rarely travel beyond your borders these days, so, you wanted to see me for some reason. Tell me. Getting married again? I would be happy for you, truly.

That was a blip on the radar, Sharon. Long gone. I think you know that.

I don't keep tabs on your love life. What then?

Well, I was thinking... he started to say.

What? she repeated.

I was thinking maybe enough time has passed.

Enough time for what? she asked.

To spend some time together, he answered, and smiled, sheepishly, obviously wary of her response.

What are you talking about? So, there is a reason you're here. Must be terribly important to make the trip. I cannot believe I didn't connect the dots.

Maybe you don't know me so well.

Seriously?

Just a simple observation, he said.

You don't observe simply, you deconstruct the complex. So please, deconstruct, for me!

Can't I enjoy dinner with my ex-wife? he asked.

My lord! I wasn't a fan all the years I had to extract what you were thinking and I've no patience for cat and mouse now. Please. Spill the beans.

A flush rose in his cheeks. He drank half a glass of wine in one gulp, refilled the glass and gripped the stem as if to hold him in place, then hung his head like a kid who blew the play that lost the game. An atypical pose for a man of his stature and customary certitude.

Sharon felt the knot in her stomach she always felt when he was in distress. Work overwhelming or finances stretched, or one of his younger brothers was having a hard time and he wanted to make it right.

She sat up taller in her chair, bracing herself. *I see it's important Red. Spit it out.*

He leaned forward, staring at her with a penetrating gaze. *All right. It's stage 3 lung cancer. 3B, to be precise. Inoperable and incurable. Enough spit?*

Sharon froze. She leaned in closer and saw how pale he was under the flush. This would also explain the weight loss. Tears sprang to her eyes, which she swiped away. Not now, she thought, reaching for his hand, which he gripped, gratefully, the first time since they'd split.

Tonight he welcomed her touch, as if nudging ajar the coffin lid to breathe.

Sharon saw tears gather at the rims of his eyes, something so rare it tore at her heart, and what she saw in those eyes were the joys and challenges of a marriage: the strands of a long-braided relationship, frayed, although never fully unraveled.

Simultaneously, rage swelled in her chest. How dare he invade her well-constructed life? she thought. How dare he bring this dark cloud to her door and elbow his way back into the center of her universe.

It's not as bad as it sounds, he said.

Sharon bristled. Oblivious. Never able to read her mood or her expression until she blew.

For the moment it's in...

Remission? she asked, withdrawing her hand.

More like submission. After an excoriating round of chemotherapy, even a virulent cancer can be tamed, for a time, but gone, no. Lurking, so to speak.

I hope you're not in pain, she said.

Could be much worse. Like something is stuck in my chest and I cannot pull it out. I don't have the tool.

A waiter appeared with salads and the white wine, and before Sharon could object, he drained the last of her first glass into the second. She hates mixing the tepid into the cold, the old with the new.

He lifted his glass. *To longer lives than expected.*

Again, she welled with tears, and again, with resentment, this time for what her sons will face.

Sharon's mother suffered for twelve years with cancer and succumbed when Sharon was eighteen. If she could have protected her sons from anything, it would be the premature loss of a parent, and worse, witness to the horrid disintegration of a life force.

There must be a trial? Immunotherapy?

I'm already on a gene therapy and my doc is on top of it. He delights in presenting scans, explaining the tumor is a lesser evil now by virtue of size, not virility. The shapes remind me of cartoons where the dark ominous dictator of a fictional third world country looms over the smaller, the powerless. Quietly deadly. Sort of like our marriage at the end.

Sharon might have defended herself, but she held her tongue. *There must be another treatment?*

Not yet, but in the pipeline, he said.

And the boys? You've just seen them. They don't know? she asked, although certain Brady would have called, no matter an oath of silence. Elder son, Jamie, is more inclined to share only good news.

Red shook his head no. *I timed the visit after treatment. And I'm already bald.* He chuckled, sadly. *I hate this for them. Maybe the worst part.*

She nodded, although the fury of a protective mother roared. *If you had quit smoking thirty years ago when I begged you to. And twenty years ago. And ten...*

I wondered how long it would take you to go there. Well, I've quit, for whatever that's worth. Maybe too little too late, but I have, he said.

Sharon clung to her outrage, her dark blue eyes glaring into his paler blue, what he once described in a romantic moment as the dusk to his dawn.

Sorry, she said, yielding and sighing sadly. *I am, I'm sorry. Pointless now. Out of order.*

That expression, out of order, was their code for when their sons' arguments went too far or when their own angry silences persisted too long.

I'll tell the boys next week. Not looking forward to that. I don't suppose you would come with me.

At one time, she might have relented, but she cautioned herself to maintain a safe distance.

I'm midway through fall term. I have no time off. With the sabbatical coming up, I have a lot on my plate. Go to Philly. Brady will come. Use the same subterfuge you used with me, business. I'll be there in spirit, and if they want to see me, you'll spot them the fare, right?

Sure. Can't take it with me, he answered.

Sharon was shocked by the irrevocability of that remark. Her stomach churned. She forced herself to eat a few bites of salad and took another sip of wine.

She reached for a basket of warm crusty bread that had discretely appeared, slathering butter on a slice and handing it to Red, before buttering her own.

He took a bite and munched happily a moment.

Nothing like French butter. Perfect ratio of salt to fat. People think it's the bread we crave, and good bread is, of course, divine, but bread is a carrier, you know, for butter. I'm talking real butter, the good stuff.

A smudge clung to his upper lip, and she had to resist the urge to swipe it off.

How slowly habits pass, she mused. How little changes, far less than expected, in habit or rhetoric. Red has remarked on the bread-and-butter equation often – plays well at dinner parties – and she was once charmed by such commentary, until she grew weary of his repertoire.

He wiped his mouth and leaned forward. *There is something you can do for me.*

His hangdog expression reminded her of the day he brought home a puppy. A rare spontaneity that delighted the boys. She was furious. The responsibility would fall to her, she cried. Dogs must be walked and fed. She was already stretched. Her reasoning fell on deaf ears and as she watched Red and the boys frolic with the pup, the big man tumbling with three kinetic creatures, she caved. How could she deny them? In the end, the dog curled up to her at night, as if it knew she needed comfort, and she was bereft when it died.

Beyond moral support, what can I do?

Well, I was thinking…

Red searched for the right words.

What? Sharon snapped.

I was thinking, maybe we might…

He paused.

My Lord, like pulling teeth. Tell me, please!

Let's go someplace warm for the winter, he sputtered. *Like snowbirds. We once said we would.*

Flabbergasted, Sharon knocked her knuckles on the tabletop. *Earth to Red! Have you noticed we're not married anymore?*

I know, I know, but since you're on sabbatical next term, we might, well, we're divorced, but friends, right? We can be good companions. I was thinking a casita in Mexico, on the Baja or the Oaxacan coast. I'll swim and fish, while you finalize your dissertation defense. I'll make sure you have good office space and reliable internet. I'll grill the fish. We'll consume gallons of sangria. I'll pay for everything. And the boys can visit when they have time. We can all be together, now and then, before I'm gone.

She stared at him in disbelief, so he went on.

I thought we could just, you know, do what we never got to do because we got caught up in all that stuff. We never got to coast into retirement together.

Sharon sat back in her chair and recoiled with renewed antagonism.

You still think the failure of our marriage was stuff? Kids, business, menopause! I remember what you said. What ruined our marriage was negligence. The painfully steady demise of a relationship that was a mistake from the start.

A mistake, you say? That's a new one, he said.

Sorry. I don't know where that came from.

Unfinished business, apparently. I had no idea you're still sifting through sand.

I'm not sifting anything, Red. I've moved on. And now you bring this to me, you bring it all back…

Mea culpa.

He held up his hands again, feigning surrender.

She stood, too quickly, as she had to grab the chair to steady her wobbly legs. *I need a moment.*

Red started to stand, but she waved him down and hurried to the restroom, where she had a rushed silent cry in the stall and then stared at herself in a mirror over the sink. Unforgiving light made her face sepulchral, cheeks sunken these days below the bone.

When she was a child, Sharon's mother claimed she had a cherubic face – chubby cheeks and an overbite, like a beaver, a nickname bestowed by a local bully. Puberty and orthodonture created sharper bone structure, although she has never had an illusion of beauty. More owl than swan, she prefers to think she's earned sophistication, like Virginia Woolf or Simone de Beauvoir: gravitas preferable to aged cherub.

She dabbed a damp paper towel under each eye to sop up streaked mascara, washed her hands with vanilla-scented liquid soap and slipped them under a ferociously loud dryer, echoing the churning in her stomach and, in the subsequent silence, the ache in her heart.

She took a few deep breaths, cautioning herself to remain calm. This is not the time for marital wrath. Certainly not dispassion. She can do better. He's come to confide in her. He wants to spend time with her. Touching, even if incongruous.

Dinner had been served. Red stood to welcome her, gazing at her gratefully, as if she might have fled. She sat, lay the napkin on her lap and spoke slowly.

Listen, Red, I'm heartbroken, I am, and I'm glad you came all this way to tell me. I want to be helpful, but my life is on track. I will have my degree at last. I will teach, hopefully here. I have friends. I even date occasionally. Now, you show up and hit me with this awful news. What did your brothers say?

I haven't told them yet, he admitted.

My Lord, keeping everything to yourself. Hiding from the people who care about you. Isn't this a good time to give that up? she pleaded.

I wanted to tell you first. I know it's bizarre, but I feel, still, when a life altering event occurs, a man first tells his wife. I know I didn't always tell you everything right away, certainly not setbacks. I've always wanted to come to you with solutions, not problems. Maybe you could cut me a little slack? I never accepted our divorce as gracefully as you.

Sharon was again stunned by his confessional tone. *Is it worse than you're saying? Do you need a caregiver, is that it?* she asked.

I don't need taking care of yet and I won't ask that of you, he answered, his own irritation showing.

The boys will want to spend more time with you.

I know, I know. I cannot make all our lives about me. My blueprint. I remember that lecture. He took a sip of wine. *I see your new life hasn't tamed your temper.*

Sorry, but it's a lot to deal with all at once.

He nodded. *Okay, I get that. But a thing like this knocks the guard down. I thought nothing could be worse than the separation, but this has done me in.*

She had never known him to admit to fragility, certainly not regret. Has the old dog learned new tricks after all?

I'm glad you told me, in person. I am. Thank you.

Well, I'm glad to see you, he replied.

A strained hush shrouded the table, the sort of silence they suffered their final years, when they lost their way. When there were no words left to say.

They picked up their forks to eat, but then Red leaned in, as if to confess a secret she should know.

Let's face it. I'm the man you married. I never changed. I know who I am. I'm an engineer, always in my head. Always in my orbit, as you alleged. Guilty. Ironically, I was trained to expect the unexpected, less what is as what might be, but when something like this happens, I'm blindsided, like when we collapsed, you and I, and now, this cancer, I'm knocked off course with my compass stuck in place. Remember that old saying, you don't get older, you get more so? Being sick, that's a whole other layer of more so. I just want to be with you, while I'm in one piece. After all, we invested thirty something years in each other. We should have a better finish. He banged one palm against his temple. *Call me crazy. Maybe the cancer has already hit the brain. I was hoping for a few months together, hell, I'd be happy with a few weeks. You always loved a beach holiday.*

Sharon was again stunned by his tone, and by the import of that monologue.

Tell me true, she said. *How much pain?*

Not so bad, really. I've got meds, and medical-grade marijuana. I've never slept so well. Might become a stoner in my old age, although now I'm wondering if this cocktail is hallucinatory.

He shrugged his shoulders with a boyish grin, and she was reminded how taken she was with him at first. She laughed at his critical analogies, admired his determination and, most of all, the core decency. When did she lose sight of all that?

Let's eat, smells delicious, Red said, squeezing lemon generously over the fish and then shaking salt over the fries so heavily the grains fell like hailstones.

She picked at her meal while he devoured every morsel, shoveling his food like he used to when he came home from work late, starving for dinner.

Let's have dessert, he said, like a kid on holiday.

Looks like your appetite has held up, she said.

During treatment, no, nothing stuck, but now, everything tastes good, he said, with a broad smile.

He ordered the restaurant's signature dessert, and when a chocolate ganache arrived on a bed of lavender cream, they admired the classy presentation. Red offered her the first bite, before he dived in, and, in a matter of moments, the plate was empty. An empty space between them as well.

I do wish I could do something, she murmured.

Red reached for her hand and pressed it to his chest, to his heart, and Sharon almost pulled away, as if she might cause him further harm.

Maybe another dinner some time? Maybe a few?

Of course, she said.

Red scribbled in the air to signal for the check, and once settled, they made their way toward the exit, where he stopped to face her.

I hate to say good-bye, he said.

Sharon felt the tears well again. How she might have cherished that sentiment at the end of their marriage. If he'd said, *I don't want to lose you.* If he'd said, *I can do better.* On the other hand, might not have mattered. She was inured to him by then.

Soon, she realized, he will vanish. Divorce is one thing. Death, unfathomable.

Let's have an after-dinner drink, she suggested.

An excellent idea!

The lounge was overflowing with people waiting for tables, and then, as if on cue, a couple vacated the stools where they first sat, and they grabbed seats.

What's your pleasure? Amoretto or Tia? he asked as they sat.

The custom of another time: sweet liqueur with sunset on winter holidays in tropical locales.

A lifetime ago, she said.

BC, he said. Another code: Before Children.

She smiled. *Amaretto sounds good.*

The bartender delivered two tumblers filled with the picante amber cordial poured over a huge ice-cube. They waited for their drinks to cool, slowly, like sand drifting through an hourglass, and while they waited, despondency flowed through them as well – the sorrow between lovers who gave up on each other.

They clinked, and as Sharon sipped, an excerpt of a poem by Christina Rossetti came to mind.

And all the winds go sighing,
For sweet things dying.

Red, she said, heart aching, resistance faltering. *I know you're eyeing Mexico, but maybe a beach town on the southern California coast? Closer to home.*

*Y*ou are what? Hank cried in astonishment.

Sharon laughed. *You heard me.*

You are going to live with your ex-husband for three months?

At most, maybe less. I'll see how long I last.

Correction: for an uncertain period of time, you will cohabitate with your emotionally detached, self-absorbed ex-husband, the man you left behind years ago and, as far as I can tell, have lived happily without? Hank recited, as if an analysis of research data.

We're still friends, Hank. He's ill.

Okay, but that's a lot to ask, no?

Yes, but how can I not? We've been together most of thirty-eight years, Sharon argued.

Simple. You say no, Hank stated flatly.

Easier said than done, and besides, I can afford a little kindness, why can't you? Sharon pleaded.

Sure, I feel for him, and I feel for you, of course, and for your boys, but to go away with him?

They were sitting across from each other at a crimson red painted wood table in Hank's kitchen, in a condo not far from Sharon's cottage. Glasses of wine and a platter of dates and mixed nuts were set between them. Hank sipped at a tall glass of red wine, waiting for Sharon to continue, or come to her senses, gaging, as she's been trained to do, what her friend is feeling. Hank knows there's always more unsaid.

Steadfastly single, devoted to work and friends, and political activism, Hank is tall, wiry, and younger looking than her sixty years. Tight curls gray at her temples, lips are naturally pale pink, and a penetrating gaze of dark eyes makes students sit up at attention or betray deep secrets, a formidable skill for a Dean of Students at a community college. A wizened espresso face is leathery, like her hero, James Baldwin. She too lived in Paris when she was young, and describes with joyful nostalgia, especially after a couple of glasses of wine, her sybaritic lifestyle there. But that was then, she will say, and this is now, although she still favors, in most things, the edges to the center, tempered only by the discretion of age.

It's a very big step, don't you think? Hank said.

I do feel some buyer's remorse.

I should think so!

Nevertheless, I said I will go, and I will, Sharon insisted. *A warmer winter will be nice, and I insisted on booking the rental, so we'll have the right space. And an ocean view will be a treat. I've never lived at the beach. Carte blanche, he said.*

It will be warmer, yes, and calmer off season. Summer is mania in Laguna Beach, Hank remarked.

You've been?

A lovely long weekend with a lovely woman, ages ago, but that's not a town that changes much.

When they first met, Hank was involved with a male architect and more recently a female biochemist. She claims to crave men equally to women, although she frequently rails against the patriarchy. Sharon has never known anyone who shifts gears so fluidly and she admires her friend, for this and for the many ways she inhabits her life to the full, while never taking more than she gives.

Sharon bit into a date and sipped her wine, its astringency countering the sweetness of the fruit and the dissonance she was feeling about her decision.

What I will miss is our end-of-the-week happy hour, she said, and Hank nodded agreement.

I'll be on sabbatical anyway, so what difference does it make what café I sip my coffee in while I work? At night, I'll read, not much different than nights here. And the boys will love it. Certainly better than visiting their sick father in Chicago and me so far away.

Perfectly rationalized.

Hank, you might cut me a little slack. I seem to remember you saying just the other day that no one you've ever truly loved is totally past tense.

Hank smiled. *Ever the scholar you are – a mental file cabinet filled to the brim.*

Only comments that matter, Sharon replied.

I am not dispassionate, Hank said. *I hear you. You're a good woman, Sharon, but do you really want to march into that den of inequity again, just to be kind?*

Nice turn of phrase.

Hank laughed. *Inequity seems the right word.*

I'm better at boundaries now, Sharon argued.

Like going away with your ex because he's sick?

I would like to believe that doing what's right for those you care about is still right, Sharon said.

And I would say devotion stops when passion comes to an end, Hank said.

This is not devotion. It's compassion, with an all-expense paid sabbatical. And I will have time with my boys, together, a rarity. I would say that's a win.

There is that, Hank agreed. *But, I must say, and forgive, once again, my big mouth, but deep down in you lies a woman who has the makings of a rebel. More contemporary than Victorian, and more Mary Shelley than Elizabeth Gaskell.*

And who would you be? Sharon asked.

Toni, of course, Hank replied, mimicking the deep tenor of the voice of Toni Morrison, another idol.

Sharon chuckled. *Of course.*

Just keep in mind, you have the right to what's right for you as much, more than, what's right for him.

Sharon sighed. *I do and I will, but I could not live with myself otherwise. And, well, there's another factor.*

She paused, hesitant to make a confession she had never professed before.

Hank popped a few nuts into her mouth and as she looked up, she noticed Sharon trembling, and she placed her hand on her arm to ground her. *My friend, you can tell me anything. Something weighs heavy on your heart, I see that.*

Sharon had the sensation she has often had she might collapse under the weight of benevolence.

I said something once, to Red, something truly awful, which I have always regretted. One of too many arguments about smoking that spun out of control. Now that memory has reared its ugly head.

She described how she had lobbied relentlessly for years for Red to give up smoking. He had promised to quit when they married, an empty pledge. She grew increasingly intolerant of the smell of smoke on his clothes. An acrid taste on his lips. Middle of the night coughing spasms. There were wasted tongue lashings by his physician. Belligerent in his defense, he argued he needed no lectures on addiction – his father was an alcoholic. That day, he shouted at Sharon to leave him be. He called her a shrew, asserting, vociferously, he never wanted to hear another word.

Fine, okay, smoke yourself to death, I yelled, she confided to Hank, despairing of her behavior that day. *Then I said, I roared, in fact, when you get lung cancer, which you will, don't expect me to nurse you into that good night. There's nothing poetic about dying. Can you believe I said that? I mean, he was already diagnosed with emphysema and lung cancer runs in his family. And, well...*

Tears slipped down her cheeks.

I could not bear the thought of him going through a slow death, or me going through that again. Way too close to my mother's long losing battle with cancer.

I can't lose you like that, she bellowed that day. *I cannot go through that again. You will be on your own!*

You won't have to deal with it. If cancer comes to my door, I will disappear, he vowed. *No one will have to watch me die.*

Disappear? she shrieked. *You cannot disappear on the people who love you. What are you thinking?*

Disappearing will be an act of love, he protested.

Sharon, shocked by his words, was speechless.

I mean it, Sharon, no more about this, I'll handle it when the time comes, he said. *Not another word!*

Do you think Red wants to disappear with you? Is that what this is? Hank asked.

I doubt he remembers that screaming match. I think he's just trying to reclaim something or restore some dignity before he dies.

Or settle something?

I hope not. After I acquiesced, I insisted this was no more than a holiday, what he's calling our retreat.

Hank smiled. Retreat from what, one wonders.

From winter, is the articulated intent, and maybe an escape from loneliness, although he does well alone.

I am reminded of a story a colleague shared with me, Hank said. A calculus professor who looks like an Italian actress: voluptuous, with flawless olive skin and fiery eyes. Gorgeous. Her classes are always full.

Sharon laughed, grateful for the comic relief.

The professor, Isabella, said her marriage had years ago gone flat. They had drifted apart, staid was her word. She compared them to a Venn diagram, the overlapping circles narrower. So they planned joint sabbaticals to travel, rekindle the fire. And then, he was diagnosed with cancer, which stopped them cold.

Different situation entirely, Sharon interjected.

Yes, but listen to what happened. The illness restored their marriage. She said daily proximity, long talks to pass hard nights, middle of the night showers and afternoon naps, these things wear down conflict like river over rock. I get that. I took care of my youngest brother when he was dying, and we mended a lot of fences in those months.

I'm so sorry, Hank, I didn't know, Sharon said.

Years ago. Smart guy but drank through what resources he had. Someone had to care for him. No one should die alone, Sharon. We talked, we read poetry, and we watched films about dysfunctional families. We restored sibling solidarity. Anyway, Isabella told me they listened to audio books, the books neither had ever had time for. They played long games of Go and curated music playlists they titled for philosophers. And here's the punchline: they fell in love all over again, just as I reconnected with my brother. There's something to be said for the long good-bye.

Sorry, I am resistant to the long good-bye. I spent a lifetime saying good-by to my mother, never knowing when she would pass. Red has asked for three months, three good months, I hope. That's all I've signed up for.

What happens after three months?

Spring. That's what happens.

Spring is the season of renewal, Hank said.

No way, Hank! The door is closed, Sharon cried.

Isabella's story is a testament to how feelings age, and change, as we all do. Cancer will not alter anything in the past, Sharon. Only what's to come.

Point taken, Sharon said.

When you screamed at Red, you wanted to make him see how upset you were, Hank said. *You wanted him to understand how debilitating it was for you to lose your mom so young. Don't be so hard on yourself.*

I was cruel, Sharon whimpered.

People argue. We say awful things sometimes. We apologize, we forget. Is this penance?

In part, I suppose, Sharon acknowledged.

Hank leaned back in her chair and studied Sharon intently, as if she were a troubled student.

What? Sharon asked.

Are you certain you're not a little bit curious about what could have been? Hank asked.

I gave up that ghost ages ago, Sharon replied.

Seeking closure? A fallacy, you know. There's no closure beyond closing the door.

I know, I do. That's not what this is.

Good, because woulda coulda shoulda is a fool's game, Hank pronounced.

Sharon nodded. *Agreed.*

What have your sons had to say? Hank asked.

Red is visiting with them next week, but I know what they'll say. Jamie, the elder, the stoic, is like Red. He'll be devasted, and hide it. Brady, my tender boy, will say what you said. What are you thinking, Mom?

And they'll counsel with each other?

Brady will try to make sense of it. Jamie will feign indifference. NBD is his favorite expression since the last girlfriend left. I thought she was a keeper, and I know he's broken hearted, but all he says is, it wasn't meant to be.

If it's meant to stick, it sticks, it's that simple.

Is it? I'm not so sure, Sharon said.

And there's the birth order thing, Hank observed.

The older threatened by the very existence of the younger, the younger forever trying to impress or keep up with the elder, right?

Nicely simplified, Hank said, with a smile.

Jamie is still angry with me over the divorce.

How do you know, if he doesn't say?

Sharon nodded, sadly. *A mother knows.*

And Red was a first born too, right?

Yes, by several years.

Where were you again, in the birth order?

In the middle, Sharon said.

A pleaser, yes, Hank said.

More mediator than pleaser. My brother and sister were always at odds. She's tough as nails, he's a softie, And you? The elder, right? Sharon asked.

The elder, not the first born, Hank replied.

Sorry? Sharon replied in confusion.

I had an older sister, but she died when I was two. I have no memory of her. Then the boys, one after another, like a little marching band, and my mother was always working, so I was the lieutenant mom.

Which makes you a good listener, Sharon said.

Which makes me impatient with needy men! Hank laughed. *Your brother in London, is he gay?*

No. An unusually astute thoughtful heterosexual.

You've told him about all this?

Yes. And I'll tell my sister at Thanksgiving.

With the boys? Hank asked.

They're with Red this year. I'll go to Florida. She hates to fly. I'll visit my brother after the defense, to celebrate, I hope.

Sounds like plans are in place. The holidays will fly, as they do, and then you'll head south, like a bird. You'd best keep me posted on this madness.

I must be mad, Sharon muttered.

At last, we agree!

Any more words of wisdom? Sharon asked.

Don't look back, stay on track, Hank answered.

Should be a bumper sticker, Sharon said.

Good idea! My grandfather, who lived his whole life in the shadows, he made me promise to never go back, not to places I've lived, not jobs, not lovers either, Hank explained.

And you've kept that promise, right?

Hank smiled proudly. *I never look back.*

I wish I could say the same. In this, I am not going back, not forward either, it seems, but suspended in time. Briefly.

How long does he have, does he know, or has he shared that? Hank asked.

He's assured me he's stable, Sharon replied.

Oh yes, cancer is so predictable, Hank said.

Okay, okay, but he's good for now, Sharon said.

Being with you will surely extend his lifespan.

I hope so, Sharon said, with a sigh.

So, I have only one last question, my friend. Once you're there, will you be able to leave?

WINTER RETREAT

Perhaps the wind wails so in winter
for the summers dead,
And all sad sounds are nature's funeral cries
for what has been and is not.
George Eliot

Red is on the phone with his one good friend Barry. Neither are men who have close friends. They spend time with colleagues, fellow fathers who coached their kids' sports teams, golf or tennis partners, perhaps a confessional neighbor. These two bonded in graduate school. Both self-assured and self-directed, they interned at the same firm, shoring each other up at the start of their careers, and in the same year Red established his engineering firm in Chicago, Barry launched his development company in Dallas. Red is godfather to Barry's daughters and Barry to Red's sons. With their families, they have vacationed and celebrated holidays together, and their spouses became friends by default.

People have often observed that they look alike: similar height and broad chests. The sort of men who stand tall, as if they shoulder the weight of the world.

Barry has been designated power of attorney and executor for Red's estate, the paperwork recently updated and digitized. Before he took off on retreat,

Red told Sharon, his sons, and his physician, that his house is in order and, when the time comes, his friend Barry will step up and take care of business, he said.

Morning has broken in southern California, the air fresh and cool. A determined sun rises beyond the eastern hills and will warm the living area facing south and west throughout the afternoon. Red wears one of two sweatshirts he brought with him: black, with an MIT insignia. The spare is maroon, with a University of Chicago emblem, his undergraduate alma mater. Completing his retirement uniform: gray sweatpants.

After researching winter weather patterns on this coast, he packed for fall, then, in an unusually spontaneous moment, ordered sandals for the warmer spring weeks. Son Jamie insisted locals in SoCal wear flip-flops or sneakers, period. Much as he would have preferred to spend the entire time in shorts and T-shirts under a perennially warm Mexican sun, this day is far superior to the freezing gray skies he left behind.

He has showered, devoured a toasted chunk of bread topped with Nutella, with a side of orange juice, and holds a second mug of coffee in hand. With his cell phone in the other, he stands before a wall of floor-to-ceiling glass that bends at the corner to a sliding glass entry door. At that door, facing a sizeable patio, he was greeted on arrival by a voluminous bird of paradise sprouting from a huge clay pot, its macabre feathered buds rising on long necks. The first of many pleasant surprises in this landscape, as nothing blooms in the Midwest before the summer solstice and the blossom period short, albeit a reward to gardeners.

What he failed to notice, until some time later, when Sharon points it out, is that the patio is bordered by an abundance of these plants, which will continue to bloom, and condense, into an aviary moat.

He arrived three days early to make sure the place was right and ready. He likes the space a lot and already harbors hope they will stay longer, although the landlord's one proviso was they must vacate by Memorial Day, when a regular summer tenant arrives – an end date beyond Red's projected timeline and, he's certain, long past Sharon's willingness to stay.

The patio connects to the street by stone steps adjacent to a garage with a pull-in parking area, where Sharon will park later today. The house is in walking distance to town, so they've agreed to the one; they can rent another if needed. The garage is overloaded with leisure supplies - bikes, picnic baskets, beach chairs and towels – also blue striped cushions to fit the two lounge chairs and six dining chairs on the patio.

On either side, very different architecture, what one might call eclectic, Red describes to Barry.

Or jumbled, Barry says.

That too. They've excavated into the hill, and at higher elevation, so we have a terrific view of the coast above the rooftops below. With my binoculars...

You remembered them?

You should know I never go anywhere without binoculars, or reading glasses, these days. By the way, although palm and eucalyptus trees line Pacific Coast Highway below, I can make out froth at shoreline, what they call a white-water view, Red reports.

Barry chuckles. *Well that sounds just dandy.*

The stream of traffic is steady, but not hard to tune out. Worth it for the view.

White water and white noise. Quite a theme.

Red laughs. *In the middle of the night last night, I swear I heard the crash of waves. Nice surprise.*

Red used to sleep deeply, through the night, but these days he awakens a couple of times, stirred by discomfort, and here, by strange surroundings. Other than a trip to the bathroom, he goes back to sleep quickly, as a rule, but last night he listened to the surf. He is not by nature meditative – focused, yes, and fully absorbed by a project or a book, and, of late, obsessed with the increasingly bizarre news. Nevertheless, he found the ebb and flow of the ocean reassuring, its ferocious beat exerting authority, as if to say, no matter the death knell, there is continuity. There is purpose. An engineer leaves no loose ends.

Sharon is on her way, with a car packed to the brim, she said. She felt the need to pack a teapot, her own pillows and a favorite quilt, she said, also a box of books, research notes, and two suitcases of clothes.

This town caters to visitors. If you've forgotten anything, you can buy what you need, he told her on their first call after he arrived.

She ignored his comment, preferring not to be caught short and, at one time, Red admired this trait.

They had agreed he would head out at the new year, and she would follow soon after. She started on the Freeway and made her way west to Highway 101 for a more scenic second day, a total of 422 miles.

While doable in one drive, she stopped for the night roughly halfway, taking a respite on the road to the respite, she told Hank. A pleasing meander, she told her sons, who share her fondness for road trips.

Red looks forward to her arrival, although he has enjoyed scoping out the terrain on Google maps. He walked into town and back on alternate routes, testing the local coffee on the way, as he relies more these days on the caffeine to boost his flagging energy.

You should have gone to Mexico, Barry says.

The boys were disappointed too, Red answers.

Good fishing down there. Good food too.

Yeah, yeah, but Sharon wanted to be able to get back to Berkeley quickly, if needed, and it is easier for the boys to fly more often on domestic flights. She spent a weekend here once after a conference at UC Irvine and she liked the laid-back atmosphere. She said the town has a homey quality, whatever that means.

Sharon's top priority was proximity to medical care. With a hospital close and medical centers nearby, she will worry less. She urged Red to contact a local oncologist and forward his records, and he assured her he has ample medication, and oxygen, only if needed, and this too took some pressure off, making their plan, as maniacal as it is, a little less daunting.

Red reminds Barry of an oft-repeated refrain to clients: *a good idea is only as good as its execution.*

This beach town has an artsy history, which of course appeals to Sharon, Red says. *Many galleries and resident artists. They're listed on the city's website. A museum and an arts college as well. But for my money, it's the coastline, punctuated south and north by Dana Point and Newport harbors.*

Red has had in mind a memory of a weekend with his father, when he was nine years old, fishing all day on Lake Michigan, sun sparkling on still water, barely a word spoken, the silence broken only now and then by the pull of the line.

Sounds good all around, Barry says.

So far so good, Red says.

Well, Sharon's not there yet, Barry says.

Very funny. The apartment, the flat I'm calling it, is just right, and the weather warm enough. I came in on a van through Laguna Canyon, an impressive visual, a little like the old west. Surprisingly green.

That part of California is opposite what you're used to. It's brown in summer, Barry says.

Something to be said for off season, Red says.

I'm sure you've mapped the grid, Barry says.

Not much of a grid. The so-called downtown is a few streets. Tudor roofs next to Spanish tile. Touristy shops. Has its charm, but not a Mexican village.

Postcard worthy, Barry says.

You can say that. The stretch along PCH covers seven miles, seventeen coves, lots of rocky shoreline. What they call Main Beach marks the center, at least for visitors. To the north and east, upside is the jargon, like the Amalfi hills, minus antiquity. These oversized houses hang on for dear life.

Mcmansions, Barry says. How many residents?

Just under twenty-five thousand living in, wait, I wrote it down: 10,542 households, Red reports.

I knew I could count on you for detail, Barry says. *But will there be enough to do?*

If not, we're nearly dead center LA to San Diego. Lousy traffic, but there are trains, Red replies.

And you're sure this is the right thing to do?

Never more sure, thank you, for the thirtieth time.

Okay, I'm a cynic, but you could be playing golf in Palm Springs or hiking the Himalayas.

That ship has sailed, in more ways than one. Let's face it, I'm past adventure, my friend, Red says.

No one should ever be past adventure, I mean, without undue risk, of course, Barry says.

Cancer is a street sign signaling a steep incline: slow down. Not a full stop, not yet. And there is a golf course nearby, nine holes, can you imagine?

I played a classy course on Newport Coast, at a conference at a chic resort, forgot the name, Barry says.

Already scoped that out. By the way, I'm looking out at Catalina Island right now. Looks close enough to swim. A little hazy, but there it is. When the boys come, we might sail over there, Red says.

Have you met the landlord? Lives upstairs, right?

Haven't heard a peep, except music. She sent us an email to confirm, and the door was unlocked, keys on the table, with a binder filled with notes about the house and a restatement of house rules: no drugs, no late-night noise, that sort of thing.

I guess she doesn't know what druggy party people you are, Barry says, and laughs.

I'm holding a fair measure of cannabis right now. Vape and gummies, Red responds.

You took pot over state lines?

Of course not. This is California, man, Red says, in a hippie voice. *The town won't allow distribution, but they allow delivery, in a nod, I guess, to Timothy Leary.*

In Laguna Beach?

He was arrested here in the late sixties. I might become a wino too. The landlord left two bottles for us, one red, one white. I sipped the red last night at sunset, damn stunning, deep saturation, the sky I mean. Wine was well saturated too. Turned out to be Two Buck Chuck, three bucks now. Trader Joe.

Barry laughs loudly. *Not great taste in wine.*

Maybe not. But she's done everything she said she would, and the place is spotless. I wanted to thank her. Music was loud, but no one answered either door, not at front, the street side, or from the balcony above. And all the curtains were drawn. Why would anyone block this view? No one can see in up there.

A little strange, no? Barry says.

Who knows. We were instructed to communicate via text, and I paid three months' rent in full. She just doesn't seem chummy, Red answers.

Just as well. What time do you expect Sharon?

Not sure, she'll call when she's close.

And until then? Barry asks.

I'll read The Economist.

You might want to pick up better wine!

Done.

Wow. You should blog. The late life post-divorce getaway under the strangest circumstances in history, blog. I'm sure the domain is available, Barry says.

Red laughs. *I'm just keepin it real, pal,* he says as he hangs up, delighted with himself, the flat, the view, all of it. Looking forward to Sharon's arrival and hopeful for the first time in some time.

Sharon stopped for the night in San Luis Obispo, a picturesque college town near the Paso Robles wine region. After settling into a boutique hotel, she stretched her legs on a late afternoon walk along the river and then treated herself to fish and chips at a busy bistro, before curling into plump pillows in the center of the large cushy bed for her first good night's sleep in weeks.

Perhaps, she pondered over coffee this morning, she's prepared now for this retreat. The fishing retreat, she and the boys call it, in jest, having heard Red talk about fishing with his dad only once, before a fishing excursion with the boys on the Yucatan coast, while Sharon reclined on a hammock with a book.

The only passion Red has ever pursued, other than sports, was classic cars. He used to haunt auto shows, captivated by a 50s Chevy with shiny grills and shark fins, or an original Ford Roadster with rumble seat and leather steering wheel. He took photos at all angles and obsessed over the car for weeks. During rare journeys with the boys on the open road, he urged them to search for antique cars and they debated the provenance. Nevertheless, he believed owning such a vehicle was impractical and he drove a Volvo sedan all his life, one after another, denying himself the pleasure of the extraordinary.

He also lacked an interest in travel to distant shores and Sharon still regrets not lobbying more often to take the boys abroad. Road trips had to suffice and, as a result, the boys share her wanderlust. She comes by it naturally. Her father, an ethics professor, buried in a book or deep in thought much of the time, on an occasional impulse, bordering on mania, gathered the three children from home in Newton, Massachusetts, inspired from his easy chair to venture, when the spirit moved him, beyond the horizon.

Into the car kids, we are going to Georgia for pecans, he would shout, which he pronounced pee-cans. A lesser drive than a previous trip to Wisconsin for cheese or St. Louis to see first-hand the remarkable arch and its birds eye view of the Mississippi River. Sharon's bag was always packed and under the bed. Her favorite trip was to Niagara Falls in the dead of winter, where they braved the frost and marveled at the icy rim.

Her mother always begged off, to keep the home fires burning, she claimed. Later on, Sharon realized it was the one time her mother had for herself, a respite between bouts of intensive treatment to keep her alive. She also figured out her father took them away to give her mother quiet time, without seeming so.

Sharon, her younger brother and older sister, were herded into the family sedan, stopping only for fuel or food, sleeping in motel rooms off the highways, three kids crowded into a double bed, opposite where their father sprawled and slept very little, as if on alert, or, in warm weather, camping, counting stars like sheep to sleep. Her father dropped them at school the following week, with apologies to the principal for what he described, every time, as a family emergency, which to his mind it was, and a perfectly honorable use of time, he would insist.

Many long holiday weekends, also in summer, Sharon took her sons to cities with history etched into their sidewalks – Charleston, Philadelphia, Baltimore, DC, Memphis and New York – memories as precious for them as for her.

This morning, along Highway 101, a winding scenic route, she is equally enchanted by the dramatic coastline at Santa Barbara as its layered topography. Before long, she whizzes through Ventura County, only to confront a morass of traffic in Los Angeles. Staring at the bumpers ahead, she puts on another podcast, hoping to resist the introspection that came over her at dinner last night.

The bistro was crowded and she was too hungry to wait for a table, so she took a seat at the end of the bar. The young bartender was attentive and flirty and put her at ease. Dinner was tasty and filling, local wine pleasing, and the clamor of a jovial crowd reassuring. Between bites, unable to focus on a literary analysis she was reading, she did her best to resist sliding into navel-gazing, which she considers self-indulgent. She rarely relents. She's not old enough yet, she thinks, for such melancholy, although too many pleasures have gone the way of supple skin: babies, career, erotic escapades. The prospect of a PhD earned at last makes aging palatable, and, as fiercely independent as the Victorian writers she admires, she refuses to dwell on what's been denied. She's strong in mind and body, she owns a little house. She has pleasing pastimes, good friends, and she has survived the challenges of parenting, as well as a disappointing marriage.

She abhors the mindset of seniors who bemoan chronic natural aches and pains, fawn to excess over grandchildren or take up mindless hobbies to pass the time. She's happier on the road ahead.

Rather than slog on the freeway, she turns west to Highway 1. Stop and go traffic lends an opportunity to scan coastal towns, all offering glimpses of an ocean said to be tumultuous, and colder than the Atlantic.

She calls Red to say she'll land mid-afternoon.

Should I stop for food or supplies? she asks.

All taken care of, he replies. *Just drive carefully.*

Okay, she says, dumbfounded. Red never took on domestic chores besides mowing s lawn or dumping trash, and he handled house repairs like engineering assignments. She cannot imagine what supplies he's laid in, but she'll find out soon enough.

Not the first time he's surprised her lately. Can he have changed so much in their years apart or, she wonders now, did she ever know him as well as she believed? She relied on presumption or expectation. On the other hand, does anyone really know even the most intimate partners if they don't wish to be known?

Traffic flows slowly through the city of Newport and down past a ritzy shopping center above a beach called Crystal Cove. Sweeping cliffs rise to dramatic vistas. Entering Laguna Beach at the north end, she's greeted by a welcome sign and an electronic banner pronouncing a smoke-free zone. She laughs. A ban on smoking? Is that even legal? she wonders. Good news for Red – his compromised lungs will not be further polluted by secondary smoke.

She passes hotels, restaurants, galleries, and a museum she makes a mental note to visit. A handful of men wearing sweatshirts and shorts play basketball on a court flanking a beach, bordered by a boardwalk along the coastline. Volleyball nets sit idle on the sand like ancient ruins. Only a handful of tourists cross at a traffic light, and, while stopped, she scans the water, as if a whale might breech in welcome. Son Brady told her gray whales migrate on this route this time of year, so close to the shore she might see.

An eponymous iconic hotel is boarded up like a broken surfboard stuck in the sand and an ice-cream shop seems forlorn. A beach town hushed off season.

Not so different from the beach towns in Cape Cod where she spent summer holidays with her family, or the towns on the Narragansett Rhode Island shore where she took the boys when they were young. There were also summer visits with Red's family at Delevan Lake, Wisconsin. The summer she moved west, she adopted Bodega Bay as her go-to beach town, with its windswept coastline and film-set charms.

She has the thought all beach towns look alike, in season: sun high in a blue sky; blankets on the sand lined up like color chips at a paint store; the rumbling of small planes and loud car radios competing with the call of seabirds. She can picture shiny beach balls tumbling in the wind, serrated fringes fluttering on kites shaped like lobsters or gulls, and wispy clouds drifting by, setting the pace.

She recalls fondly the frenzied ambiance by day, muted at last under the nighttime sky, and she smiles at a sweet memory of folding her sons' bodies in towels at dusk, both squeezed onto her lap at the sunset, and, when they finally fell asleep, hanging bathing suits to dry before she too collapsed for the day with the sweet exhaustion unique to summer season. The heat, the busyness, the pleasure of togetherness, a tonic.

When Brady called yesterday to make sure she was safely on her way, he described off season as the calm after the summer cyclone.

That's when the locals enjoy a lower frequency, he commented, with the insight of an urban planner. *They breathe more freely and the landscape breathes as well. It's restorative. I prefer beach towns off season.*

Sharon can see what he means. The hills in the distance are surprisingly green. Magenta bougainvillea pepper the landscape. A gentle wind blows through her open window and there is palpable quiet. No crowds, no frenzy.

Today is January 5th. Throughout the world, there is great expectation for 2020. The number has a good ring to it, people say, despite the political battles that will take center stage.

She heads up a long hill and at the top, one last turn toward their retreat house. The journey is over, the clock set for three months. Surely, she thinks, they can avoid stirring the stew of discord and enjoy what pleasures will be found here.

R ed guided her around the rental like a realtor. He pointed out a bench at the entry door where blankets and tablecloths are stored, the carved fireplace mantle, wainscotting in the hallway, and, he said proudly, as if he had installed them himself, recessed lighting overhead, pointing to a remote on the wall. *Operated by gadget, like the ceiling fans.*

He also groused over rusted hardware here and there, joints askew, and a few cracks in floor tiles.

Signs of settling, wear and tear. One expects this of houses on hills, and in this climate. Otherwise sound.

Sharon smiled, pleased with the space. Sparse decor for her, cushy enough furnishings to satisfy Red. Clean and in good condition, thankfully.

The vacation rental occupies the lower half of a glass-front home, with two bedrooms and baths, an expansive view, and a flagstone patio spanning the breadth of the house, surrounded by lush plantings. A typically California open floor plan – living, dining, and cooking – align to a glass wall facing west, bedrooms set to the back, separated by closeted walls to buffer sound. A long deep couch upholstered in gray tweed anchors the living room, with throw pillows in shades of sea and sand. Two oversized pale gray chairs face the sofa, flanking the fireplace, with a widescreen TV mounted above. On a large round coffee table, a pile of oversized art books, and on shelves on either side of the fireplace, a hodge-podge of paperbacks left behind by previous tenants. In the corner, completing the living area, a square pine table with ladderback chairs, and on the patio, a larger glass-topped table.

The listing claimed that sea breezes and ceiling fans were sufficient, even in summer heat, certainly in winter, and, although Red would have preferred air-conditioning, in case, Sharon favors fresh air. They will not likely need cooling off season anyway, she said.

He pointed out the efficiency of construction on the hills – houses positioned vertically to optimize the view, with narrow setbacks between. For privacy, he explained, north and south, mature olive and pepper trees serve as screens.

As they made their way through the galley kitchen, with stainless-steel appliances and tall white cupboards, he opened a closet door at back, slowly, like a magician hiding a rabbit, to reveal a stacked washing machine and dryer, with cleaning supplies.

Handy, Sharon said, before inspecting each of the cabinets and admiring the essential provisions.

Nice floors. Earthy, she remarked, of the terra cotta tile in the kitchen. *Nice contrast to the plank wood in the other rooms. Maybe reclaimed woods?*

Seems so. You know, you can never be sure with a seasonal rental. I mean, that it will be as pictured. But we, you, hit the jackpot, he said, with satisfaction.

What she's sure he failed to appreciate in his perusal of structural elements are the handwoven rugs scattered about and bold colorful paintings. All adding texture and contrast to pearly white walls and gray furniture, like stained glass in a church.

These paintings seem to be the same artist, same style, she commented, peering at the unusual artwork, trying to decipher the signature.

I hadn't noticed, he replied.

He stepped closer to a landscape painted with exaggerated tree branches set against a golden sky.

Reminds me a little of Matisse, Sharon said. *And lit by natural light,* she murmured, turning to gaze at sunlight filtering into the room.

Red followed her gaze. *Quite the view.*

Sharon was again reminded of his penchant for stating the obvious, although the view was sufficiently grand to emphasize. He also seemed nervous, and try as she might not to be, she was too – the strangeness of the arrangement now fully realized.

She moved toward the glass wall and craned her neck to look up to the balcony.

Shades, in part, the lower patio in the heat of the day, Red said. *Upstairs, where the landlord lives, the only sound, all day long, is music, which complements the flow of traffic below.*

Can't hear the waves, I guess, she said.

At night, late at night, yes, he said.

Lovely.

You did good, Shar, he said.

I'm so glad you're pleased, she answered.

I am pleased. It's perfect!

Perfect! That's a word I can get behind.

They used to respond in that way to pay a special compliment, or in condemnation. She accused him once of being a hermit in his own home and he responded, *hermit, well that's a word I can do without.*

You've mapped the town, I'm sure, she said.

The highlights tour. More to come, of course.

With that, there seemed nothing more to say, and Sharon wondered again, *what were they thinking?*

I'll let you unpack, Red said. *I've got a good size piece of Halibut, should we marinate?* he asked. *The grill on the patio works fine. Or better in the oven?*

You've become a chef in your old age? she asked.

The boys turned me on to all recipes dot com. If you can read, you can cook, he said. *What I mean is, you can put a meal on the table, not great or gourmet, but edible,* he added, quickly, to avoid offense.

That's all we need. What else? she asked.

One of your mixed salads will do nicely. I have a lot of fixings, he replied. *We can go out of course, plenty of places to try, I just thought you might be tired. You might want to unpack and...*

I don't mind cooking these days. No rushing from work to housework to starving boys or worse, non-stop eating adolescents.

Red chuckled. *I get it.*

Another pause hung between them until she said, *thanks for setting us up. I won't be long.*

I'll catch up with the news and I'll show you how to use the TV later, it's a little tricky, he said.

Sharon refrained from saying she was sure she could figure it out. After all, gadgets are his bailiwick.

Red turned on CNN and lowered the volume. He remembers Sharon's easily rattled by loud TV chatter. He only half-listened, seated at the corner of the couch where he had a glimpse of her shadow through glass French doors to her room, shaded by opaque fabric panels. He tracked her silhouette, listening to drawers slide open and close, the swoosh of clothes unfolded and the scrape of hangers on the rod. The sounds a woman makes day-to-day, which today sounded like a symphonic swell. He nearly wept with pleasure, this music denied to him so long, although he was rarely there to listen when they lived together: gone early, home late, in his home office often well into the night. That thrum of home and hearth, and companion, have been conspicuously absent in recent years, the silence often maddening. He sighed, loud enough for her to hear, so she came to the doorway.

Everything all right? she asked.

Standing there, in the shadow of the afternoon sun, Red recalled their honeymoon in Greece, as if it were yesterday. And all the years since, stirred by the soft curves of her body. Her solid stance on sturdy legs. As happy as he is to be with her now, he wonders, not for the first time, whether he loved her as much as he was glad to have captured her. Gratitude, admiration – are these the components of love?

I really appreciate that you've come, he said.

Sharon smiled, the smile he's missed more than anything else, and returned to unpacking.

She will have to get used to sounds of him. The constant commentary. And he sighs, loudly and often, especially in the shower. An involuntary action, like blinking. Over time, she imagined sighing was his way of exhaling feelings he could not express, but she never got used to the noise, like the distant drone from the television of an insomniac neighbor.

I'm almost done, she called out.

Room in the garage if you need storage.

I didn't bring as much as I thought.

Maybe you want to be able to make a quick exit?

Sharon took a deep breath. She will not take the bait. Passive-aggression is tolerable in small doses.

You promised sunsets with wine, she said.

And a promise is a promise, he replied. *Wine in the fridge, good and cold.*

I'm impressed. I'll just take a quick shower.

Sharon gazed again at the panorama of sea and sky: a gift, no matter the circumstances.

It's a great place, Red. How lucky we are, she said, and closed the doors until they snapped shut.

Red sighed again. At the end of the day they will close doors, like roommates do. Spouses often slam doors, until, for the less fortunate, they close for good. He knows she needs time to adjust. He hopes she will ease into the pleasures of retreat, as he already has.

Sharon surveyed her room. Queen bed, layered with several colorful quilts, with plump pillows pressed against a wicker headboard. A chest, a small desk, a couple of bedstands, with reading lamps with off-white linen shades. Nothing more, no more needed – a room designed to return to at the end of a pleasant day. She sighed with relief.

In the shower, however, she was overcome with emotion. Sprays of water cascaded over salty tears.

She's stepped off her path. The only man she ever loved is ill. Living together will be challenging. No one slips into a past life, no matter the familiarity. No matter a lovely flat with an ocean view.

She chided herself to focus on the beauty of the place – light-filled rooms, a soft color palette and bold artwork. She must concentrate on her priorities.

After dinner, she will conclude the nesting. Plug chargers for easy access. Set the Wi-Fi code to log into devices. Arrange toiletries by the sink and pile books on the desk.

Tomorrow morning, she will get back to work on her dissertation defense. She's not on holiday, and not completely off her path. Red promised her freedom to work, and she promised companionship.

So it shall be.

Red is reading on the patio in what has become his favorite spot and his favorite time of day: early afternoon. Most of his life, at this time of day, he was consumed with work, rushing through the closing hours to polish off priorities in time to catch the late train home. In retirement, back in Chicago, he would fill this time by catching up on the news, the stock market, and the handful of magazines he reads – a bridge between morning sport and evening TV. On retreat, these afternoon hours pass undetected, other than a pang of hunger or the ding of the phone alerting him to the rare message. Each day winds down by the slope of the sun.

Time here seems an artificial construct meant to define lives that require definition, which Red no longer requires.

He reclines on one of the two chaises, his bones cushioned by a blue and white striped pad, shaded by the balcony above and fanned by sea breezes. The weather in winter here is pleasingly temperate – most days the temperature in the low 60s, with a precipitous drop as the sun sets. He heats up more quickly in the afternoon sun than he used to and chills more easily later, which he's not sure is age or disease, also could be the medication; whatever the source, he has worked out the minimum delta at this time of day.

The landlord's music seeps down the stairs like a snake. Every day, the same sequence: Latin jazz through the mornings to late-day classical. A timepiece as consistent as the trajectory of sunlight and as calming as the ebb and flow of the waves below.

He confessed to Sharon last night he hasn't let down so fully in years and she said she's not sure he's relaxed like this in his entire adult life. He had to agree.

A week has passed since she arrived. He might have deluded himself they were back in time if their daily schedule was not so different. He rises early still, his body clock fixed, but no longer jumps up at dawn to get to work. She languishes a little longer in bed, a luxury she never had, awakening to birds chirping and his bare feet padding from the kitchen to dining table, where he reads the morning news before hiking. He moves slower now, and as quietly as slowly, largely a concession to her sensitivity – she startles like a traumatized veteran – what she calls Mother's Ears. A perfect description. She heard every babble, whimper and nightmare, and when the boys were adolescents, heard them tiptoe up the stairs after curfew. Red, who slept fewer hours, slept deeply, so he never noticed a commotion. He also never worried, because Sharon was, as he liked to say, on the case.

Back then, he started his day as if everyone were awake, or should be – the buzzing of an electric razor and electric toothbrush, and the pounding of a shower enough to rattle them all, even deep-sleeping adolescents. Here, he sets up the coffee pot at night to percolate at sunrise and then makes a fresh brew for Sharon. He waits for sounds of her before his morning ablutions.

Last Saturday, the first break in Sharon's work schedule, they strolled to the Farmer's Market in town. They tasted fruits and coffees, and took home a still-warm sourdough bread she toasted and topped with avocado mash, chopped red onion and dill, and a fried egg. Their first brunch on the patio. She served mixed fruit from a bowl she replenishes often for snacking.

She's a convert now, she told Red, to the writer Michael Pollan's mantra to *eat real food, not too much, mostly plants.* She contends this is crucial for a robust immune system. Red, who prefers bagels smothered in cream cheese, pancakes drowning in syrup, or bacon and eggs, saw no reason to argue. He's happy to be fed filling meals, whatever the menu.

The air was warm that day, the sun nearly at its apex, and they lingered at the patio table, she reading an e-book, he the local newspaper.

Listen to this, he cried, reciting from an article about a battle over a bird's nest discovered on the grounds of a nearby school.

The bird, a gnatcatcher, is too important to be disturbed, so the construction project has been halted until they figure it out. Ridiculous.

Why is that bird so important? Sharon asked.

An endangered species. Seems development has diminished their natural habitat.

What exactly is a gnatcatcher?

Red scanned his tablet and clicked a few times to find a good description.

Small gray bird. Insectivorous, feeds on bugs, also worms. Apparently hides in coastal sage scrub. An isolate. Doesn't travel in a pack, he explained.

Got it, she said, thinking that might perfectly describe Red, but also, in truth, herself.

And, interesting factoid, they don't bathe, they clean their feathers using moisture collected on leaves.

So why not move the nest? she asked.

Too fragile, so they say. Environmentalists may be well intentioned, but they can be obstructionists.

Just yesterday you were singing the praises of all the open space preserved around here. Who do you think made that happen?

Red ignored her question. *Well, I hope they come to some sort of compromise, although conservationists are not known for concession.*

And you thought SoCal might be boring!

Red smiles at this conversation now, watching a hummingbird dive bombing a lavender bush. Sharon left early today, after a few spoons of yogurt, a handful of blueberries, and a cup of coffee. She has signed up for Pilates class three mornings a week at a studio on the north side. On alternate days, she walks to the center of town to stretch her legs, but she says she has little interest in the hiking trails Red has staked out. They take too long, she argued, and she likes perusing beach houses and gardens.

Post-exercise, at one of two cafés she's adopted as her workspace, she reviews findings and notes that require additional research. She has become, in her advanced age, she says, a café scribe, like the eminent writers and artists who long ago populated Paris and London. She enjoys the parade of colorful outfits and voices raised in debate, or laughter, although, she told Hank, the crowd in Laguna is hardly as sophisticated as in Berkeley and she misses boisterous students.

When Red asked how she can concentrate, she answered that the din is her version of white noise.

He already begrudges the hours she works and resents her lack of interest in spending more time with him, as if he's parenthetical. He had hoped for time together beyond cohabitation. On the other hand, he promised nothing would interfere with her sabbatical intention. If pressed, he would admit he admires her work ethic. He will have to be patient.

For him, the best part of retreat, thus far, other than evenings with Sharon, has been exploring trails in a greenbelt circling town. They flow like tributaries into and across voluptuous hills and he has yet to tire of the views, although he keeps one eye on the ground to avoid divots or rocks. He stops occasionally to catch his breath, which he hopes is the elevation more than his increasingly fraught lungs.

The first week he was here, he hadn't gone far before he was huffing and puffing like the little engine that could. He felt the same on the first walks to town, facing the nearly half-mile incline back to the rental. Every day since, he breathes with greater ease and has greater stamina. Diligence pays off.

When a hiker recommended a trail at the top of the world, Red thought he was joking, until he noticed one of the small public transport buses that run routes around town with a destination sign reading TOW. He hopped on one yesterday and, as the name suggested, he felt he might touch the clouds.

Lovely morning. Have a nice day, hikers call, and Red responds the same, while laughing at himself:

the workaholic engineer hiking the trails. One of many things he never imagined in his youth, or just a few years ago, and yet, suits him perfectly right now.

On return to the flat, he showers, pours the last of the coffee over ice and grabs one of the protein bars Sharon has stocked. He reclines on a chaise in a state his sons describe as blissed out, and because he is feeling so good, he has postponed the next round of treatment, harboring hope companionship, good food, and regular exercise might prove healing.

Miracles have been known to happen.

At this moment, after a satisfying walk, and as the sun moves into the afternoon arc, Red is as pleased to have convinced Sharon to join him on retreat than any achievement of his career or personal life. It's too late, he knows, to make up for 12-hour workdays and skipped vacations, or what she contended was a lack of interest in her aspirations. She never got that he had to be on the job – his name was on the door. Standards must be set and kept.

He wonders now if he has something in common with a gnatcatcher: an endangered species of a sort.

He surrenders to the fatigue he feels this time each day, ready to nap – another new ritual – and he's not sure how long he has slept when he's awakened by humming coming from the far side of the patio.

A woman is clipping flowers in a slow hypnotic motion. Shapely, petite, she wears tight jeans and a body-clinging white T-shirt which exposes generous cleavage. A wide-brimmed straw hat partially blocks her face, dark wavy hair curling to the nape of her slim neck. Tapered arms are tan and toned. Her jeans stop at the knee, revealing muscular calves, slender ankles. So perfectly proportioned, she could be a blueprint, he thinks. He's mesmerized by these glimpses of skin, like poets inspired by the sight of flesh. Reminds him of his youth, when any chance to glimpse any part of the female body was an imperative.

The tune she hums is 60s rock, although he cannot be sure. Maybe the Beatles or Rolling Stones, neither to his taste. She lines up long stemmed flowers onto a flat basket, like a character in a fairy tale, and now he wonders if he's dreaming. No matter, he thinks.

From the shadow of the balcony, his eyes study her curves. This is the body of a woman who does not often sit still. The sort of woman who walks around at home naked, he imagines.

Sharon was never satisfied with her shape and rarely wanted to be seen half-dressed or wear revealing clothing. In bed, however, she opened her arms and her body to him. She was always warm to the touch. When the boys were teenagers, out with friends on a weekend, she forsake modesty and seduced him into what she called an afternoon delight. A fond memory.

When their sex life came to a halt – fewer engagements, a plethora of excuses – he attributed her ambivalence to a menopausal diminished libido. He thought it best not to press her. By the time he understood his mistake, the damage was done.

Today, much to his surprise, watching this lovely woman, his body stirs with desire, although he was told arousal is not easy after chemotherapy.

No arousal without intervention, the doctor said, handing Red a prescription for erectile dysfunction.

Barry urged him to get the meds as an act of optimism. *Why not be prepared?*

Red knew it was foolish. He's not delusional. He accepts that sex, which he enjoyed for many years with several partners before Sharon, and a few since, is past tense. Something of a leading indicator to mortality.

In this moment, watching this alluring female, he fantasizes cupping her firm derriere with his hands, pressing his lips to the swell of her breasts, wishing she might lean over him, invite him to her. He imagines her skin is silky and warm. Defying medical expertise, he feels himself swell – a penetrating desire he hasn't felt in ages, with an erection worthy of a younger man. Perhaps, he thinks, an erotic response requires only a stimulus like a glimpse of a sexy woman within reach. He's never been one for pornography, although it has occasionally served its purpose. He is a man, he would say in defense and, if he were alone, he might have finished this off. At the same time, he begins to feel too much a Peeping Tom, so he presses himself down his pants and stands to greet her.

She startles. *Oh my, I didn't know anyone was here. You're staying here?*

I am. I'm Red, Red Mervyn, the winter tenant.

He extends a hand to shake, but as her hands are taken with the gardening gear, he withdraws.

Tammy, she says. *I am so sorry to show up without warning. It's not always rented off season. How long have you been here? How long will you stay?*

We arrived early month, plan to stay three months, maybe longer, he answers.

Fabulous. Snowbirds? she asks.

Sort of, yes. From Chicago.

It can be cool here, but not frigid, no frost, and will warm up for you before you know it, she says.

I don't like it too hot anyway, he says.

Not me. The warmer the better. I dress summer all the time, as you can see. She spreads one arm to display her attire, as if he hadn't noticed. *Just a few more degrees and out with the shorts and flip flops.* She laughs. *Rosa has given me carte blanche to cut from her garden. I love having fresh flowers to start the week, and it's good for the plants, a pruning, you see, so I'm a little like her flower gardener. I'll leave plenty for you.*

No need, although, my wife might like that. We're enjoying flowers in winter, and the succulents, they're fascinating, he says.

The aliens, I call them, she says, and laughs.

Some of them seem so, he answers, and smiles.

He enjoys how easily delighted she is.

You picked a good spot. I'm sure Rosa is pleased.

I hope so. We've not met. She keeps to herself.

Tammy explodes in raucous laughter. *That's the understatement of the century. I'll have to tell my hubby that one. Where's your wife?*

Uh, she, Sharon, Red stammers, *she's in town. She takes a fitness class and then goes to Zinc or some other place, to write. She's a PhD candidate at Berkeley.*

Robbed the cradle, did you? she asks.

Only by six years. She's a late bloomer.

Really? Tammy says, skeptically.

I mean she was the home minister, raising kids and working. She taught high school, so finally getting around to the college level, he explains.

How wonderful! I was on one path my whole life. I've just taken retirement and my kids are grown too. I think I was born to be retired, she says.

Red is surprised, as she seems too young. *Took me a bit of time to adjust, but I'm good with it now.*

Tammy steps closer to fist bump in solidarity. He can see her clearly now – a heart-shaped face, dark brown eyes, and full red lips, like Snow White. Her skin is taut, just a smattering of laugh-lines and crow's feet. She's aging well or she's had some fixing, he cannot be sure. He's never been good at gaging age.

Tammy sees the ravages of time and bad habits, also a gray pallor to his skin. She can always tell when someone is ill, although not whether deadly or chronic.

Come for happy hour, she says. *If I'd known you were here, I would have invited you sooner. Take my number and text me yours.*

My sons arrive Thursday, for a long weekend, but then we're free agents. Most kind of you, Red says.

We're headed to Mammoth tonight, the slopes are calling, but only a few days before Dave hears the call of the water.

As Red pulls out his cell phone, Tammy grabs it to enter her name and number into his contacts.

Make contact, she says, and then she extracts a few flowers from her basket: long stems with thin white petals and dark purple centers.

African daisy. Get them into water, surprise your wife, she says, reaching to shake hands.

Her grasp is firm, skin as soft and warm as Red imagined.

Tammy can feel the heat in his palm. She can tell he's aroused. She doesn't mind. She likes men. She thinks they're misunderstood. She has three brothers.

Red watches her as she leaves. She sways as she walks and he imagines, again, the warmth of her, but no response this time. That anomaly has passed.

He would enjoy meeting neighbors, but he's not sure Sharon will, given their odd circumstances. They will have to concoct a pretense why a divorced couple is here for the winter. Something believable but vague, to avoid gossip, or pity.

J amie and Brady landed for their first visit at Orange County Airport, named for actor John Wayne, which elicited a contentious comment from Sharon.

Macho and racist, she exclaimed.

Red dismissed her comment. *No one cares what an airport is named, besides politicians or namesakes.*

So we should keep statues of confederate heroes up too? she argued.

No, not all, but some have historical significance, he retorted.

Some well-known figures should simply not be lionized, she insisted.

Agreed, he said, ending the argument.

He drove to the airport while Sharon prepared lunch, and when the boys arrived at the flat, they greeted her with whoops and hollers, like conquerors.

Sharon was struck, as she so often is, by how robust her sons are. Striking and sturdy. Quick with a smile. Broad shouldered and long-legged, like Red, but with her dark hair and wide eyes. They could be heroic characters, like Captain America or Superman. She's particularly proud of the way they have handled their parents' separation, although she worries about how they will deal with their father's death and how she will possibly compensate for his absence. He has been a good compass, a model for accountability and decency, if not intimacy.

Red is having similar thoughts, pleased by his boys' equilibrium and sense of purpose, although he also knows they see the world in millions of pixels via a far wider lens than he could have imagined when he was young. They are the products of good schools and loving parents, also satisfying. His job is done.

After lunch on the patio and after they check in and drop bags at the historic hotel Red has booked for them, they drive north along the cliffs above the beach historic Crystal Cove, park and then walk through a tunnel under the highway toward the ocean.

At the turn of the last century, tents filled with Hollywood outliers populated this beach in summer, where a series of cottages were subsequently erected. Palm trees were transplanted in 1917 to simulate the South Seas for the film *Treasure Island*, convincing movie-goers the setting was paradise.

Today, for Red, is indeed paradise. His energy is good, nearly his healthy self, he exclaimed to Sharon this morning, and he's exhilarated by a family reunion. Today is the sort of day he wishes would not end.

They explore the information center and then stroll down the beach, where they burrow into a dune. Brady and Jamie remove their shoes and run toward the waves, seafoam tickling their toes, then race back, again and again, before rolling up their cuffs to make the game more daring. They bounce from damp to dry sand, laughing, relishing abandon like kids.

Sharon and Red watch them, smiling, visions of their childhoods gathering like sugar plums the night before Christmas.

When the boys tire of play, they plod back to their parents, looking up at them as they once looked up to them on beach days: their bedrock, their ballast.

They embrace a willing suspension of disbelief that they are, here and now, as happy a family as they once believed: an image of what seemed to be, as well as what might have been.

They dine at a café on the sand, spiced by sea breezes and seabirds, watching the sky turn from pink to orange, then to a brilliant crimson, the sun sinking steadily behind Catalina Island until out of sight.

Once back at the flat, Red and Brady flop on the couch. Sharon and Red take the easy chairs.

This sort of room should have couches opposite each other, bracketing the fireplace, Brady comments.

But then watching television would be awkward, Jamie retorts.

Good point, Red says.

If it were up to Mom, there would be no TV at all, right Mom? Brady says.

True, she replies.

But how would we watch football? Jamie asks

But we don't have TV stations, Sharon says.

Mom, it's called streaming, Jamie says.

Right, of course, but the seating ignores the view.

I guess the thought was at night, no view, Red comments.

Sharon nods. *Good point, although the lights along the coast are equally impressive.*

Who cares about city lights when there's football? Jamie says, and they all laugh.

Red's eyelids start to droop, like a flag at half-mast. She gestures to Brady to shift to the end of the couch to give his father more room.

Brady instead drops to the floor.

Red, startled, says, *no, there's plenty of room.*

Dad, I'm a floor hugger, Brady says.

Just where he belongs, at my feet, Jamie says.

Sharon is reminded of the constant affectionate needling between brothers, not like the antagonism between her brother and sister, although this banter has been known to slip precipitously into contention. Today, gratefully, not. They are on their best behavior, she thinks, and happy to be here. In that moment, so is she.

Brady turns the television to Netflix, searching for an early episode of *The West Wing,* a family favorite, to revisit a fantasy of politics committed to the greater good. Red sleeps, stretched on the sofa end to end, his head against a plump pillow. Sharon unfolds a throw blanket over him, and the boys' eyes meet, touched by the gesture, also because Red is snoring, a low decibel wheeze they enjoy for the same reason those vibrations satisfy Sharon at night: life affirming steady breath.

Brady pauses the TV. *How's Dad doing, Mom?*

Remarkably well, she answers.

Truly? he whispers.

Truly.

Neither of them, albeit hopeful, are convinced.

Truly, Sharon repeats. *He hikes, he eats well, he rests on the patio. He's never been a napper, but all this fresh air is relaxing. So far, so good!*

And you, Mom? How are you doing? Brady asks.

I'm fine, honey. I'm sticking to my work schedule. We watch movies at night. All good right now.

And how long will that last? Brady asks.

Jamie kicks his leg, and he grimaces.

It's all right, Sharon says. *You have the right to ask. We agreed to three months and a deal is a deal.*

And then what? Brady asks.

That remains to be seen, she replies.

I think Dad would like to stay longer, Jamie says.

What makes you say that? she asks.

The way he talks about being here. He's just, I don't know how to explain. Brady, help me out here, Jamie says, nudging his brother again with his foot.

I know what Jamie's saying, Mom. Dad raves about the views, the hikes, the air. He's loving all this and who can blame him? Brady says.

Did he say he wants to stay longer? she asks.

Not in so many words, Jamie says. *I wouldn't argue with him if he did. I wouldn't say, you may need intensive medical care. He doesn't want to think that.*

Neither do I, Brady says.

Sharon sighs. *Of course not. And it's premature.*

But we will have to consider those things, right? Brady asks, his eyes beseeching Sharon for guidance.

That's up to your dad. Listen, I know you want to be helpful, but let him take the lead. He's the one to decide what and when, and right now, he's happy here. Let's go with that, shall we? Besides, dad's a planner. He may even have plans we don't know yet. Let's cross the bridges we have to cross...

When we get to them, the boys chime in.

They all chuckle and then Jamie shifts subject.

So, you guys find movies you both will watch?

Or have you finally seen the error of your ways when it comes to action thrillers, Mom?

Sharon smiles. *Plenty of choices in between.*

The boys glance at each other with a knowing expression and Sharon sees they doubt their parents' potential to stay in sync. She'd hoped time and the perspective that comes with maturity would help them make greater sense of their parents' split, but they would still rather reverse the clock. She feels again the distress she often feels for prioritizing self-preservation over their well-being, when every other decision she's ever made has been in their better interests. She was convinced then her own best interests were theirs as well, but remains forever uncertain.

And what's the deal with comida? Brady asks.

And the wine tasting! Jamie adds.

Sharon laughs. *Ah, yes, the comida. Long late afternoon meal, Mexican style. Lovely ritual.*

Like happy hour for old people? Jamie quips.

Not exactly, she retorts. *We take time to prepare and enjoy good food. Healthy food.*

Together? Jamie interrupts, incredulous.

Yes, she answers. *And your father has been shopping! Imagine that!*

Do wonders never cease? Jamie says, echoing an expression of Sharon's.

And the wine? Brady asks.

A California thing, she says. *When in Rome!*

The boys nod agreement and Jamie grabs the remote to return to the television, preferring to resume a passive repose.

Red lifts one eyelid, and then curls deeper into the blanket, happy to be folded into his family without having to engage.

Sharon hopes she has impressed upon her sons how easy retreat has been so far. Her concerns have been dispatched. They have carved out a good groove, each with destinations and intentions. Red has good energy after a nap. He's attentive. He's agreed to listen to one of several podcasts she follows – not the book reviews or story readings, but the political or historical – while they prepare the comida. They have interesting conversational codas. They have caught each other up on family members and old friends, agreeing that the passing of time is measured in the aging of the children who filled their lives – their boys, and their friends, as well as the children of friends and neighbors.

At dinner the other night, Red inquired about her dissertation, and he posed thoughtful questions, although, by the blank expression on his face, she knew he had no clue what she was talking about. No matter. He showed interest and she was pleased.

On their recent phone chat, Hank said they are getting on well because neither have anything to prove.

Essential to co-existence, she said.

I hadn't thought of that, Sharon said.

Well, the food and wine, and sunsets, those help, Hank remarked.

I've never seen sunsets like these. They light up the sky like Matisse, or Van Gogh, Sharon gushed.

And then? After dark, Hank asked.

He cleans up, I catch up on emails.

That's it?

He lights the fireplace, for warmth, Sharon said.

Makes for a cozy ambiance, Hank said.

No, Hank, Sharon argued. Warmth. And then we watch movies from a shared queue. Honestly, feels like we've slipped into an old married couple's lifestyle, without having earned it.

Interesting observation. And you're not a little bit lonely, without your people? Hank asked.

It's fine, for now. Most people would love to be in this situation, strange as it is. Who'd a thunk?

Still no sight of the landlord?

Nope, however Red met a neighbor who's invited us to happy hour at their place. I'm not keen, but he is.

Socialization might be good for you both. After all, you're on sabbatical, not seclusion. Only hermits hide indefinitely, Hank said.

An observation that will resonate in the weeks to come.

*N*othing wrong with being friendly, Red argued, when Sharon balked at Tammy's invitation. *Sure, okay, but please, no misrepresentation,* she demanded. *Say you wanted a break from winter, which is true, and I was on sabbatical, also true, and our kids will visit now and then. No need to say more.*

She needn't have worried. Tammy and husband Dave were clearly more interested in local gossip and also serving as ambassadors for the community.

They are gathered on a deep deck traversing the width of their 2-story home, two doors from the flat, taking in the same view but more breathtaking, Red comments, as their living area is at higher elevation.

Like many houses built on these hillsides, the architecture is upside-down: kitchen and dining, living area and den, at street level, with two bedrooms below. Spanning a street-to-street lot, a deep and wide lawn is bounded by flowering bushes, also fig, lemon, and orange trees.

I'm spending most of my third stage, so to speak, gardening, which I had to put on hold when I worked and when the kids were home, Tammy says, in response to Sharon's admiration of the grounds. *Although, in truth, I always found time for the greenery.*

We bought the place twenty years ago, when property could be had by the middle class, Dave says.

We lived in Costa Mesa then, on the wrong side of the tracks, Tammy adds.

Until Mr. Segerstrom stepped in to dress the town up, Dave explains.

Quite the philanthropist, I've read, Red says.

Quite the businessman, Dave says. *He turned family farmland into commercial gold. Richest shopping mall anywhere. And first-class theaters.*

South Coast Repertory has a superb reputation, Sharon says.

Yes, but we rarely go. Too busy partying, Tammy says, with a schoolgirl giggle.

By partying, my lovely wife means we spend a lot of time in clubs following local bands we like. Rock, blues, a bit of country. We also wine and dine here at home with friends and neighbors, like you, Dave says.

Much appreciated, Red replies.

Sharon smiles, but with little enthusiasm. Their lifestyle, as described, is not to her liking. She's also not sure what to make of Tammy. She's never known an older woman who dresses like a Hollywood ingenue and giggles like an adolescent. On the other hand, they seem as content a couple as she's met in a long time.

Dave, in contrast, seems average to the point of ordinary – not tall or thin or heavy. With all-American features and hazel eyes, his coloring suggests he was blonde before graying, and skin blushed by the sun makes him appear younger than he must be, despite deep creases around eyes and lips. He could be a fireman, a truck driver or a gym teacher: an everyman, the only exception being wavy strands of hair dangling to his neck like a rock musician. From a trim waist, his upper torso rises to broad shoulders in a reverse triangle, like a swimmer, which he admits he was, in high school and college, and that center of gravity serves as a stabilizer for surfing, a lifelong passion.

I'm in the water most days at dawn, he says.

His voice has a nasal quality, with an upspeak, like a Beach Boy.

Dave's a great surf guide, Tammy says proudly. *He taught the kids and most of our friends' kids.*

Happy to take you out, Dave says.

I think that ship has sailed, although, who knows, I might give it a try, Red says.

Sharon is alarmed by Red's response, and she wonders if, given the diagnosis, he's decided to throw caution to the wind. He's always been a careful man, never a risk-taker, certainly not reckless, and she's not prepared for otherwise.

You're on, Dave says, with a smile in his eyes.

Red might have said he prefers sports played on solid ground and with defined boundaries. He played baseball and basketball in school, then switched to tennis, and of late, golf. Neither the artistry of a surfer, nor the shifting playing field of an ocean.

Nevertheless, he understands the lure of the water. He stopped just the other day at a surf break south of Laguna and sat on a rise to watch. A pageant of wispy clouds crested at the horizon, mirroring lacey froth in the distance. Winter waves, they're called – what a novice might long for. He watched, mesmerized, as archetypal utopians patiently awaited the perfect wave, the right moment, and then, whether they ride or wipe out, paddling out for another round, defying Einstein's theory of madness – repeating the same action, again and again, expecting a different outcome. The epitome of persistence, even more than fishermen.

Sharon, in that moment, pictures Dave not as ordinary, rather like the Kahuna of a primordial tribe. He may ride the waves, but he's unlikely to make them. He's the stem to Tammy's bloom. She cannot help but feel a touch of envy.

I was with the County, public works, Dave says. *Forty years in Santa Ana, but we preferred to live in CM. I've worked with some of Segerstrom's people, an exceptional command of infrastructure, and I was all about infrastructure, which is why I love to surf. Sounds odd, but there is a configuration to the water and to the experience. It's not, as people think, a freefall.*

I'm an engineer, retired, but with a small army of civic and mechanical engineers on staff at my firm, Red says. *So I know what you mean. By the way, what's your opinion on this gnatcatcher impasse?*

Sharon smiles. Leave it to Red to establish his professional expertise as well as common ground. Then again, that's exactly what such a gathering is about: the prosaic, not the profound.

Dave nods, with knowing resignation. *Standard issue. The architect lives nearby, by the way, and he's good. but preservationists rule in this part of the world. Will take a while to resolve.*

We rented this place out for eighteen years, Tammy says, picking up on the previous conversation as if weary of development talk. *It was just the upper level then and not in great shape, but habitable, and when we finally moved in, we renovated the upstairs and excavated downstairs, literally, and finally, the landscaping. Dave served as general contractor.*

A good investment, Red says.

Dave slugs ale from a brown bottle. *We're like lots of people in town. Land rich, cash poor.*

And where are your kids? Sharon asks.

Portland and Philly, four grandchildren between them, Tammy answers.

You cannot be old enough! Red says.

Sharon might have been taken aback by his flirtation, but Red has always been attentive to pretty women, and at his best in casual conversation.

We have a son in Philadelphia and one in Boston as well, Red says.

Ooh, I love Boston, Tammy croons.

Sharon and I went to school there and lived there until the first was born, Red replies.

But way too cold. Nearly as cold as Chicago, right? Tammy says.

Minus the wind, Red says.

Tammy goes inside to retrieve appetizers, which pleases Sharon as she's acclimated to early dinners.

On a platter shaped like a leaf, figs and almonds surround chunks of cheese, with scattered crackers. A matching plate holds sizzling samosas, radiating a tantalizing scent. Dave puts down a bowl of tortilla chips with guacamole, an avocado pit at the center. Plates and utensils are already on the table, napkins imprinted with images of seashells.

Help yourselves, Dave says.

We nibble with booze, Tammy says, as if she'd invented happy hour. *I never cook serious meals and Dave mostly grills.*

I'm a nibbler by nature, Red says.

How politic he is, Sharon thinks, knowing he'd be happier with a slab of steak and a baked potato smothered with butter and chives.

Tammy tops off Red's glass of red wine, and her own, then Sharon's white from a bottle nesting in an ice bucket, and when she replaces the bottle, a bit of melted frost drips down her arm, which she swipes away. She smiles coquettishly at Red, who's watching her, obviously enchanted.

And what did you do before retirement? Sharon asks Tammy.

I'm a nurse, she answers.

In the OR, Dave adds, with spousal pride.

Thirty-five years, Tammy adds.

Sharon cannot reconcile this frivolous woman with the image of an operating nurse. She pictured her a shop girl or a cocktail waitress.

A noble calling, Sharon says, scolding herself for the rush to judgment.

Red smiles, redeemed – the sexy woman exalted by nobility of service. He knows Sharon had written Tammy off as beneath her intellectual standards.

Tammy certainly does not look the part. She wears a peacock blue, low-cut shirt that tugs at her breasts and clings to her hips. She glitters as she moves – a diamond engagement ring is set within two platinum bands and thin gold chains around her neck and one wrist. Foundation and bronzer sets her face, black mascara and eyeliner adorn nearly round eyes, and crimson lipstick finishes the look on full lips.

Sharon suddenly feels like a gnatcatcher in comparison to Tammy's plumage. She's in a billowy white linen tunic over black leggings. She wears little make-up, a pale pink lip gloss and simple silver jewelry – the one nod to style her favorite dangling earrings, dotted with turquoise.

Tammy continues to expound on nursing.

Surgery is the best part of American medicine, and the doctors used to ask for me in their theater – they still call it a theater, the OR, at least the insiders do. I like to think I was a star!

Did they ask for Nurse Tammy? Red asks. *By that I mean, is Tammy short for something?*

Two answers to that question, Tammy says.

Dave smiles at the onset of a familiar response.

I like to tell people my name is Tamara, elegant, biblical, and middle eastern, where my grandparents come from. Means date or palm tree. I spent most of my formative years in Los Angeles surrounded by palms, so there's that. But the truth is, Mom named me for Tammy Wynette, the country singer! She grew up in Nashville but was lured to LA by my itinerant father.

Itinerant? Red asks.

Not a migrant worker. Not military. Just highly distractible. My poor mother was forever juggling what bills to pay and where I would go to school. We moved a lot. Like twelve times in my childhood.

Must have been hard, Sharon remarks.

That's one of the reasons I fell for Dave. I could tell he was a solid citizen. More importantly, a man who appreciates a good woman. And he's cute!

As Dave leans over to kiss Tammy on the neck, Red sees him slip a hand to her ass, likely a squeeze. Red would have, he thinks. And unlike other women, who might have shrugged her husband off for the sake of decorum, Tammy smiles in appreciation. Red thinks any man would be melted by that smile.

Sharon too witnesses the exchange. She would have to admit she admires Tammy's easy-going nature – a woman who takes pride in what she can do, without dwelling on what she cannot. She seems to have no artifice and even after many years immersed in disease, disaster, demanding surgeons, and raising children, she's light-hearted. Impressive.

Then again, attractive women always have an edge, Sharon thinks, and Tammy has a husband she can count on. A man so facile in the waves must also be a force between the sheets.

Red too is wondering what it might be like to live with a perpetually agreeable woman, like Tammy, although who knows what she's like behind closed doors. And, he thinks, who knows how each of them have tempered expectations over time. To an engineer, the glass is neither half empty nor half full, rather the wrong glass for the drink.

By the time they finish comparing notes on northern California versus south, Philadelphia versus Boston or Portland, why Dave and Tammy hope to visit the last of the Hawaiian islands they haven't seen, and why Sharon hopes to see Asia, and other wanderlust talk, the sky has turned dark, and flickering lights illuminate the wavy coastline below like an airstrip.

Sharon eyes Red to telescope a message it's time to leave, just as Dave asks, *What about you, Sharon? I hear you're a PhD student. Online?*

Well, no, I'm... Sharon stammers.

Sharon has been living in Berkeley, for a while, and now she's on sabbatical, Red interjects.

You stayed in Chicago? Dave asks.

A matter of timing, Red replies. *Better for Sharon to be on campus while she puts the finishing touches to her dissertation. She's an assistant professor there.*

Sharon was often annoyed when Red answered for her, but right now she's relieved. She never knew he was such a facile liar, however, although he hasn't misrepresented them. When their eyes meet, she sees sincerity in his, or is it optimism? She has a disturbing thought he believes what he's said, hoping her move west was merely transitional. As if she might return to him once her goal is achieved.

I've enjoyed Berkeley, she answers Dave. *Smart people. Great culture. Nothing like the beauty of the bay bridges, although you guys have the climate.*

Maybe the best in the country, Dave says.

They all nod as they munch on the still-warm fudgy brownies Tammy has presented with aplomb.

My older daughter has a PhD in environmental studies, Tammy says, licking a smudge of chocolate off her lips. *She wrote a dissertation about synthetic coral reefs. Too complicated for me. I'm no good at science. Nursing is more about instinct. What are you writing about, Sharon?*

Impressive, your daughter's work, Sharon says.

My focus of study is rather esoteric. Elizabeth Gaskell, a Victorian writer. I also teach a class on Mary Shelley and there's a surprising linkage there, so that's integral to my thesis.

Frankenstein? Tammy exclaims.

She's known for that, but she's much more. They both wrote about intimacy. About creativity. Also the dark side of modernity.

Like? Dave asks.

Inequity? Poverty? Suppression of women.

Dave nods. *What's so special about Gaskell?*

For one thing, she was prolific. She wrote eight novels, thirty-two short stories, and more. She was the forerunner of what we know as the social novel.

I guess there's a lot of writers people like us don't know, Tammy says.

I doubt there are many great writers Sharon doesn't know, Red asserts.

Not so, Sharon insists.

She despises the *isn't my wife special* comment.

Tell us more, Dave says.

About Gaskell?

Yes. Think of us as your students, Dave says.

Sharon smiles. *She's called Mrs. Gaskell. Quite formal, some say up-tight, and passionately concerned about the underclass. Three novels were BBC series.*

Like Jane Austen? Tammy asks.

She was less interested in the mannered life than the hardscrabble. Her mother died when she was a year old, and Mary Shelley's in childbirth, by the way. Reflects in their work, I mean, in the search for meaning.

So sad, Tammy mutters.

Yes, but tragedy was a catalyst for the writing. And, although Gaskell married a minister, and played the dutiful wife, she chronicled the challenges women faced in her fiction.

How did she get known back then? Dave asked.

Dickens, whom she met through mutual friends, invited her to submit to his magazine, called Household Words. She published a lot of her early work there. He called her Scheherazade.

Him, I know, Tammy says.

What, or who else do you teach? Dave asks.

George Eliot. Middlemarch, of course, and Adam Bede, my favorite.

Couldn't read Middlemarch, Tammy says.

Sharon hears this often, a stake in her heart.

Shelley influenced them all, Sharon continues. *She's been labeled science fiction, but she wrote gothic before it was a genre.*

Storms and haunted mansions? Dave asks.

Gothic has more to do with the battles within the psyche. The meaning of existence, Sharon says.

Wow. I can see why you're at Berkeley, Tammy says. *I went to Cal State, that's where Dave and I met, and barely got out with my BS, but it got me to the OR.*

Talk about gothic, or mysterious, Red says, in an abrupt segue. *I'd like to know more about our landlord.*

Sharon isn't sure if Red has given her a way out of the writer-talk or if he's tired of the subject, or both, but she too is curious about the landlord.

Oh, Rosa, Dave says. *She's legend around here.*

Dave has a thing for Rosa, Tammy says.

A fascination, not a thing, Dave responds. *But I only met Matt a few times.*

Matt? Red asks.

Mateo, Tammy says.

She leans the back of her palm to her forehead to mock a dramatic swoon. *Beautiful man. I met him toward the end, he was already sick, but he was still a looker and quite the charmer.*

A painter, Dave elaborates. *And he designed the house. His studio was where you are now. Whenever we had a new tenant, I would let the neighbors know, in case there were problems. We chatted a few times.*

And were there? Red asks. *Problems, I mean.*

Only once. We've been lucky, Dave answers.

How well do you know Rosa? Red asks.

No one knows Rosa well, Dave says.

Their relationship is a mystery, Tammy explains. *She never speaks of him, not that I know of. She called, about a year after he died, to ask me to advise the daughter of a friend about nursing. Elena, the girl who shops for her. You'll meet her. Sweet thing. We had tea and Rosa looked exhausted. Pale, painfully thin. That's when I noticed the garden needed tending, so I asked permission to cut them now and then. She was oh so grateful. Very dear, she is.*

We haven't met her yet, Sharon says.

Your instinct is to wrap your arms around her to protect her, comfort her, but she's tougher than meets the eye, Tammy says.

Mateo took good care of her, Dave says.

She took good care of Mateo, Tammy counters. *There are definitely secrets there, maybe gothic, if I get your drift, and I can tell you a bit more, but that subject requires more than wine. How about some weed?*

Indeed! Red says, nodding elatedly, like a child who has discovered he can reach the cookie jar.

Sharon is struck dumb. Medicinal cannabis is one thing, but marijuana with total strangers?

Dave jumps up. *I'll get the stuff, honey.*

Tammy picks up the food plates, nestling them in the crook of her arm like a waitress and waving away Sharon when she tries to assist. *No worries. Dave's the dish man,* she says. She drops them at the sink and then shoos them down the stairs to where four blue-painted Adirondack chairs surround a brick fire pit.

Sharon instantly recalls roasting marshmallows over fire pits on summer holidays, when she was a girl, where such chairs encircled a lawn facing a lake. She sits back happily, relishing the nostalgia.

Tammy lights the fire with a long butane lighter, which she then hands to Dave, who holds a plastic bag filled with what could be assumed to be tea leaves. She pulls blankets from a pile by the stairs and hands them around, wrapping one around her with a flourish before she sits.

Dave packs the grass into a pipe bowl and, once satisfied, he lights, fanning as if igniting a campfire.

On the rare occasions Sharon tried marijuana, in college, she smoked joints. She hasn't seen a bong since and such paraphernalia seems like a 60s movie clip. Whatever her first impression of these neighbors, she would not have imagined them stoners, although she knows she's naïve. Nevertheless, a former nurse and a civil servant getting high in the backyard is unexpected and she also thought people this age more often use gummies, or vape. She has to stifle a laugh as Red leans forward in his chair, fixating on Dave like a puppy awaiting a treat.

Dave passes the bowl, but Sharon demurs.

Not for you? he asks.

Makes me mellow. High is not high for me.

Depends on the stuff, Dave says. *This is what you might call pot-light. Like an after-dinner drink.*

We have liqueurs in a cabinet, I think, if you'd rather, Tammy suggests.

I'm good, thanks, Sharon answers.

She cautions herself not to go grumpy, which she will do when she feels out of place or excluded, even if by choice. She pulls the blanket tighter to her chest and leans in closer to the fire, while the others lean into the warmth of the psychotropic.

Flames in the round fire pit bubble at the center like water boiling in a tea pot. They don't evaporate. They don't wax or wane. Not at all like a furious fire in a fireplace – no sparks, no wood scent. Nevertheless, Sharon is captivated. She stares at the flames as if they might reveal a deep dark secret.

Rosa must be upset about the refugee situation at the border, Dave says.

If she even knows, Tammy says.

She must, Sharon says. *It's all over the news.*

She only listens to music, Tammy says.

Has she been here long? Red asks.

Like, twenty something years, Dave answers.

She's not illegal, is she? Red asks.

Why do you ask? Tammy asks.

Well, people stay under the radar, Red replies.

He sucks smoke deep into his lungs and holds, as if he's been doing this forever, then exhales volubly, and at the same time, coughs, vehemently, turning red in the face until the spasm passes, and when it does, he smiles, sheepishly, and sighs.

Dave chuckles kindly, as Tammy watches Red, intuiting more than he would like her to know.

Sharon shudders at the mental image of smoke strangling Red's discolored lungs.

Why would it matter if she's legal? she asks Red.

You don't want ICE showing up at the house, do you? These are strange times, he answers.

Dave says she's been here for many years, she can't be on anyone's radar, Sharon argues.

She's legal, Dave says, ending the dispute.

Mateo made sure of it, Tammy adds. *However, since he passed, she has been reclusive, as if she is in hiding. She never goes anywhere.*

Nowhere? Sharon asks.

Not that we know of, Dave says.

What about shopping or church? Sharon asks.

She used to go to church in town, that sweet little one, but not anymore, Tammy says.

Elena, the girl Tammy mentioned, delivers her groceries, and our postman, who, by the way, holds an excellent supply of dope and is happy to share, leaves her mail at her door, so she doesn't even have to go out to the street, Dave explains.

I noticed a young woman the other day, Red says. *I was dozing, she might not have noticed me. She just ran up the stairs, dropped the bags and was gone. I thought I was dreaming.*

Didn't wake you like other people? Tammy says, giggling, giddier now, the effect of marijuana, Sharon suspects, although she drank a fair amount of wine.

And I am so glad you did, Red sputters, as he too giggles, an unnatural sound coming deep from his throat, like gurgling.

When Sharon notices a loopy expression on his face, she cannot help but smile. The relaxed setting, tasty food and drink, and the weed, have stripped him of age. She would have to admit, the evening has done him good.

One of the day workers knew Rosa well, Tammy says. *Carlos, remember, Dave? He used to visit her at lunchtime, but when I asked about her, he shook his head and said, tan triste. So sad. When I pressed him, he shrugged and went to work. They protect their own.*

Day worker? Sharon asks.

There's a site in town where laborers are hired short-term, Dave explains. *Hard labor. Heavy lifting. Protected from dishonest contractors, mostly.*

And when they didn't have lunch with them, I made sandwiches, Tammy says. *You can't imagine the gratitude – you'd have thought I served them surf and turf. There's an English teacher there too.*

Well, that's brilliant, Sharon exclaims.

We hired a few during the remodel, Dave says. *They worked long hours. Meticulous attention to the project. Anyone who buys the myth Mexicans are lazy has never worked with one.*

And we have a food pantry in town, for the poor, Tammy announces. *Dave volunteers there.*

Was Rosa a day worker? Red asks.

She was Mateo's housekeeper, Dave answers.

And now she owns the house? Red asks.

My lord! Sharon cries. *Are you worrying we're renting from a squatter?*

Dave said there's a story, Red insists, glaring at Sharon like a frustrated husband, and she looks away, dismissing his disdain like a bored wife.

Dave passes the bong a third round.

Rest assured, he says, *the house belongs to her.*

Sharon watches as they continue smoking, one by one, gazing at each other like teen co-conspirators. When she stands, they look up at her in surprise.

Sorry, it's getting late, and I've got an early call with my advisor.

Sharon might have said, Red needs his rest. It's past his bedtime. He seems suddenly weary. His eyes are bloodshot. She hopes he's grateful for a reprieve.

To be continued, Dave says, standing to escort them to the street.

With obvious effort, Red wrests himself from the chair, swaying some on his feet. Sharon and Tammy move close at once, until he steadies himself. At the stairs, Tammy ushers Sharon ahead of her, then nods to Dave to follow Red to shore him up if he slips.

At the front door, Tammy turns to hug Sharon, a warm hug Sharon appreciates, and then she stands on tiptoe to hug Red. When they hold the cinch longer than etiquette, Sharon wonders if he has seized an opportunity to nuzzle into her lovely body, or she may be propping him up.

When they release, Tammy smiles at Sharon, knowingly, and Sharon suspects Tammy suspects his fatigue has more to do with poor health than weed. Red's secret may not be safe after all.

Low clouds pull on the sky and a crescent moon sheds little light. Sharon slips her arm through Red's to lead him past the jumble of parked cars, inching like caterpillars until they arrive safely at the side stairs to the flat, and once inside, he stumbles to his room with a wave and mumbles goodnight.

Once she has slipped out of her clothes and into a nightshirt and boxers, she stands at her doorway, listening for his sleep breathing, and only then she closes her doors and flops into bed. This will be a night to remember, she thinks, as she too slips into a deep sleep.

osa Zyanya was born in 1980 in Teotitlán del Valle, thirty miles east of the city of Oaxaca, Mexico. The family name, in Zapotec, means always: a promise of devotion to loved ones and values, and the centuries-old weaving tradition for which the village is celebrated. Bus loads of visitors travel to the countryside throughout the year to watch fabrics dyed and spun into rugs they will take home to step on or hang as a memento to mark their visit to this historic puebla, nestled into the Sierra Madre mountains.

Rosa was a naturally talented weaver, skilled at extracting a coveted red dye from the cochineal, a tiny nut-shaped insect that feeds on cactus. Subtler tints were derived with the addition of lime, and with a hint of ash, reds became purple, greens turned to gold. Yellows were yielded by marigold petals or the edge of a pomegranate, and the shells of local nuts produced distinctive shades of browns and oranges.

The yarn, spun from maguey and palm leaves, is typically boiled over a fire and then threaded on a loom or a wheel into ancient patterns.

Rosa whirled designs more like the Persian or Turkish, which she'd never seen, and by the age of sixteen, her rugs caught the eyes of merchants in the historic center's commercial plaza, the Zocalo, and soon after, by importers from the U.S., where weavings would be priced-up tenfold and sold in upscale shops.

When a retailer from California took a particular interest in her work, Rosa's father, Balam, rejected his overture, insisting indigenous art remain where it is made.

Let the buyers come to us, Balam said, proud of his family legacy and unwilling to compromise.

Rosa's mother, Nayeli, a curandera, renowned in the village for her healing powers and prescience, predicted at Rosa's birth her destiny would take her far from home.

This girl, she told Balam, *holds a sovereign spirit. Before too long, you will have to let her go.*

Although he respected his wife's wisdom, Balam insisted Rosa wait until she came of age to take flight.

What Nayeli never told him, or her daughter, was the shadow she saw hovering over the girl's lifeline – intersecting threads of profound sorrow, subject to one ascendant man. This alone would not have been disturbing; after all, life is hardship. Love demands. However, although Nayeli saw clearly that Rosa would flee her roots before long, she could not see the path of her return – only a dark sky without definition.

With no way to protect her daughter, she would beseech the spirits to guide her.

Rosa was seventeen when the rug wholesaler returned, and she asked her mother to intercede with her father. Nayeli studied the stars and, assured that the merchant was not the danger, asked Balam to give his blessing, and he acquiesced.

Rosa, anxious to take flight, and trusting in the inherent goodness of humanity, consigned her future to the merchant.

Hundreds of thousands of Mexicans migrants made their way north in the latter years of the century, although their journey was arduous and required a guide. Coyotes, named for their stealth-like qualities, smuggled the hopeful over the border, and were known to prey on them. The merchant convinced a trusted guide that the innocent girl was a talisman for her people and if she was harmed, he would be targeted by wolves. The ruse was effective because Zapotec honor the mystical and because the guide was promised a generous bonus when Rosa arrived safely.

The night before the journey, Nayeli made an offering of her most colorful rug to the god of justice, Kedo, and the creator god, Coqui Xee, who represented infinity, beseeching them to ensure her daughter's safe passage and, sooner than later, reveal her true path.

Rosa took her best rug with her for luck – interlocking threads of deep orange and sapphire blue, with a golden fringe – which she has kept close since.

They traveled north on a stuffy smelly bus, then another, bypassing the guarded border crossings to a junction farther west. For the first time in her young life, Rosa felt afraid. Not a fear of thunder or the earth cracking under her feet, but fear of the unknown. She slept in bursts only when she could not keep her eyes open. She subsisted on dry bread and berries, or an avocado fallen from a dusty tree. Exhaustion made river crossing more chilling – more than once she was certain she would drown. On arrival in Texas, before she had a moment to savor the bright blue sky, she spent days struggling to breathe in a windowless van, then another bus from Arizona to California, landing at last in Los Angeles, weary but grateful. Her faith in the gods had been rewarded.

She was housed in a dingy apartment with five other laborers, assigned a sleeping space in a bed with an older woman who shunned her, at first, the way an older dog repels a puppy.

By day, she was overwhelmed by strange street noises, and at night, nauseated by rancid food strewn by alley cats. There was little more than weaving and sleep, although workers dined together and sometimes laughed together, bonded by culture and language, and long workdays in a stuffy warehouse. Over time, Rosa was accepted, but not embraced, and it was here she first learned how to be alone.

The rugs they wove were marketed to buyers as authentic, although they were blended with synthetic dyes and threads. Although Rosa had fled her village limitations, she was ashamed to betray her family tradition. Trapped in that dilemma, she decided to forge another path, although it took two years to exit.

She studied English watching sitcoms on TV and on Sundays, after mass, she wandered galleries or museums, mesmerized by fine art from other worlds.

At an exhibit of paintings by a Peruvian artist, she overheard a conversation between a gallerist and a collector. They were debating the definition of art. Rosa listened attentively and, without realizing, she nodded at their words. When she murmured under her breath, not meaning to be heard, *art is the revelation of the spirit*, the men glanced her way.

As the gallerist approached, Rosa was mortified, and about to flee, when he introduced himself. He had kind eyes and invited her into their discussion.

Simon Oliva was middle-aged, with mocha skin and a tightly trimmed beard. He was taken at once with Rosa's artistic purity and sophisticated aesthetic. Surprised to discover she had no formal training, he suggested she attend classes at one of the city's art schools. Rosa nodded, as if she might, not confessing, although he suspected, she had neither means nor time for schooling. When he asked if she created art of her own, she said only that she was a weaver of rugs from Oaxaca.

Detecting in this diminutive girl a creative force, Simon invited her to spend a week in Laguna Beach and offered her a small sum to teach the art of weaving at his gallery there.

But where would I stay? Rosa asked.

Simon assured her she would be safe in a cottage on the grounds of his weekend home, where the Mexican woman who managed both his property and gallery resided.

Because he reminded Rosa of her grandfather, she trusted his good intentions, and when she asked him to swear on the life of his mother, he complied.

A month later, as the day grew longer and the sun moved into the summer sky, Rosa waved good-bye to her comrades and left an explanatory note for the merchant who had facilitated her journey. She never mentioned to anyone where she was going, or why. She already knew she would not return.

She was captivated by the bustling beach town with open-air summer arts festivals held in sweeping spaces reminiscent of the Zocalo. Painters, sculptors, ceramicists, photographers and jewelers displayed and sold their wares, and, in her off hours, with a pass gifted by the gallerist, she wandered the grounds until closing with her new roommate and mentor, Sylvia.

Although she was raised less than 200 miles from the Oaxacan Pacific coast, Rosa had never felt the sand, and the surf was as foreign, and exciting, as arts festivals. Late at night, in a little room carved out in the back of the guest cottage, like an afterthought, she leaned against a headboard painted with sprays of lavender listening to waves break at the shoreline. She slept soundly and awoke with the sun to take slow walks on wet sand. She sent postcards to her family to share the sweetness of her new landscape.

Nayeli understood then why she was not able to see Rosa's destiny – the sea is vast, its secrets hidden beyond the horizon.

Rosa began to hope she might someday reside in her own home by the sea. She was not one to give up without trying, so, when the class ended, and when Simon handed her a train ticket back to Los Angeles, she asked instead if she might remain for a short time, and he agreed. She did not say she hoped to find work and reside for a time in the beautiful beach town.

Before long, however, she realized she could not afford to rent without employment and, not wanting to take further advantage of his generosity, she slept on the beach, capturing sweet dreams under moonlight.

The night police descended on the sand, Rosa ran as fast as her short legs would carry her, until she found shelter under the lower branches of a pepper tree. At sunrise, she made her way to a park where breakfast was served for the needy. She never asked for help, fearing she might be repatriated. Instead, she continued to sleep under the trees, where an image of her father's disapproving face haunted her.

The gods smiled on her one day as she walked around town and noticed a *For Hire* sign at a small hotel. The manager, a fellow émigré, recognizing Rosa's innocence, and determination, offered her employment as a housekeeper, and instructed her to do the work without interacting with guests.

The hotel turned out to be a flop house for the poor and drug addicted. Rosa was deeply disturbed by the degradation she witnessed. She moved about her days like a shadow, ignoring the detritus. No matter how tired she was, she never napped on the job, but she stole hot showers when possible in vacated rooms. She kept her belongings close at hand and at dusk, made her way far from the hotel to sleep on streets bordering large, elegant homes, accepting hardship as inherent to her path from lonely immigrant to artist.

One day, although she knocked and announced herself, when she entered a guest room, she discovered a man still in bed. The scent of urine and sweat filled the air. She apologized and turned to leave, but then she noticed he was shaking. His eyes were glazed. She wiped his brow with a damp washcloth and dripped droplets of water to his lips. He begged her not to tell anyone; however, fearing he might die, she alerted the front desk manager. Within minutes, the man was carried by gurney to an ambulance and the manager, to her surprise, commended her for her action. Seizing on his kindness, Rosa confided she was a weaver and asked if he could help her connect with other artists.

He laughed, loudly, as if she'd made a joke. *Of course. Everyone in this town thinks they're an artist!*

When Rosa lowered her eyes in humiliation, the manager had the thought, perhaps, she might be more than she appears, and he promised to ask around.

One month later, about to give up and make her way back to Los Angeles, or return in shame to Mexico, the manager approached her with an opportunity to be a housekeeper for a local artist. She would be paid a small salary, he said, with room and board, on a street not far from town. Rosa jumped at the chance.

To impress the artist with her skill, she brought to the interview the rug she had taken from home.

Mateo Perez was sixteen years older and already respected as a modern Fauvist painter. Born to Cuban refugees, and despite dialect differences, he was able to communicate effortlessly with the shy urchin from Oaxaca, although he could never have imagined how their relationship would evolve.

He invited her into the house he had designed, the house with the broad sweeping view of the sea, where Sharon and Red would reside on retreat twenty years later.

The lower level then was Mateo's studio, and it was there he fashioned living space for Rosa, removed from the busyness and eccentricity of his personal life, but close at hand.

She never left.

Sharon is on her way from town and although she's running late, she stops at the bookstore to inhale the scent of bound paper and purchase a guide to the southern coast. Red prefers GPS, but she likes printed matter in hand, and she's curious about day trips that might be of interest to the boys.

The store décor is beachy, anchored by a replica of a lifeguard tower. Display tables are filled with titles catered to tourists – escapist fiction, surf culture, local lore – and at the register, souvenirs and gifts. When she asks where she will find the travel section, the salesclerk points to the back. On her way, she briefly peruses the fiction shelves, then heads to the travel. Moments later, the clerk joins her, nodding when she comments on the trifling selection, and launching into a lecture on California, north to south.

The young man is scrawny. Clothes barely hang on his frame. He reminds her of students who inhale nourishment from the air rather than consume good food. Dark wavy hair gathers in unruly curls around his head, and because he wears black-framed glasses, he bears a resemblance to Harry Potter.

This state is not a state, it's a country, he says. *It's larger in acreage than many countries. Largest population in the U.S. and the largest GDP, the sixth highest GDP in the world, just behind Germany and India. So vast, so economically and politically diverse, there's a movement to break into three separate states*, he explains.

Two customers look up from their searches and smile, as if they've heard his commentary before.

But there's way more than three, he continues. *Begin with the Northern region, way north, might be called the State of Mind. It's populated by aged hippies who drifted north from Santa Cruz and the Bay, toward Mendocino and beyond to the Oregon border. The air is rarefied, truly, also permeated with the skunky smell of marijuana.*

He laughs and Sharon laughs with him, happy to be reacquainted with the ebullience of a student.

Next is the Vino State, Sonoma and Napa, might as well be one place, and the Bay, Marin to Palo Alto, gentrified suburbs to San Jose. The State of Technology may be the term. Then on to the capital, Sacramento, the Capital State, obviously, although if we stretch into gold rush territory, used to be Nevada, might be another state of its own. Dense forests, tall trees. Still gold in those hills, I imagine.

At this, one of the customers chuckles. A warm smile spreads from his lips like an oil spill, through a stubble of gray along the jaw. A stocky man of medium height, he wears a gray sweater with weathered jeans that bag at the knees.

The clerk says, *be right with you, Sam.*

No rush, the man named Sam answers. *Always fascinated by your thoughts.*

Thank you, kind sir, he answers, with a bow.

What about Berkeley, Sharon asks.

Berkeley is in a class by itself. Throw Oakland in for good measure, maybe the last truly diverse city in the state, and we'll call that the State of Enlightenment. From there, west to the Monterey State, Santa Cruz to

Carmel, an eclectic confluence of surfers, golfers, and classic car collectors. Below that, from SLO down the central coast and inland toward Paso Robles, into the central wine valley. Middle Ground might be the name.

Ah, but wait, Sharon interjects. *I have it on good authority that's not actually the middle of the state, you know. San Francisco is nearly the center.*

Sharon makes a mental note to tell Hank that her tutorial on California, delivered the night before the drive, has come in handy.

The young man's face brightens. *You are SO right! Let's say In-Between, meaning between the more notable, I would say more interesting regions. And then there's the Valley, the agrarian heart. Important, in a flat affect sort of way.*

Some locals might object, Sharon says, *but go on.*

He shrugs. *Santa Barbara might be the Oprah State now, then down to Ojai, a jewel, so maybe the Gem State, and at last to Malibu, through LA. The State of Pretense, which should include Long Beach because it doesn't fit anywhere else. Then we arrive in Orange County. Used to be the Red State, as in Republican, except for Laguna Beach, which used to be true blue, not now, but the county went blue in the mid-terms, so maybe purple. And the Surf State, from Huntington Beach to San Diego, all vying for the title of surf city, except Laguna, the arts town.*

The customer named Sam chuckles again, but the young man ignores him and goes on.

I might group most of the inland cities together as the Inland State. Julian and Big Bear too, although up there might be called the Hiking State, or, because of the desert towns, the Windmill State. So how many is that? Eleven? Twelve? He counts his fingers.

You should build an app, Sam calls out.

I've thought of that, but I've got more important things to do with my time, the clerk says.

Your description reminds me of one of my favorite novels, North and South, Sharon says, as if he might know it. *Only in the geography,* she adds.

Civil war? he asks.

Victorian. Elizabeth Gaskell.

Not my era. I'm strictly 20th century lit.

Not the new millennium? Sharon asks.

Wannabees. What's so great about North South?

North and South. Your 20th century writers are the descendants of this writer, among others.

What's it about? he asks.

Hard to summarize, Sharon answers.

The Wiki version, he says.

Well, about doing the right thing. About fairness. Duty. Compassion. Also a love story, she explains.

Are you a professor? he asks.

Something like that, Sharon replies.

I could tell, he says, with a smug expression. *Maybe a book group will want it, or maybe Sam.*

He points to Sam, who nods in the affirmative, although she suspects tolerance more than interest.

And this is all the travel? Sharon asks.

The young man sighs, as if a personal failure. *The only guides we have are North or South Cali and a couple of maps. Travel lit is better. Steinbeck, Stegner,*

Hammett, Mosley. Or Didion, he says, handing Sharon *Slouching Toward Bethlehem,* the paradigmatic essay collection she's read a few times.

Remember, he says, with dramatic flourish. '*The center will not hold.*'

Sharon nods, yes. Didion: essayist-philosopher.

She also said, I think these are her exact words, 'a passion for the documentation of irrelevant detail is characteristic of the afflicted,' Sharon quotes, affirming herself as a supercilious academic.

The boy is speechless at first and then bursts into laughter. *A fellow cynic for sure. I can't say if Lady Joan would argue for secession, but she would get it.*

With that, he returns to the counter up front to help customers waiting patiently.

Sharon peruses a moment longer, then lines up at the register behind a woman standing behind Sam, who turns and smiles, as if partners in crime. His eyes are a pale gray, nearly lavender, like Elizabeth Taylor's, reputedly, and he gazes at her as if he knows her or would like to.

When she realizes she's blushing, she lowers her eyes to page through the books she holds, and by the time she purchases a story collection by TC Boyle and the Didion, Sam is on his way out the door.

At dinner that night, Sharon recounts what she recalls of the young man's diatribe. Red is delighted by the theory, and afterwards, he maps the state online, checking with her now and then on the clerk's geographic stipulations, which he shares in an email with Barry.

Sharon has the distinct feeling she has betrayed the young man, although he cannot have invented this notion. Perhaps she feels protective toward him, as a student, or a son, as silly as that is, and she's bothered by Red's appropriation of the narrative. He's done that before when someone relays a fascinating take on something otherwise obtuse or unusual. He takes it on like an engineering project – tweaking this or that to optimize. A habit of his that rankled and then festered: mole hills to mountains.

Once she turns in, an image of the man called Sam invades her mind's eye. A charmer for sure. She wishes now she had looked more closely at what he was reading.

She tosses the decorative pillows off the bed and her clothes into a hamper, pondering Hank's treatise on relationships. How few stick for long. Perhaps the better plan is one love at a time and many over time. She should have been promiscuous in her youth. She wishes she had been more demanding and daring, and less Victorian.

In my next life, I'll forsake devotion or solitude for precocity, she muses, as she closes her eyes; however she sleeps restlessly, like a runner before a marathon.

R ed reclines on a patio chaise, bundled against the chill in his black MIT sweatshirt and comfy sweatpants. He stands to reposition the chair to better capture the sun, and as he feels rays spread across his face, he is reminded of the sun porch at his childhood home: sunlight and warmth analogous to hope and the sense of opportunity infusing his youth.

Each week on retreat passes quicker than the previous, and uneventful, other than deliberations in the news about a coronavirus incubating in China. The CDC has begun screening for symptoms at the airports where passengers from Asia land, and tens of millions of Chinese nationals are already in quarantine. NIH experts suggest this may be no more than a nasty flu, while medical pundits fear a malicious mutation of SARS or MERS.

Red has had his flu and pneumonia vaccines, and that night he told Sharon he's glad they no longer live in a big city.

Density is the enemy, for communicable disease, and why the Chinese will be hit so hard. Our retreat to a small town may prove our salvation.

Sharon wondered what he meant by salvation.

Here's the strangest part of all this, she told Hank on their latest video chat.

As if everything about retreat with your ex isn't strange? Hank asked.

Point taken. But I had an aha moment yesterday, a revelation, that in my long history with Red, I've gone from attracting him to pleasing him, to frustrating him, and he frustrating me and, over time, begrudging him the disappointments, the feeling that lingered and could not be tamed. One end of the continuum to the other.

Longevity is over-rated, Hank said.

Oh yes, I remember that speech: no two people are meant to mate for life, Sharon recited.

Exactly. Like machinery, wears down over time.

Okay, but here's the thing: having moved past what ruined us, and because here we're on our best behavior, I have no traction. We've been disenchanted for so long and now we're accommodating, so it's foggy, like mornings on the Bay. Here too, you know.

We have fog, you have marine layer, Hank said.

You are a sourpuss today, what's up?

Hank sighed. *Sorry, go on, this is enlightening.*

What I'm trying to say is we've entered a parallel universe. Without discord or discontent, I have no center of gravity. No compass, Sharon explained.

Dare I say, a bit gothic, Hank mused.

Gothic would be far more interesting.

It is an existential dilemma, yes?

Not from a literary perspective, Sharon said. *No prophesy, no creation myth. No decay, no spirits, no creaky mansion. Only a lovely glass house with a view, surrounded by a plethora of birds of paradise, which can be scary in the shadows but otherwise exquisite. Maybe I'm the madwoman in the attic!*

There is the mysterious landlady, Hank said. *And the mist, the waves lapping against the shore…*

Mysterious yes, not threatening. Hardly a peep, besides the music, all day long, and thankfully she has good taste in music. I am curious about her, of course.

She could be mad, Hank said, punctuating the comment with ghoulish sounds.

Sharon laughed. *Muted decor, lush gardens. No, she's no threat. The signs of a gentle hand.*

Or the hand of the late painter? Hank posed.

Could be. Either way, more spiritual than gothic. If there is a story, it's Austen not Shelley.

You're the expert, Hank said. *Gotta go, sorry. Yet another meeting. I'll never get anything done today.*

She hung up before Sharon had the chance to say good-bye or probe into what's got her in a snit.

She left early this morning for her walk to town. She's always been a street walker, in the best sense. She walked everywhere she could in Boston and then, in Chicago, exiled to a suburb, she drove into town and parked her car at a central location, walking the rest of the way. She rarely strolls, rather an urban stride so rapid her sons had to hustle to keep up. In Laguna, she ambles along side streets perusing the mishmash of architecture: beach cottages with pitched tile roofs abutting mid-century moderns with flat roofs and tall windows. She peers around garages to get a closer look at ocean-facing monoliths. Growing familiarity with these streets makes her feel less an outsider, although she once fantasized being a stranger in strange lands. These days, in late life, fly on the wall seems preferable to trespasser.

Red, having returned from his hike, eases into the afternoon heaviness that descends over him, his eyes as weighted as limbs. As he's about to slide into sleep, a young brown woman emerges at the top of the stone steps from the street. She wears green hospital scrubs cloaked in a dark brown sweatshirt with a gold Cal State logo, and shoulders two canvas bags packed with groceries. Before he has a chance to speak to her, she climbs the stairs. A long braid swings behind her as she trots, despite the heavy bags, which she plops on the balcony, and then bangs on the glass door.

Lo siento, Madrina. I'm on second shift, she calls.

He cannot hear the landlord's response, but the young woman answers, *igualmente. Hasta pronto,* she says, and skips down the stairs.

When Red jumps up, she recoils in alarm.

Sorry to frighten you, he says. *I'm the winter tenant. I just wanted to say hello.*

The girl regains her composure and smiles.

I know you are here, she says.

You are a friend of our landlord? he asks.

I am Elena. Rosa is my godmother.

And you shop for her?

Yes, twice a week. Something I can do for you? she asks.

Red is touched by her generosity. *No, thank you, I shop here. Is this what you do? Shopping?*

I shop for Rosa because she's family. I am a nursing intern at the hospital, she says.

Good for you. At the hospital in town? he asks

Yes. Mission, Laguna, she answers.

Mission Laguna, Red repeats. He laughs, and then, recognizing Elena's confusion, explains.

Sorry, I am on sort of a mission here in Laguna, so the name tickled me. He laughs again.

Elena smiles. *Forgive me, sir, I have errands.*

Wait, before you go. I'd like to meet Rosa, but she doesn't answer the door. Is there any way to connect or something I can do for her?

Elena pauses, as if considering what she might divulge, or not, so Red tries to coax her into revealing more than she may be inclined.

We're so comfortable here, my wife and I, and we'd like to invite her for a glass of wine or a meal. She's right there, upstairs. He points upward, as if the girl needs a visual. *We're neighbors as well as tenants.*

You are most kind, sir, but Rosa requires privacy. She's glad you're here, she likes to have people in this part of the house, and you can text her to say you're pleased with the accommodations.

Red nods. *I see. I might drop off a bottle of wine. A liqueur? Is there something she especially likes?*

She doesn't drink alcohol. She has all she needs, and she requires only tranquility to paint.

She paints?

She is an artist of many talents.

What type of art? he says, encouraging more.

I cannot explain, she answers. *I'm not an artist.*

Although she maintains eye contact, she seems anxious to leave, but also withholding. Protective.

Does your mother visit her as well? he asks.

My mother is with God, sir, Elena responds.

Oh, I'm so sorry.

Thank you. No need. I will see her again. But I must go now. Nice to meet you, she says, turning to leave, back down the stone steps to her car.

A pleasure to meet you, Elena, he calls to her.

Adios, she calls back to him.

Red realizes he never introduced himself. Next time, he thinks, as he looks up to the balcony, all the more intrigued by the landlord's mysterious presence.

Red has never known anyone so intentionally removed from human interaction. From a larger world. Despite his inclination to solitude, he cannot fathom how she manages nearly total isolation.

The sleepiness has passed. He won't nap now. Instead, he'll turn in earlier tonight. He decides to walk toward town to pick up croissants for tomorrow's breakfast. He's grown fond of a hole-in-the-wall bakery off PCH. Perhaps he will bring one for Rosa, he thinks, and although he knows he shouldn't, he tiptoes up the stairs, lured as if to a snake charmer, to peek into the grocery bags to assess her tastes. Nearing the landing, he sees the bags are already gone. The slider, however, is open.

A gravelly voiced singer croons loudly to a Bossa Nova beat, the rhythm pulsing like a human heart. Red has never been much of a dancer – too leggy and awkward in his youth and, later in life, self-conscious. This music permeates his body like a drug. He would like to have a partner in his arms. He longs for the gyration of hips, the heat of a woman's body. Sharon liked to dance at special events with bands or DJ's, but he demurred. If they had stayed together, they might have taken dance lessons. One of those things aging couples do to reacquaint themselves or prepare for a family wedding.

He swivels slightly to the hypnotic rhythm, as if he's somewhere else, somewhere with spicy aromatic foods and women wearing colorful tops that slip off the shoulder to reveal smooth skin. The music he prefers is symphonic – a feat of engineering, he likes to say – but this music makes him want to sway.

He peers through the screen door into a large open room illuminated by rays of sunlight spreading across the floor like floodlights. Shopping bags sit on a counter near a dining table in the corner, where two chairs perch on a right angle. He hears humming, and the shelving of groceries, out of sight.

He sees no other furniture. Instead, three easels with three large canvases line up roughly six feet apart along the center of what must have been a living room. From his vantage point, none of the paintings seem completed and all feature a path diminishing into the distance. On the first, a narrow road snakes through grassy hills bordered by wildflowers. The second, a dirt trail winds through tall trees, shadows crisscrossing like a spider web. The third seems cobblestone, like an English country road, flanked by small houses with red or purple walls, steeply pitched roofs and narrow doors, but no windows.

Red is not sure what category of art this is. He can no longer recall the lessons of art history class in college, or the weekends Sharon dragged the family to exhibits at the Chicago Art Institute. These are hardly traditional landscapes, what he read recently in the local newspaper is called Plein Air painting, as if only if painted in the open air is a landscape a landscape.

The colors are bold but blurred at the edges, like reverie. He wonders if these are studies for a larger work. Maybe they will form a triptych.

The images remind him of blueprints: elevation, scale, and dimension. The unfurling of a new concept, without conclusion. Perhaps there is a message he's missing. He knows he's no good at subtlety.

Below the easels are used paint cans filled with brushes and paint tubes, also a palette with a blunt-edged knife. The wood floor is carpeted by white sheets splattered with paint, like a Pollack. His curiosity is piqued, and he would like to see more, but he cannot without exposure, so he eases back down the stairs. As he reaches his patio, the sliding door above closes and the music volume is turned up. He fears he's been detected. He'll have to explain, when they meet, which he hopes they will, if only to understand why a talented artist has tucked herself away from the living. She must have had the desire, or need, to disappear, what he once promised to do under the circumstances he's now in.

As he makes his way to the bakery, he's struck by the many ways to withdraw, not the least of which is to bury oneself in work, as he had, or in children or latent aspirations, like Sharon. Rosa, for reasons yet to be gleaned, has vanished, in effect, in plain sight, hiding from the outside world, soothing her spirit with music and solitude, painting paths to nowhere.

He has a thought there are worse ways to live.

M ateo painted six hours a day, six days a week, accompanied by classical music. As an image came to light, he hummed to a Chopin piano sonata. When accentuating, he swayed deftly to a Mozart string quartet. The more melodic the music, the louder the humming and the thicker the pigment. Nearing completion, in that moment when a vision comes to fruition, he switched to the Cuban classical guitarist, Leo Brouwer. On the rare occasion he was unhappy with the outcome or uncertain of the finish, he warbled arias by Puccini or Verdi at the top of his lungs to beseech the muses.

Vinyl albums played start to finish as they were recorded on a portable stereo his mother purchased for him when he was nine years old, the year before she died. She was the one who shared with her son her passion for classical music. His father, who died years later, but before he knew how successful Mateo would become, was devoted to Latin jazz.

Mateo mourned his parents in part in song, even as the music inspired his art.

He had vowed as a young man he would devote himself to painting and personal pleasures. Nothing would get in his way.

No waiting tables or menial labor, his friends heard him proclaim, even when times were tough. *No diversion by the bourgeoise.*

His first two years in California, he drifted from couch to couch, sand to green. When he at last landed in Laguna Beach, he felt a connection to its bohemian persona. However, his paintings were not at all like the traditional landscapes and beach scenes exhibited at weekend or summer art shows. Buyers looking for a souvenir of their visit were confused by Fauvism, with its bold colors, thick brush strokes and exaggerated features, or landscapes bordering on abstract. Only an occasional sale covered expenses. When a developer new to town asked him to create a larger piece for a new hotel inland, and then others, these commissions made it possible to rent a room up a steep hill with a sliver of an ocean view. One year later, he moved into a studio apartment he furnished with art supplies and an easel, sleeping on a mat on the floor when not in the bed of a lover. At last, he captured the attention of a gallerist with clients who prided themselves on being avant-garde and he commanded higher prices.

Before long, he had saved enough to move, and soon after, acquired a small parcel of land where, years later, he would design and build an artist's sanctuary, and subsequently, a home for Rosa.

The second he laid eyes on the short brown girl clutching her rug, he believed she had been sent from a spiritual realm. Perhaps another time on his lifeline. Her purity, and her trust in destiny, seemed a gift from the gods, and she tugged at his heartstrings when she presented her weaving and explained her technique, as if to proclaim, *I too am an artist*, words Rosa would never have said aloud.

She spoke softly, eyes downcast with humility, although shoulders squared with innate confidence, and he was taken by her inherent gentility, as a child might take a stranger's hand when lost.

Rosa might have been the sister lost to him long ago, the wife he would never have, or his patron saint of forgiveness. Perhaps, redemption.

For all the people who were kind to him over the years, and there were many as he made his way from talented outlier to respected artist, not one embodied compassion as absolutely as Rosa.

In his later years, he would speak of her in the words of Charles Dickens, of whom he was a great fan. *'She was so pure and beautiful that earth seems not her element, nor its rough creatures her fit companions.'*

To his amazement, she managed his household like a drill sergeant, assessing daily whatever required tending and who might do the work. Cupboards were filled with supplies ordered and delivered. Laundry and cooking were handled expertly, without comment, despite the fact Mateo's home was something of an inn where friends old and new gathered. She grilled meats and installed a comal, Oaxacan style, for tortillas. She learned to prepare Cuban dishes, like black bean soup with sweet onions, and Mateo's favorite, pescado en escabeche, a pickled fish in an onion and pepper stew. She mixed pitchers of sangria or margaritas to start and wines were open and breathing for dinner.

Rosa infused into every act her gratitude and affection. In turn, Mateo was inspired by her diligence and patience, and grateful, over time, for her devotion.

He questioned her only once, a few days after she arrived. She was still learning the routine and he told her there was no need to make his bed, because he didn't mind crawling into rumpled sheets.

In fact, wrinkles can be aesthetically pleasing. There is an elegance to the folds, no?

Rosa smiled the half-smile that would become her hallmark. *Would you begin a painting on a messy canvas?*

He never questioned her again and she never pestered him with her curiosity about his art. Instead, she studied him like an apprentice. She watched how he selected and applied paint directly from the tube, embellishing with brush or palette knife. She observed his method for augmented faces or houses suspended on hills, stacked like lovers. Late at night, she scoured similar images in the books she borrowed from Sylvia: masculine women with jagged jawlines and triangular chins, magnified eyes framed with inverted eyebrows, bold blots of red in lieu of cheeks, elongated noses, and lips curled as if awaiting a kiss. Male figures were often depicted with stubble on their chins or beards as mangled as birds' nests, their faces angular and eyes glaring. They too had dramatically wide shoulders and wore the same seductive clothing as women.

Sylvia, pursuing an art history degree, took a special interest in Fauvism.

Fauve means wild beast, from the French. La bestia salvaje, si? Not savage, not in art, but liberated. Nearly feral. Passion without restraint, she explained. *Matisse, the master. His range, the color, the intricate detail, like no one else. Dufy, exceptional. Early Braque, yes, a cubist, all born of post-impressionism, after Van Gogh. Ordinary subjects are extraordinary. Color from the tube seduces the spirit, right?*

Rosa stared at these paintings as she stared at Mateo's art, as if she might be embedded in the paint, awaiting her moment to emerge.

Sundays, she walked to St. Francis by the Sea for morning worship. The antiquity of that chapel reminded her of home. She made a few friends there, although she rarely socialized off church grounds and rarely went anywhere else except to visit Sylvia in the cottage by the water. Most Sundays, on her return, as she climbed the stone steps, she would find Mateo on the balcony sipping coffee with friends or a man who might live there for a time.

Rosa was too naive to understand his passions. She saw only the beautiful man who had taken her in and smiled when she passed as if her very existence made him happy.

When Sylvia stopped by one day with nopales from a Mexican market in a nearby town, Rosa inhaled the scent and felt an overwhelming longing for home. These cactus paddles convey health benefits touted by curanderas like her mother, as well as being breeding ground for the cochineal. As the women of her village do, she stripped, soaked, and chopped the nopales to marinate in lime juice, added red onion, tomato, garlic, and cucumber, a handful of sea salt, cilantro leaves and chunks of avocado. She put her nose to the clay pot and joyfully breathed in her roots.

When Mateo and guests retired to the living room to play chess or continue a heated debate, she cleaned up and returned to the lower level, where she looked up words she had heard but not understood in a dictionary bequeathed to Mateo by his father, which now rested on the bedside chest atop her precious rug, surrounded by photos of her family. Mateo had gifted the dictionary to her in honor of their shared language and her desire to master their adopted idiom.

When at last he turned in, or when he was out for the night, Rosa moved through his studio like a thief, examining canvases in progress. She floated her fingers over his paint strokes, following each one from inception to completion. Practicing his technique, she learned to bring life to her imaginings, although she never painted on her own until after his death.

Rosa was an observer. She learned to weave by watching the elders. She learned to cook at the side of her grandmother. She learned to paint by studying Mateo. She would never have labeled herself in this way until she heard him expound on his theory that all humans fall into three categories.

We are participant, catalyst, or witness, he said one evening to a friend.

But aren't we are all three? the friend asked.

One is preeminent. Like being right-handed or left-handed. Few of us are ambidextrous, right?

True.

Living require participants, the doers, who need catalytic agents to do what they do, and we all require witness – the lens of the living and keeper of intention.

Rosa contemplated his words. She knew at once she was a witness. She also understood that without fellow participants or catalytic agent, a witness has no intrinsic value. Paints do not blend on their own, fire cannot ignite without fuel, nor a story take flight without words. What purpose does she serve if not in service to others?

When did you know you were a participant, a painter? the friend asked.

The moment I was born, Mateo answered, *when I opened my eyes to an azure sky.*

That was the night Rosa knew she was in love with Mateo Perez. Her purpose would be to bear witness to his life and devote herself to his well-being. She would derive satisfaction from this alone.

No wonder, once Mateo was gone, she was lost, taking his place at his easel and using his methods to paint paths going nowhere, desperate to excavate a route to a future she could not envision without him.

The last evening in January, sea breezes shifted to balmy winds, the scent in the air shifting too, redolent of summer, despite the calendar.

A change in the wind, literally, Red remarks, as he carries dinner plates from the patio to the kitchen and emerges with tumblers of liqueur.

Your digestif, madam, he says with a bow, as he hands her a drink, and then sits opposite, shaking his glass to spread the ice and chill the drink.

As sweet as cake, he says, after the first sip.

Sharon nods, and sips, the sweet-bitter almond flavor coating her throat like a rich dessert.

As the last of a dusky sky turns dark, moonlight appears on the water. Red gazes out as if hypnotized. Sharon watches him. He seems thinner, which she hopes is hiking, as his appetite is good.

Rain coming later this week, I hear, she says.

Why don't you hike with me before then? The views are breathtaking from these hills, he says.

Not so bad right here.

Triple that. Seriously.

But I work mornings, she insists.

Early, instead of Pilates, or an off day, he says.

I know the hiking is great, but I can get in and out of class quickly or stretch my legs walking to town. And I concentrate better in the morning, she says.

Once, tomorrow maybe, before the rain? Or once a week would be nice. You'll like these trails, he pleads.

Sharon nods. *I'm sure I would, but I must stay on schedule to be ready for the dissertation defense by May. You appreciate a work ethic, I know you do.*

Red nods, more resigned than amenable, as he shakes the glass again to settle the melting ice.

Maybe I'll go surfing with Dave, he says.

Maybe that ship has sailed, Sharon retorts.

Why?

Well, aren't you a bit on in age to take that risk? If nothing else, your lung capacity is compromised.

I am well aware of that, Sharon, but this could be a kick. Maybe better than fishing. He chuckles.

Right, fishing. I thought you were planning a trip out to Catalina some time, she says.

Yes, I will, but I might surf too, he says.

Fishing is safer, although I'm sure Dave is a good guide. You're doing so well, Red. Why push your luck?

He bristles. He'd forgotten how severe her scold when she thinks she knows what's best.

Sharon leans back in her chair, as if the conversation is over, and that too rankles.

What's the benefit of not pushing my luck? he argues. *I spent my life playing by the book. This may be my last chance to get out of my comfort zone. What was it you used to say? I play by the book, you read the books. Well, no playbook now. What have I got to lose?*

Sharon shakes her head but smiles. Leave it to Red to recall a random comment to fit an argument. Playing by the book has been his way of keeping chaos at bay, so she's surprised by this sudden willingness to test unknown and potentially dangerous waters.

To get to where you want to go, Red would advise his colleagues, and his sons, as a strategy for problem solving, *identify the destination, the goal, then work your way back from there to the source. Delineate the hypotheticals: what if, what then? Like a draftsman or a sketch artist. Until the last leaf on the last branch of the decision tree. That's the path to the solution.*

The more successful he was, the more linear, the less spontaneous, and the less like the man she thought she had married. The man who in their first years together composed and printed on yellow post-it notes, in neat block letters, for which he was infamous among family and colleagues, sweet rhymes or Haikus he hid around their apartment so she might stumble on them and smile. Although she'd been drawn to him for high-mindedness and reliability, she was delighted by such contradictions, and these made him far more attractive than the junior consultants, ad executives, or aspiring editors she dated, young men who drank too much, talked over each other or were quick to label everything and everyone with a synopsis or soundbite.

Sharon, where did you go? Red asks. *I repeat, what have I got to lose?*

You have a life to lose, which is your choice, but you will deprive you sons of what time remains, she replies, regulating her breathing to control her temper.

My life is coming to an end. All lives come to an end. I just happen to hear the ticking of the clock.

She hears the grumble in his voice and sees the frustration in his eyes, which aggravates her own, but she says no more to avoid escalating the dispute.

I would say you have an unnatural fear of death, and you should deal with that, he reprimands.

That's not so, I don't fear death, she counters.

I think you do, he says.

I do not! I fear illness. I don't want to be sickly. I want to go to sleep and not wake up, that's all.

Wouldn't we all? But that's statistically unlikely.

Is it?

She is immediately sorry she asked. Red stores statistics for moments like these and delights like a child at the cookie jar at the chance to share.

87% of deaths in this country are from disease, non-communicable disease, like cancer, followed by the less common communicable diseases like Aids and TB, then alcoholism and drug addiction. At the lower end, by suicide and accidents. So much for death by fatigue.

Red sits back, triumphant. He's scored a major victory, he thinks. Sharon, however, is confounded, not for the first time, by how much he knows, yet how little he understands.

Where do you get these statistics? she asks.

I make it a point to know because information makes for an informed decision.

An informed argument, you mean.

Yes, exactly. We never know what's next, do we? The World Health Organization has declared a global emergency, the virus is not yet a crisis, but who knows. Strange times demand strange decisions.

Well, I don't have a decision to make, other than to do whatever I can to stay healthy as long as possible and avoid being miserable way too long on the way to death. I'd rather skip that, she says.

Lots of luck, my girl.

I am not your girl, please do not use that tone.

What tone? he asks, with genuine confusion.

The patronizing tone you use when you're trying to bully me. When you talk at me, not to me, she says.

Ridiculous, he retorts.

Not ridiculous. And you're doing it again!

Sharon cautions herself again to hold back. No point to rock their boat with a meaningless argument. She sips her drink to calm her nerves, and they sit silently for a few awkward moments.

Look, I'm sorry, I didn't mean to make a fuss. I just wanted you to walk with me, Red says.

And if I don't take a hike, you threaten to surf and maybe get hurt, or worse, and then what? Who do you suppose will take care of you?

Well, I guess I'll call Nurse Tammy, he says, with an ingratiating smile. *Or Elena, the budding nurse.*

How nice. You're lining up your team. Really Red, you promised this would be a retreat, not the death march. And, well...

Well, what? he cries.

I worry about you, that's what, she says.

He sighs. *I don't mean to worry you and I won't interfere with your work. Forget hiking. I'll hike and nap and wait for you to show up.*

I waited years for you to show up, she says.

So this is payback?

Of course not, she says, in a conciliatory tone.

A short angry silence falls between them, until Sharon speaks, hoping to restore peace.

Lord, we're right back in time, aren't we?

You stand your ground better, Red replies.

Thank you. I'm working on it, she says.

Why? Why now? he asks.

I guess the better-late-than-never thing, although not surfing, she says.

Red doesn't respond. He drinks the last of the Amoretto in a steady stream, thinking, no matter her concern, it's never too late to surf. He stands to return to the house, taking her glass as well, and then washes them in the sink, placing them on a towel to dry.

Sharon follows him to the kitchen.

Tell me this, are there other now or never things I should know about? she asks.

I just wanted to hike with you. But, I will say, after watching surfers, I think it's worth trying. I'd like to think I have the chops.

Red, you are not a careless person. You respect your limitations. Please, think of your sons, she pleads.

And you? Will you be sorry when I'm gone?

She's stunned by the question, and he stares at her mournfully until she speaks.

We lost each other years ago. I mourned for you while we were still married and for a long time since. I will grieve for you, yes, of course I will, but it's no longer about us. The boys need you, for as long as you can be here for them.

The boys are solid, he mutters.

So? Sharon cries. *Did you notice how happy they were here with us, in family mode. They're solid but still young. Still in need of parents. I was eighteen when my mother died and a mess for years. You never got that.*

I do get that, but the boys will be fine, he insists.

Is that all you want? To be sure we're fine when you're gone. We will be, sure. That does not mean we're ready to let go.

But maybe drowning is a great way to go, he says, and chuckles, even as he shakes his head sadly.

Red! What an awful thought.

It's not about surfing, he insists, *although it does look like a rush I've never had. It's that the same is just the same. Know what I mean?*

Sharon nods. She's sorry she's boxed him into a corner, forcing him to face the endgame. Why should he? He has time. He's living every day to the full.

He retreats to his room, calling out *sleep well,* and she echoes the same, although she's too tense to sleep. She hates these rifts and no matter the detente they've achieved, mismatched dispositions do not fade. They intensify, like paint strokes. Even minor rumbles rekindle angst. They have been doing so well here, she hopes they don't slide backward. She cautions herself to stay on course. After all, it is his life to live, whatever responsibility she feels for him. On the other hand, two more months may be more than she can bear. She too has nothing to lose, but what is there to be gained?

February arrives. The shortest month of the year. The passage between blustery winds and rain, in many places snow, and the promise of spring. They used to take the boys on winter holidays to a Caribbean island or the Mexican coast, where sun defrosted the frigid Chicago winter embedded by mid-February into their bones. The moment they stepped down the airstairs from the plane, they were welcomed by a blast of hot humid air and, by week's end, thawed and tan, they trudged reluctantly back up the stairs to return to winter.

This winter, the rain southern California relies on has not delivered sufficiently. Neither are the mountains snow-capped. Fear of fire burns well before fire season here – drought a perpetual plague.

Beyond climate concern, the first death from COVID-19 was reported in Wuhan and China has been accused of withholding information, as if harboring the key to the genetic code.

Hank related to Sharon that administrators are debating B, C, and D plans, should they decide to close schools for periods of time. Few faculty members have lesson plans fully digitalized, nor the training to teach from a distance. The American university system relies on group classes, unlike the Europeans who proctor reading and independent study.

Panic and disorder in the ranks, Hank said. *It's either the end of the world or a killer full moon.*

Very funny, Sharon said.

Seriously. Mercury is moving toward retrograde, the first of three, which portends a hard time for many.

Sharon laughed. *If I have a choice, I choose the moon over the end of the world,* she said, hoping to offset the strain in Hank's voice.

You can laugh, but these things prove out, over and over. The universe has had us on high drive since mid-January and more crazy skies on the way.

I do concede the power of the moon, Sharon said.

Since puberty, and more so since menopause, Sharon has felt a draining fatigue at the onset of a full moon and an energy boost at the new moon. She's sexually aroused at both, like an animal in mating season, and she awakened just last night in thrall to an orgasm, as if stroked by moonlight. A moment she would have liked to have a man in her bed. However, what she's been feeling of late is not sensual, and not enervated, rather jittery, as if on alert, like birds who take flight before a storm. Antsy, she used to say, when her sons flopped around the house as edgy as languid.

Moon or plague, the signs are ominous, Hank said. *We're strategizing how to manage a mass exodus.*

A mass exodus? Sharon echoed, in disbelief.

Could be. Even if not a pandemic, we have to prepare for contagion, and no one, from the very top of government through public health, to college admin, is prepared for this. How will we handle students going home mid-semester? What if too many teachers get sick or can't work from home?

Yikes, Sharon cried.

Trustees are worried about the price tag, but I'm worried about the kids. They need structure or they'll sit on social media all day. Brains and bodies will rot.

This is worse than I could have imagined. Maybe I should come back, Sharon said.

Why? You're on sabbatical. Be glad of it. Stay out of the fray. Faculty on campus will get the brunt of it. If they need you, they'll call you, for sure, Hank insisted.

I'm glad you're in charge, Sharon said.

In charge? Now that's funny! Hank cried.

Sharon deliberates this strange state of affairs as she walks back from town. Birds of paradise line her path, as if tracking her, ready for take-off. They seem to bloom much of the year, and, as if to argue seasons, they go dormant at the time when visitors descend on their habitat. An odd contradiction, she thinks, although she's developed a fondness for these plant-creatures, and sees them less gothic, more like ribbons of color offsetting gray skies.

Red is not in his usual place on the patio and when she enters the flat, she finds him glued to CNN on TV, a rarity midday. He's so engrossed, he doesn't notice her. When she drops her bags, he startles at the sound and turns in alarm, before nodding hello.

Like watching the Twilight Zone, he says. *Or a movie I saw once, don't recall the title.*

Maybe Stranger than Fiction, she says, referring to a favorite film about the writing of a novel.

No, something about contagion, he says.

Glancing at the TV, Sharon shakes her head in disgust. *Like lions tearing their prey to bits.*

Red nods again, absentmindedly.

I'll shower to wash off the catastrophizing, just as contagious and as troubling. I'll be quick, she says.

Red looks up. *Sure. Sounds good. By the way, I stole lemons from a tree down the street, already on the ground, for the fish.*

Cool, Sharon remarks, as she closes her door.

Although a shower refreshes, she's still agitated as she preps a filet of salmon, which Red flops onto the hot grill with equal preoccupation. The sizzling scent triggers their taste buds, but when she sees him shiver in the evening air, she sets the inside table and quickly tosses a salad. At dinner, she shares Hank's account of the goings on at school and her greater concern for students. Red tells her air travel is already restricted in most parts of the world.

We should talk to the boys, she says.

They know as much as we do, I'm sure, he says.

To his eye, she appears calmer than when she arrived, despite the new anxiety. She knows he would like to be helpful, but no broken pipes to be repaired or a street made safer with a median or roundabout.

Having trouble with the dissertation? he asks.

No more than usual, why?

You seem, I don't know, less enthusiastic.

Just antsy. All this virus business is troubling.

That's for sure, he says. *Anything else?*

Nothing of note, she says, shaking her head no.

She won't admit she misses her life in Berkeley, or she's had a strange sense of longing of late, for what she cannot say.

Okay, let's watch something diverting, Red says, grabbing his phone to scroll through their watch list, but to every suggestion, she frowns.

Sorry, I am distracted. You choose. Nothing to do with the end of the world, please.

After they clean up, as Red continues to search for a film to please, Sharon goes to her room to retrieve notes from the morning's research review. She might focus better, she thinks, on work.

She's gone only a couple of minutes, but when she returns, Red greets her with a critical expression.

I thought you had turned in to read, he says.

Have I ever turned in without saying goodnight?

No, he acknowledges. *But you like to read in bed.*

The comment seems innocent enough, she does not detect sarcasm, but there is dissent in his voice.

When she was a child, reading was encouraged, but not after hours. In adolescence, once everyone was asleep, she often tiptoed downstairs from the room she shared with her sister and curled into her father's reading chair, where he would find her in the morning. In her twenties, she read aloud to her first boyfriend in bed, both before and after lovemaking, and from then on harbored a fantasy of reading to her husband, to her mind the epitome of intimacy and the best possible foreplay.

Red insisted a bed is meant for sleep or sex, nothing more.

A good reading chair is worth its weight in gold and a bedroom is no place for books or TV, he declared.

They were on the eastern shore of Cape Cod on their first weekend away together. They had spent the afternoon strolling the town of Chatham and stopped for dinner at a seafood restaurant on the water. Waves lapped the shore and beach grasses waved in the wind. The summer day, the lovely setting, and a few drinks with dinner, were as soothing as sunset. Sharon was happy to share a respite from their busy lives and, hopefully, take their relationship to the next level.

They retired to their room at the inn, also overlooking the water, and when she commented that inns were sexier than hotels, he laughed.

She persisted. *There's a sense of history in these lodgings, lives lived, passions shared, don't you think?*

Red was charmed by her romantic nature.

After they made love, she suggested they watch a movie. How fun, she urged, to watch on a big screen from bed, but Red was already yawning and fell asleep in a matter of minutes. Sharon turned off the lights and curled close to him, warming to his warmth and the pleasure of intimacy. When the surf pounded too loudly to sleep, she didn't mind. She lay awake in a post-coital glow. However, his comment about reading in bed weighed heavily on her mind. She could not imagine how anyone compartmentalizes life so rigidly. And, when he commented on the nobility of the bed chamber, she was sure he was joking – an eccentricity, perhaps, despite the austerity.

She believed then, and for years, he would come around, just as she would accommodate his quirks. He never did. All the years of their marriage, drained by the demands of the day, she read in bed while he read or watched TV in the den, or spent the evening in the garage workshop. She gave up hoping for more, although, after a time, he offered a concession.

If you use a focused reading light, I'll sleep. Won't bother me a bit, he said.

Nevertheless, most nights, by the time he came to bed, she was asleep, and, over time, the half-empty bed became symbolic of the chasm between them.

Red sits in one of the armchairs and Sharon sits on the couch, but before he settles on a film, he turns to her and clears his throat, to get her attention.

I'm a little antsy myself, he says. *Let's spend a day in San Diego. We could use a change of scene.*

We're inhabiting a change of scene, she says.

I'm talking about recreation, he says. *There are museums at Balboa Park, and a Japanese garden. We can have dinner on the way back, make a day of it.*

She hears the loneliness in his voice, despite their companionability. Perhaps it is the off season that ails them, she thinks, its flat affect contagious. Maybe nothing to do with the phase of the moon or the stars, nor a virus threatening the globe.

I'll scope it out, Red says to her tacit agreement.

A voice in her head urges her to keep her nose to the grindstone. Still, a day is just a day, she thinks.

Just give me two or three days, until the advisor meeting coming up. I need to be prepared, she says.

Good. Great, he answers, obviously pleased.

Sunday, Red grumbles over botched Superbowl plays, while Sharon pours over dissertation material. This will be a good break point, she thinks. Nothing like a little road trip and cherry blossoms to bolster the spirits, which they seem in need of right now.

The next morning, the sun hangs on the edge of a cloudy sky like a nightlight left on overnight. Sharon zips a black fleece and ties a gray scarf to her neck. She is wearing comfy rubber-soled brown clogs and black leggings. Her hair has grown in some and she likes the tickle of fringe against her neck.

Red has just returned from an early walk. He stands with coffee cup in hand watching her head out. She balances a canvas tote, heavy with books, on one shoulder, and a slouchy purse off the other. She walks tall, with a sense of purpose. Well-balanced, he has often thought, like an iconic scale of justice, although today, he would say balanced, but not always just.

She's foregoing Pilates this morning in favor of getting right to work. When she arrives at Zinc Café, she orders a latte and finds a seat at a small table off to the side, but soon she's uneasy, unable to focus on notes, so she pulls Didion from her bag for a diversion.

Slouching Toward Bethlehem. The book title was taken from a poem by Yeats' *Second Coming* and interpreted as impending apocalypse, the fulfillment of prophesy. Written after WWI, the tenor reflected the ambiguity of the post-war period, despite the triumph of victory.

'Mere anarchy is loosed upon the world.'

Sharon leans to a different meaning: the fallacy of normalcy. Nothing reverts, Yeats might have said.

Didion took the allegory a step further, exposing in her essays the dark side of the 60s in a state extolled as a paragon of self-actualization – America's devotion to reinvention embedded in California gold.

The center was not holding, the opening line of the title essay, catapulted the collection, and author, to fame. Sharon is second to none in her admiration for Didion, despite an often-didactic voice. Much like the young man at the bookstore, she thinks now.

She's so engrossed in reading, she only realizes someone wants her attention when a shadow looms over the page. She startles, as if a beast were slouching over her, and looks up to discover the man from the bookstore, the man called Sam.

I'm sorry to disturb, to get into your light, he says.

Sharon peers up to the gray eyes that caught her attention that day. He smiles and holds a book up: the Didion.

I was reminded the other day, when Jason recommended it to you. I thought it might be a good time to reread. Everything old is new again.

Sharon chuckles. *Truly.*

A little dated, not the prose but the tales.

Tropes, now, she says, *but then, remarkable.*

Exactly. We should have coffee and discuss. Like a book group. A very small group, he suggests.

I might take a while. I have to read Joan in small doses, she tends to flatten the spirit.

He nods in agreement *You have a lot of reading. Books piled on the table and a folder full of, what, notes? Are you writing a book? Maybe the next Didion?*

Hardly. Dissertation research. A late bloomer, she says, and shrugs.

Better late than never, he says.

Exactly.

He holds up a mug with film around the rim. *I was just going to reload. Want a refill?*

Sharon's coffee is tepid. *Definitely. Decaf, black, thanks.*

Sam returns a moment later with two steaming coffees and a scone, with butter and jam on the side.

In case you need a boost. By the way, I'm Sam Jeffers, he says, handing her the cup.

Sharon Mervyn.

Wait, I've been presumptuous. May I join you? If you don't want to be distracted, I won't be offended.

I seem to be in need of distraction, she replies, gesturing for him to sit.

He sits catty-corner to her. He's curious about her. He's glad he shaved and washed his hair.

To Sharon, his look hints at an easy disposition. He wears a navy fleece sweatshirt zipped to the chin and slightly baggy jeans like the ones he wore the other day. His silver hair is scruffy but thick and shiny, and his build sturdy, not cultivated in a gym, rather sporty.

They both wrap their hands to their coffee cups to warm. When he smiles, she sees the crookedness of teeth, a sign of age, and this too makes him seem a man who accepts what is, without driven to repair.

Sharon engages easily with strangers, as a rule, and she gets on well with men. She always has. She's not gregarious, like Red, but genial. She's considered interesting. In this unexpected encounter with a man who hasn't been introduced, she's tentative, but also flattered by his interest, although perhaps he's just naturally friendly, she thinks.

So, you suddenly show up in town and become a regular at our homegrown café. Where from? he asks.

Berkeley. Last five years, that is, she answers.

I lived there, a long time ago, briefly, he says. *Is it the school that got you there?*

Yes. I mean, I like the northern California vibe, but it was the degree I was after. I was in that place, that phase, I mean, when I needed a fresh start. I lived in Chicago for many years. Raised my sons there.

How many? Sons, I mean, he asks.

Two, grown. East coasters now, she answers.

Chicago might be the best American city, except for the cold, he says.

Truly. Extremely livable. And yes, the cold gets old, although I miss snow sometimes.

Not me, he says, emphatically. *I prefer the warm.*

Don't tell me you're California born?

Guilty. Fullerton. Moved around a lot, sowing oats, you might say. Landed here, chasing a girl who defied chasing. Thirty plus years ago. End of story.

Sharon smiles. *It is a nice town.*

Sam laughs – long exuberant laughter that makes Sharon chuckle as well, without knowing why.

How politic you are! Nice is so generic a word. Hardly urbane, just a small town with its charms.

That sums it up well, she says.

Or, if we're being honest, if Los Angeles is the place for reinvention, Laguna is the place to settle in.

And that makes for a nice place, Sharon says.

Here for the winter or relocating? he asks.

Three months. Two to go. On sabbatical.

Vacation rental?

Yes. On a street aptly named Coast View.

Oh? I live farther up that hill. Temple Hills. Wait, are you by any chance in Rosa's place? he asks.

Yes. You know her?

As well as anyone knows Rosa, which is to say, not well. I knew Mateo. Met him when he built the place in '98, no '99, he had a huge new millennium party soon after. We did the glass, he says.

The glass?

I'm a glazier. Was. Mostly retired now. Killed my back. I still own the business. I advise. The thing is, it wasn't great anymore. Maybe little is great after thirty years, but no point if it's not great, right?

Exactly right, she says, because she remembers knowing her life had to change the day she realized nothing was great anymore – not teaching, not her marriage, and her sons grown. She knew then that if she wanted a great life in the last phase of her life, she would have to make it great.

I'm also one of those people who believe if it's too hard, it isn't meant to be. Life is too short, he declares.

Well said, she says.

Anyway, these days, windows and doors are ready-made, but, as I'm sure you've noticed, there's lots of glass around here, or homeowners want thicker glass or tinted, that sort of thing. We do solar as well.

Everyone wants to look out, she comments.

Exactly, he says.

I'm sure there's an art to glazing, and much more complicated than imagined, but glass is glass, no?

Yes and no. All glass starts the same, with silica, but depending on the heating and cooling, the method of tempering, there are infinite variations in thickness and strength, also how the light passes through, and that makes a huge difference in how we see. In the end, it's the cutting and fitting that makes the difference. We make the right glass to fit.

Sounds like a slogan.

Sorry. Once a salesman, always a salesman.

No apology required, she replies. *It's interesting. How did you get into that?*

An uncle. I was a bit of a ne'er do well in my youth, sort of a counter-culture type. Never got through college. Liked lectures, well, some, and I love to read, but hated studying. I prefer to learn by doing.

What else do you read, besides Didion? Sharon asks, although she's pained by her professorial tone.

I've been on a mission to read the most important works – the Pulitzers, the classic canon, etc. Working through a list of fiction in translation now. I also love California noir. Hammett, Chandler. A few of the new.

Impressive, she comments.

I don't play golf, I don't garden. Might as well catch up on all I missed. A few years ago, I read Virginia Woolf. She was big on the window metaphor. You're doing your degree in lit, right?

She nods yes. *Victorian. Elizabeth Gaskell, who should be more famous than she is.*

Sorry to say I don't know her work.

Few do. She's the Atwood or the Zadie Smith of the 1800s, troubled by the fallout of industrialization and... She pauses. Sorry. I should have a slogan too, otherwise I go on and on.

What else makes her worthy? he asks, leaning in like a student, to express interest.

She wasn't the sort of woman not to marry, and she was married a long time, but major female writers then were single. Austen, Brontë, Rosetti. Others, like George Eliot, Charlotte Brontë, they married later in life.

Sam smiles. *The room of her own thing, I guess. Glass, you know, was front and center to the Victorians.*

Now, Sharon leans in. Now, she's the student.

19th century was the era of public glass. The gleam from the gloom, so to speak, he explains. *The exposition in Oslo, 1851, featured a twenty-seven-foot-high glass fountain. Great photos online, check it out. Moving and static glass, a marvel for the time. Also colored glass for effect. Very cool.*

Sam pauses, as if he's organizing his thoughts for a lecture, and in this way, aligns with Sharon.

When a ray of light passes from one transparent medium, like air, to another, like glass, color refracts, bending in relative proportion to the two. Similar effect to sunlight passing through shallow water. Luminous, like the shimmering on the ocean on a sunny day, or under the full moon.

Pure poetry, she says, and smiles.

Sam blushes. *Sorry, I get carried away.*

Sharon is charmed. She cannot wait to tell Hank about an interesting older man who blushes.

No apology required, it's fascinating. But why was glass especially important to the Victorians?

Glass was an engine of the industrial age. You might say they were the voices of refraction, he says.

May I quote you on that? she asks, grabbing a pen to scribble in her notebook.

All yours, he answers, clearly flattered.

So, glass is a medium…

Between seer and subject.

Like literature, she says.

Yes! The flow of light through glass, convexity or the concavity, is like reading. In fact, we talk about the grammar of glass.

The grammar of glass! she cries in delight.

Mateo and I spoke of that. He was well read.

I've heard only a little about him, but he sounds like someone I would have liked to know.

You would have fallen for him. Most women did. And many men, he says.

What exactly made him so beguiling? she asks.

An indomitable spirit. Joie de vivre. Also, to me, his clarity of vision. He understood the way things work and how they should fit together. Fantastic aesthetic.

The eye of the artist? she posits.

Sure. His eyes, by the way, were the color of raw jade. And he always looked at you head on. When he hired me to do the glass, the infrastructure was already completed – caissons and foundation – and the builder was working off Mateo's sketches, in meticulous detail, like blueprints, but not actually blueprints.

It is a great view, she says.

Mateo was less interested in looking out than the tide of the light. Yet the northern light, painterly light, is at front, street side, not central, as one would expect from an artist. Only his bedroom faces north, or what was his bedroom. From all other angles he wanted a glow of light, his words, from morning to night, moving as if he could feel the rotation of the earth. He said he wanted the colors of the sky and sea to be infused into the house. I knew at once he was a rare human.

Sounds like you were smitten, Sharon says.

Sam smiles. *The way you fall for a painting or a song, or a writer. The way I feel a special affection for some of the houses I've worked on. There's a spirit, maybe an aura, I don't mean to go metaphysical, but there is, and we're drawn to that, right?*

A friend of mine contends that every single being we encounter and every place we've spent time leaves a trace in the DNA, which we're drawn to.

Serious metaphor material there, he comments.

Sharon takes a deep breath, as if otherwise she might go into a pant. He reminds her of a professor she had in college, also with mesmerizing eyes. She was infatuated with him the way a young girl fantasizes the masculine ideal. She feels the same in this moment and takes a sip of coffee, afraid to reveal a slow burn, while Sam, anxious to hold her attention, goes on.

Another thing about glass that might interest you is that restoration of stained glass, a gothic revival, became a new art during the Victorian age. Highly controversial, a conflict between preservationists and restorationists. He laughs. *Still a conflict around here. But the thing is, glass takes forever to break down. The bubbles or ripples, or the bulls-eye indentations you sometimes notice, were created during glassblowing. They're not flaws, although there can be, and, under the influence of atmospheric toxins, the strength may wear down over time, like anything that's not quite right from the start.*

Sam gazes into her eyes, and she into his, and as she waits for him to continue, an appreciative smile on her face, he feels a pleasure he hasn't felt in years.

Early glass relied on glassblowers, as you know. Some still live in town. And when you think about their breath, their lungs, discharging air to facilitate a shift from embers to clarity. Not something to nothing, but the inert to the useful. Enduring. That's powerful stuff.

Sharon inhales the gravitas of his words before she responds. *Glassblowers, like all the people fueling the industrial age, were the underclass Gaskell wrote about. Condition of England novels, they're called.*

And Dickens published stories about glass in his magazine, Household Words, he says.

Sharon stares at him in amazement. Very few, other than an academic, know of Dickens' magazine.

That magazine put Gaskell on the map, she says.

I'll have to read her, he says, and then laughs. *You were most tolerant the other day at the bookstore.*

He was a hoot. I'm used to student tirades.

I'll read Gaskell if you promise she's nothing like Jane Austen. Please don't hate me, but I cannot get her. I didn't even like the Masterpiece series.

Sharon chuckles. *I prefer Eliot myself.*

I feel so much better now, he says, miming wiping his brow with a dramatic sigh of relief.

They smile, and hold the smile, like a first kiss. They would both like to reach out and touch each other, but they do not.

Sharon's brother once asked her to describe the perfect man. Without hesitation, she said the perfect man creates something out of nothing – a woodworker or a builder is what she had in mind, maybe a sculptor – and then comes home to the woman he loves, leaving all else behind. And they read in bed together.

And, Sharon told her brother, *this perfect man reads Proust. Now that would be sexy!*

They'd laughed at the impossibility of that man.

Now, she thinks, a glazier who reads Didion and Woolf is a close second.

The moment comes to a sudden halt when she hears her name called. *Sharon, is that you?*

She looks up to see Tammy approaching the table. She would hide if she could, to hold on to the magic, but too late.

And you, Sam! How are you? Been ages, Tammy exclaims. *You guys know each other?*

We met at the bookstore, Sam answers.

He stands to give Tammy a hug and she points to the chair for him to sit again.

Join us, he says.

I've only got a minute, she replies.

She stands with a hand on Sam's shoulder. Her fingernails are trim and buffed, with no bold color like her lips or clothes. A nurse's nails, still proudly plain.

Sharon, I was going to text Red today, I never got your number. You guys want to come over Friday night?

Sharon is perturbed by the reference to Red and she hopes Sam hasn't made note of it.

I owe you dinner. Maybe another night, she says.

Rain check, sure, but come on Friday, meet a few neighbors. You too, Sam. Always room for one more. Or is there a plus one these days?

Nope. How's Dave? Riding the waves? he asks.

Of course, she answers, with a flirtatious smile.

Still healthy? he asks, with a similar smile.

Tammy turns to Sharon to explain. *Sam told me once if anything happens to Dave, he's ready to step in.*

I had a few margaritas under my belt, as I recall, not that the offer doesn't stand, he says.

You old flirt, Tammy replies. *This boy is the best hetero in town, and yet, solo,* she explains to Sharon. *A loner,* he says, *but when he lets loose, he lets loose.*

I do like to dance, Sam admits.

And you like a lot of partners, Tammy says.

Ouch! Sam cries, without argument, and then shrugs sheepishly. *I am getting on, Tammy. Maybe it's not too late to mend my ways.*

He smiles at Sharon and Tammy notices.

Hey, different subject, he asks Tammy. *What do you make of this virus?*

The smile fades from her face. *Mixed intel. A few insiders I follow say way worse than the flu. Not the first coronavirus but spreading fast. Wash your hands, a lot. Drink tons of water, dehydration is dangerous, especially to those of us devoted to wine.*

Tammy turns to Sharon. *Keep in mind, people with serious illness can be hit hard by a malicious virus.*

The immune system is already under assault.

Before Sharon can respond, or anything more said about the virus, Tammy waves to a friend on the opposite side of the patio.

Do come Friday, she says. *Come early for sunset, although you both have a view. Whenever.*

She smiles at Sharon, kisses Sam on the cheek, and takes off like the tornado she is.

Sam returns his attention to Sharon, as if they had never been interrupted.

Tammy is quite the character, isn't she? I'm not surprised she found you. She's a good woman who loves to party and loves to be in the know, he says.

She is gregarious, Sharon remarks.

Sam nods. *She means well, keep that in mind.*

I can see that.

Well, I guess I should leave you to read, he says.

She's surprised by the abrupt retreat. *I suppose I should get back to my work,* she responds, like a child procrastinating on homework.

One more thing, if I may. Who's Red? he asks.

Oh yes, she replies, as casually as possible. *Red is my ex-husband. He gave Tammy the impression we're still married, he wasn't exactly forthcoming when they met. We're roommates for the winter, that's all. It's a long story.*

Sam stares into her eyes, searching for truth, and Sharon would like to explain, but she's promised to keep Red's secret.

Relationships are complicated, says the man with no expertise, he says. *When you feel like it, if you do, I like a good story. I've chewed your ear off about glass, you owe me.*

And I'd like to hear more about Rosa.

Ask Tammy about her, she knows what's what.

She said not, Sharon said.

Tammy likes being on the inside, but when it comes to matters of the heart, she's as tight-lipped as anyone I've ever known. She respects privacy.

I do too, but I'm intrigued about the landlord.

Well then, I'll leave a bit of mystery on the table for another time, he says, with a conspiratorial smile.

He reaches for her hand to shake before turning away, nodding to a few patrons as he departs the café.

Later in the day, Sam will berate himself for his pontification on glass. He fears he must have sounded like a pompous ass. On the other hand, he thinks, there was real chemistry between them. The sort of intellectual and sexual chemistry he craves.

Sharon, at Zinc, sits quietly, unwilling to break the spell. When she attempts to finish reading Didion's essay, she's bogged down by the fading hope of the hopeful in 60s San Francisco. She doesn't want to feel that way today. She would rather cling to this sudden enthusiasm – the thrill of meeting an interesting man who seems to find her interesting in return. Perhaps there is a second coming for her.

At the same time, she has a troubling sensation she has betrayed Red by her attraction to Sam. Worse, she's betrayed him all along – on retreat in body, not spirit. Penance more than solidarity. She must do better, she thinks. She can look forward. He cannot.

She packs up to walk back to the flat to make plans for a day trip to San Diego, as the touch of Sam's hand lingers like his fresh scent. She closes her eyes and pictures his smile. The intensity of his gaze. The warm resonance of his voice. And then she laughs with delight, the sound of her laughter a balm to whatever it is that ails her.

Rain arrived that evening and showers hovered throughout the week, thwarting plans for an excursion to San Diego. Red's disappointment permeated the flat – he moped around, flat-affected, having charted a detailed itinerary, seeking diversion as doggedly as he had planned their winter retreat.

Soon enough, she answered his grousing, trying to make light of it. *The rain cannot last long,* she said, as if pacifying a distraught child.

Red, no more interested in fanning the flame of discord than Sharon, swallowed his irritation, stewing, however, with resentment, at her dismissal.

The Friday night gathering with neighbors was also compromised by inclement weather, compounded by a communal fixation on the coronavirus. Guests arrived wrapped in fleece and shrouded in anxiety, all seeking Tammy's counsel, which, it became evident, they do often at the first sign of benign symptoms, also post-surgical advice, which she's happy to provide.

To their surprise, Tammy insisted they gather outside, despite the damp grass and lingering droplets from tree branches, dispatching Dave to wipe down chairs, and pile shawls and blankets for extra warmth.

Multi-colored bulbs strung overhead lighted the perimeter of their yard, making the setting more festive than foreboding. The group of middle-aged and older neighbors, casually dressed, huddled at an outdoor bar making the sort of small talk common at such get-togethers: rising real estate prices; the challenge to revitalize the heart of the town without compromising ambiance; pending vacation or remodeling plans; the birth of grandchildren, or their achievements, etc. The rise and fall of voices, chuckling or braying, reminded Sharon of the din at the café, and she had the feeling she should be taking notes. As she was introduced to one after another, Red was already in a huddle with two men, deep in discussion. She has always admired his ability to connect so easily with strangers.

Sam was last to arrive, tracing the cacophony of voices to the yard, where he hugged both hosts before greeting others who welcomed him like a hero returned to the fold. Sharon noticed him out of the corner of her eye while chatting with a slim woman named Annie, a property manager with aquamarine eyes and a neon smile. She told Sharon the rising popularity of short-term rentals has been keeping her busy, and then she complained that *those pesky clients* interfere with her tennis game. She laughed as nimbly as Tammy.

When Sam concluded salutations, he accepted the margarita Dave pressed into his hand and made his way toward Sharon.

Hello stranger, Annie crooned, with a smile.

Where's your better half? he asked.

There, with the gang by the bar, naturally, she replied, pointing toward one of the two men with Red, all three nose to nose, as if the fate of the civilized world rested on their prognosis.

After Sam asked about Annie's daughter and got an earful about college woes, she left to refill her glass and he whispered to Sharon, *happy to see you.*

His hair smelled of almonds and he was freshly shaved. A crisp pastel-blue shirt collar popped up from a navy V-neck sweater and Sharon imagined this is as formal as he dresses. She also thought, if this were a scene in a Victorian novel, she might have swooned.

Glad you could come, was all she had time to say, before Dave began ushering them toward a buffet set up on a table near the bar, where frosty pitchers of margaritas had been replenished and ice-filled metal coolers on the ground held wine and water bottles, beer and sodas.

One by one, they filled plates from platters of poached salmon, grilled chicken, chunks of cheeses, spinach salad flecked with mandarin oranges and walnuts, and thick slices of crusty bread. Gripping plates and drinks, they squeezed into a double layer of chairs circling the firepit, napkins on laps and glasses perched precariously on chair arms or on the ground for easy reach.

Annie and husband Tom, a medical technology entrepreneur, sat next to Red, and Sam on the other side of Sharon. A tall, white-haired financial manager named Richard, with a booming voice, debated bear or bull stock markets with Tom, while his wife, Caroline, a therapist, shared the latest book group news with Annie, who had apparently missed a meeting. Bruce, a bearded, heavyset software developer, wore a T-shirt with a *Lord of the Rings* logo, with plaid board shorts and Birkenstock sandals with socks. He sat near Sam with his stylish partner Alec, a marketing director, who told Sam he spent most of his work week in LA now, returning on weekends to *chill out.* LuAnn, the elder of the group, with long, wavy, nearly white hair, sported a necklace of colorful stones and wore a tie-dyed sun dress with a plunging neckline, exposing burnished, wrinkled cleavage. When she shivered in the night air, she turned to Sam with a coquettish smile, and he stood to grab a blanket to wrap around her shoulders. When she touched his hand in thanks, Sharon felt a pang of jealousy.

Tammy urged them to go for seconds.

You might as well enjoy good eats now. What I have to say may ruin your appetites, she said.

The tenor of the group changed instantly, and once plates were refilled, they sat like schoolchildren ready for reading hour.

Tammy stood before them wrapped in a multi-colored striped shawl, commanding attention by her solemnity – nothing like the usual party-girl persona. She waited as Dave refilled wine glasses from a bottle in each hand, like a waiter at a banquet.

I've been reading about the SARS contagion, also a coronavirus, and other viral outbreaks, like Ebola, and I'm concerned this one will be unforgiving, she said.

Hardly any cases in the states. Let's not get ahead of the horse, Tom piped up.

It has begun, Tammy said.

The severity of her tone startled them all.

Like bird flu? LuAnn spoke up, anxiety revealed in the strain of her voice. *Much ado about not much?*

Hopefully, Tammy answered. *Or this may be the big one public health officials have expected a long time.*

The big one? Richard repeated, mockingly.

The big one, others murmured, like a chant.

Caroline grimaced, obviously exasperated with her husband, and then spoke up in the kinder voice of the therapist. *You're concerned about a pandemic?*

Based on the few experts who've weighed in and given the sad state of the global immune system, not to mention lousy health care in most parts of the world, if it spreads, the death toll will be catastrophic. Rivaling Spanish Flu, Tammy pronounced.

Her words settled over the crowd like the mist and as foreboding as dark clouds overhead.

Bruce shook his head sadly, without comment, so Alec spoke for them. *Impossible to imagine another Spanish Flu.*

Times have changed, Tom argued. *We have good hygiene, advanced medicine and equipment, and state-of-the-art technology, certainly in the first world.*

At that pronouncement, they erupted into full-on debate, agreeing or disagreeing about details, while all wanted to believe it was too soon for speculation. The stoics among them resisted Tammy's dour prediction; the fearful grew more fearful.

Tammy pressed her case. *Stay out of crowds. As you can imagine, no one is sadder to avoid restaurants and bars than Dave and I, but must be done.* Her chuckle spread through the crowd like a wave.

Seriously, close quarters are the danger. Stay home, stay in the hood. Let's gather in our own yards.

At this, Dave piped up. *The food and wine here is always good and the price is right!*

They all cheered, but the rest of the evening was dominated by somber conversation.

Tammy served platters of sweets. Dave poured drinks. Tom held court on the nature of disease and how it spreads, mapping of the human genome and modern medical miracles. Red spoke up, saying he was certain a vaccine would be expedited based on current scientific advances. Alec agreed, postulating that the pharmaceutical industry would act quickly to reap the profits. Richard posited a serious economic downturn. Caroline considered the effect on families who will lose loved ones. Annie pondered how this might impact how we live at home and Sam wondered if the town would take action to curb group gatherings. LuAnn expressed fears for her grandchildren.

Now and then, someone whispered to a partner, expressing concern for children or grandparents, and one or another put a hand on their loved one's arm to soothe. Despite different points of view, they cleaved to a collective concern, friendship naturalized like weeds in the narrow setbacks between their homes. In the end, they were divided on whether COVID-19 was a looming disaster or a challenge to modern medicine.

What began as a Friday night dinner turned into a referendum on how little even educated, affluent people can control and how vague the path ahead.

A few men returned to the bar, including Red, while Sharon talked books with Annie and Caroline. Sam, corralled by LuAnn, glanced now and then at Sharon, expressing without words mutual concern.

Eventually, the subject matter, an abundance of food and drink, and fatigue, spread like a virus. One by one, they bid goodnight to each other and to their hosts, thanking Tammy for her counsel, and assuring each other they would get through this, because no alternative was fathomable.

Sharon approached Red to suggest they leave, and after expressing thanks to Dave and Tammy, with a promise to meet again soon, she waved goodbye to Sam. He watched her walk away with Red, cautioning himself not to read too much into it until he got the entire story. Nevertheless, he would have liked to be the man to walk her home.

Tammy may be a bit of an alarmist, Red said, as they made their way slowly down the street, crowded with even more cars than usual. *She's delightful, and no dummy, but tends to hyperbole.*

You're dismissing her too easily, she replied.

I'm just challenging her assumptions.

She's done her homework.

She's a nurse, not a doctor or an epidemiologist.

Nurses are in the line of fire, They have no agenda, Sharon said. *Physicians are building practices or protecting practices, bound to the AMA and the FDA.*

Exactly. AMA is the authority on best practice. FDA is the arbiter of good medicine. The CDC, the expert on disease control. Evidence, that's all I ask. Do you want nurses to make crucial public health decisions?

If you go to a hospital, you will be dependent on the instincts and training of good nurses. Just the other day, you were hoping nurses you've befriended here might be your backup medical care, Sharon retorted.

Sure, in an emergency, he acknowledged. *All I'm saying is it's too soon to be suggesting a pandemic.*

Is it because Tammy trots around in her tight bright clothes? Too female to be a sage?

I like the way she trots around, and that's not what I'm saying. She just has a dramatic personality.

Next you'll say she's got the vapors! she cried.

Red stopped in his tracks, turning to face her.

You two are night and day, so why do you feel the need to defend her? he argued.

Sure, on the surface, Tammy's not my tribe, and I'm not saying she's an authority, but she seems to be paying attention, and Sam said she's a solid citizen.

When did he say that? And where did you meet him anyway? He seemed a little familiar.

We met at the bookstore. And then I ran into him, and Tammy, at Zinc. He's a good guy, she said.

How do you know that? he questioned.

Tammy knows him well, she answered.

She started walking again and Red, even with his long legs, took an extra step to catch up with her.

We just don't know him, that's all, he said.

We don't know Tammy, but you've judged that book by its cover. She's a caring person. And she seems happily married. Imagine that!

You've said, more than once, some women are better suited to marriage than others, he replied.

True. Maybe she holds the secret to the good life. Maybe he's a dream husband. Whatever, she's seems to be in the know and she has good intentions.

No argument, she's a most agreeable woman. I just don't think she can predict a plague. At least, I hope not, Red said.

The dispute ended there and back at the flat, they fled to their rooms like boxers to their corners.

By the way, Sharon called. *Tammy told me that people with a compromised immune system will be at greater risk.*

Red came to the doorway. *Was she referring to me? How would she know?*

Nurses know. They have that sixth sense.

But you haven't confirmed her suspicions, have you? he asked.

I wouldn't. We agreed to the cover, she replied.

Yes, we did, he muttered, and closed the door.

The next morning, Red was up and out just after dawn, so when Sharon emerged, warm croissants were on the dining table, which they munched while reading the morning news, without further comment on the virus.

The weekend was uneventful – he hiked, Sharon read, they watched a BBC mystery one evening and part of a TV series they both disliked on the other, and while he caught up on emails, she returned to Didion, pondering again how moments of the past repeat and how little changes in any one life, or so it seemed.

R ed is pacing the flat, from the fireplace wall to the sliding door and back, waiting for Jamie and Brady to arrive. They're flying separately, landing within an hour of each other, *if all goes well,* Red says repeatedly, to which Sharon says, repeatedly, *they will get here soon enough.*

Once the boys find each other, they will pick up a rental car and make their way to the flat – the car to be driven on a trip north to Yosemite National Park, so Sharon will not be left without transport.

Red has meticulously planned their route and, at the last minute, snagged a room at an inn on the grounds. Rain or shine, they will hike the trails, visit the waterfalls, watch action movies and eat fast food. Sharon declined to go in favor of what she called *boy time.* In truth, she's in need of solitude, reminded of her mother taking time for herself when the rest of the family took a road trip.

Early this morning, a thick mist obscured the hills, so, instead of a trail hike, he walked a short way up the street facing the flat leading to the so-called top of the world, then to and fro on side streets, in case he had to make a beeline back if rain resumed. While he walked, moisture drizzled from a canopy of tall trees, the last vestige of the rains. Coastal desert sucks in moisture so fully after the rain, there's little left but a green tint to the hills. None of the loamy scent of New England he fondly remembers or the earthiness of the Midwest. Still, the air this morning is crisp, and he's looking forward to an adventure with his boys, as he has yet to enjoy an escape with Sharon.

He's also troubled, still, by the reproach in her words the other night. He is not a misogynist. She should know him better. He feels a sadly familiar rift rising between them which, until now, seemed pliable.

And, because of the rain, he hasn't hiked much this week. He's been pacing like a caged animal, his mother's description on wintery days too frigid even for sledding or snowball fights. He was imprisoned inside, rewarded with hot chocolate and warm chocolate chip cookies. To this day, the aroma of cookies warm from the oven feels compensatory.

Sharon baked only at holidays with the boys, when they were young, so Red made do with store-bought cookies. *Sweet is sweet*, he would say, which he meant sincerely, but Sharon took as begrudging. In truth, he took pride in a wife not tied to an apron like his mother. He should have said so.

This morning, despite the prospect of time with his sons, Red feels more alone than he has in years. He knows this makes no sense because he has had company, and because, in truth, he hasn't missed the bustle of family life. What he has missed is a sense of belonging. Being part of a whole. He feels acutely an absence of amorous affection. Then again, he reminds himself, his sons are launched, and Sharon operates independently, so he might have found himself in this situation whatever the route.

When he returns, the flat is warm and there is a sweet scent emanating from the oven, a homey scent, as if to welcome him back to the fold.

What smells so good? he cries.

Chocolate cake, Sharon replies. *A treat for the journeymen.*

Yum, he says, and heads right to the kitchen to find the cake cooling on a rack, brimming with chips like a pin cushion and sprinkled with powdered sugar.

Yum, he repeats, and Sharon chuckles.

While they wait, she ignores his panther-like pacing and puts the finishing touches to their comida: a large halibut filet is doused with lemon and garlic, and chunks of potatoes and cruciferous vegetables with olive oil and salt, for roasting. An arugula salad awaits dressing, and sourdough bread wrapped in foil to warm. She smiles with satisfaction: a meal to please even junk food-loving sons and a carnivore father.

Red checks the weather forecast on his phone. *Looks fine after midnight and clear sailing tomorrow, so to speak,* he says, looking up at Sharon like a child seeking assurance Santa will show despite a blizzard.

Will you set the table, please? she asks, hoping to distract him with a task.

Consider it done, he exclaims, grabbing napkins and utensils, and as he does, Jamie and Brady arrive on the patio with a shout and charge into the flat.

Something smells delicious, Jamie exclaims, as he hugs Sharon and then Red.

He makes a beeline to the kitchen and to the cake, followed closely by his brother, shouting with joy at the sight of the sweet, and then Brady too hugs his parents.

The prodigal sons return, Red says, pleased beyond measure to be with them again.

They chat, while Sharon roasts and preps, and then join together at the table. The boys describe the crowds at the airport while the meal is devoured, in a matter of minutes, and she insists they wait a while for dessert, eliciting a shared groan.

At Sharon's urging, the boys clean up and load the dishwasher, while Red pulls out Monopoly. Jamie joins him first and stakes out the role of the banker, piling fake bills at his place and playing cards on the dining table. As he and Red argue good-naturedly over who will claim which pieces for play, Sharon pulls Brady into her room for a quick chat.

Dad tires easily, she says. *He naps, most days, so might be best to be back at the inn by mid-afternoon, so he can rest. He dehydrates quickly too, keep water on hand. The meds. He sips all day.*

Will do, Mom, Brady says.

I'm going to text you now, so I don't forget, the link to his medical records, and medications, in case.

Okay. And then relax, we've got this, he says.

Just covering the bases, she replies.

Once a wife, always a wife, huh? he asks.

Sharon is pained again that her sons have had to juggle the parental divide. She also fears they harbor hope for a temporary reconciliation, beyond retreat, if only to comfort Red in his waning days. She pats the edge of the bed, inviting Brady to join her – a pose she once adopted when they behaved badly, and just then, Jamie comes in search of his brother.

At her command, he too sits, wondering what he might have done to warrant a reprimand.

I was describing to Brady what to watch out for while you're with Dad, she explains.

Jamie nods in relief. *We're good, Mom.*

I'm sure you are, and I don't mean for you to worry about him, he's doing well. Very well. We just want him to stay as well as he can for as long as he can, right? Do your part. He needs regular rest, he needs lots of water, and he needs to take his meds on schedule, okay?

A tear falls from Brady's eye, which he swipes at with the cuff of his sweatshirt. Sharon touches his hand. The sensitive son. The worrier. Rather than the concrete thinking expected from an urban planner, he operates intuitively, as attentive to aesthetics and compatibility as function. He was mesmerized from an early age with children's fantasy literature, even when he didn't comprehend, and she imagined he might be a writer, but he obsessed over wood blocks and Legos, constructing and reconstructing buildings and street scenes, and then tearing apart piece-by-piece to pile with the many other pieces stored in a trunk she acquired for that purpose, using these for years to fashion futuristic parks or rocket launch sites based on his own vision.

Jamie, thirty-three, three years older, and more physically agile, was the athlete. In play, he preferred to recreate than invent, the same sort of strategy he uses with clients now, advising them to build on fundamentals. Stoic and steady, like Red, he wobbles more than he admits, and, based on his track record, fails to stick with women.

Brady has been living with a wonderful young woman, Delia, who is working on a master's degree in public health, so she cannot take time for these visits. She's smart and intuitive, thus, Sharon suspects, she also knows Red and his boys need time on their own.

With a hug of reassurance, the boys return to the living room to play a marathon game of Monopoly with Red, stopping only briefly to cut themselves large slices of cake, before they finally give in to exhaustion and go to the hotel to rest.

The next morning, they arrive with exaggerated enthusiasm, shouting to each other as they pack the trunk of the car.

Water, check. Phones, check. Chargers, check. Underwear, check, which reduces them both to giggles.

Sharon laughs and Red smiles, his nose buried in his phone, downloading their route, and then scans the trunk as if they might have missed something, with a thumbs up.

Under a rapidly rising sun, Sharon embraces her sons and hugs Red. She watches from the top of the stone stairs as they drive away, Red's hand waving from the passenger seat until they're out of sight. As sorry as she is to see them go, she's glad to see them leave, but suddenly, she has an urge to run after them, to cry out, *stop, wait, come back, don't go.* She cannot imagine why.

She sits on the top stair gazing at a blue sky seamed at ocean's edge: infinity defined by the horizon. The air is warm and the forecast mild. She could take a walk on the beach. She could read all day. She could binge watch a series. Whatever she wants to do, she can do. Without warning, however, she begins to weep. Her body shakes vehemently. A release of anxiety, she suspects, largely from so much unknown. What Hank referred to once as the burden of sympathy, an odd juxtaposition of words describing what it feels like to caretake to a loved one battling exhaustive emotional or psychological struggles.

Her tears may also be because each time her sons visit, she has another glimpse of what might have been. There's no way to escape introspection when a vision of past and possibilities crash in a surrealistic present.

What's done is done, she bellows, rising above melancholy and standing to go back into the flat, wash her face, and start her first day on her own again.

Her mother told her, *crying cleanses the eyes and makes it easier to see.* She remembers that now, determined to look ahead.

She decides to stretch her legs and walk to town and when she arrives at Zinc, Sam is there, munching a currant scone slathered with dark red jam. When he smiles at her, one of his front teeth is obscured by the jam, like a child missing a tooth.

Get yourself something to eat and let's tell stories, if you have time, of course, he says.

I have time, she answers.

By the end of the first decade that Rosa lived and worked with Mateo, a few of his paintings had been acquired by museums in Orange County, Los Angeles, Houston, Chicago and Miami, as well as collectors throughout the Americas.

Rosa was by then his artistic assistant as well as his housekeeper. By taking responsibility for his home and workspace, she made it possible for him to devote all his time to his passions, which she believed, as so many do, the nature of an artist, as if creative inspiration thrives only in excess or depravation.

She made certain the studio was ready for each day's work. She scrubbed the few brushes he used. She scraped the palette knives. She ripped old T-shirts into cloths for touchups. She studied each painting in process to ensure that the necessary paint tubes were malleable or replenished. Upstairs, in the living areas, the dining table was always set for he and friends to dine, drink wine or rum late into the night, dance to their favorite music and sleep late into the morning.

Rosa had never known anyone as profligate in the off hours as he was productive in the studio.

Mateo trusted her completely and treated her like a loving guardian, urging her to master English and pursue a high school equivalency diploma. He sponsored her for a green card in order to escape the vicissitudes of migration politics. He helped her enroll at a community college, where she attended classes at night. She sidestepped mathematics and the sciences, baffling subjects of which, she insisted, she had no need, focusing instead on humanities. At last, she was indoctrinated into art history and European literature, grappling with translations of Cervantes and Flaubert, delighting in Victorian poetry, and thrilled by the tales of Chekhov, de Maupassant, and Dickens.

Bogged down with Shakespearean sonnets and Chaucer's old English, Mateo advised she read aloud.

You will hear the music in every word, he said, and, eventually, she did.

Captivated by the platonic ideal in a philosophy class, she recognized her own attachment to Mateo: a relationship elevated above romantic love or desire, and beyond friendship, to the divine. They belonged to each other, she believed, which few would understand and which she had no words to explain, nor need to.

To ensure her mobility, Mateo enlisted a reliably sober associate to teach her to drive. As they wound through narrow streets into the hills above town in an antique MG, Rosa delighted in the open air, sunlight and leaves chasing her toward the sky. Once she had mastered the stick shift, Mateo taught her to navigate his SUV for mobility, and soon after, purchased for her a Honda hatchback, which she drove until she stopped leaving the house and then bequeathed to Elena.

Sunday mornings, after church service, friends gathered at Sylvia's to watch Univision TV programs, a tether to their Latino roots. Afternoons, she phoned her family. She harbored hope to visit them someday, or bring them north; however, year after year, she declined Mateo's offer to fly her to Oaxaca at Christmas or for Day of the Dead celebrations, fearing, even with legal status, she might be denied return at the border.

By the start of the second decade, she grew ever more apprehensive about leaving him, and prayed to Kinich Ahau, the Mayan god of health, for her parents' longevity, so they might be reunited sooner than later.

She had no idea that before too long, she would pray for Mateo's well-being as well.

Wednesdays, when there were no lovers living with Mateo, he and Rosa dined alone. She used these evenings to test new recipes, the best of which were repeated for his friends. While they dined, he quizzed her on her studies and tutored her in classical music, and they debated the meaning of artistic movements and literary periods. Mateo took increasing pride in her evolution and cherished her companionship.

One evening, Rosa described a linguistics class she especially liked. *The evolution of language, from biblical time to the medieval, to now, a fascination.*

And what particularly fascinated you at class this week? he asked, exhorting her to educate him and making her feel she was as interesting and worthy as his most erudite visitors.

We examined the word infant, from the Latin, in fans. Como infante. Which means without a voice.

Si. From infandus, meaning unspeakable. Like the French word for childhood, enfance. He applauded. *And we all must find our voice, right? Ah, Rosa, before you know it, you will be a professor.*

Rosa might have said, I would never presume. She might have said, I will never leave you.

When she told Sylvia about the derivation of the word, Sylvia said, *but why do you seem saddened?*

Not sad, Rosa said. *I fear, however, that because I found my voice here, I cannot speak anywhere else.* She gazed toward the sea. *Out there, nothing for me.*

Rosa, you are young. So much ahead, especially now, an educated woman! Sylvia exclaimed.

There is nothing without Mateo, she answered.

But you know what he is, yes? Sylvia probed.

What Mateo and I have transcends the corporeal, she said, blushing, because she never spoke of matters of the heart, or the body, even with her dearest friend.

Rosa could not have known her college studies were only the beginning of what Mateo had in mind for her education. In the privacy of her room downstairs, with his orchestration, Rosa was instructed in sexual pleasure – not as a woman might naturally experience intimacy, rather through the attention and tutorial of his hand-selected lovers.

The sweet driving teacher, Antony, was the first. He visited one night in her room off the studio, greeting her with a hug, and asked her to read to him.

Whatever story pleases you, he said.

She sat on the reading chair in the corner of the room reciting a story by Hawthorne. Antony reclined against the pillows on her bed until, like a child, he slept. She whispered the last pages of the story to his sleeping body, stirred by his brown skin and muscular arms. When she tired, she shook him gently to release him. He kissed her on both cheeks and left.

Rosa inhaled his masculine scent on her pillow and dreamed sweeter dreams.

When he came to her door a few nights later, he

asked her to lay with him on the bed and she complied. She had no reason not to trust him. Again, she read. Half an hour passed before his fingertips grazed her shoulder, then her arm, wrist to elbow and back, like a spider. When she shivered at his touch, he noticed and smiled. He took the book from her hands and pressed her body into a fetal position, curling behind her. Their heated breathing filled her room, like the crash of waves in the distance. When he pressed his lips to the nape of her neck, she shivered again. When he caressed the curve of her hip, she gasped. When he burrowed closer to her body, she stirred with longing.

I want you to feel special, Rosa, he whispered.

She would never be certain if it was his touch or his benevolence, but she followed his lead.

Antony was followed by a long line of tutors. All types and orientation, they lay with Rosa: brown, black and white, thin or thickset, like brushstrokes. Some murmured endearments in Spanish or shared stories of their homelands. Others confessed deep yearnings and fears, and occasionally wept. Some read to her, or she read to them.

The glassblower brought tequila; the bartender poured mezcal. A writer arrived with a first edition of *Lady Chatterley's Lover*. Waiters delivered leftovers for late-night snacks. Painters smelled of paint, which proved to be an aphrodisiac. A sculptor made love to her with his eyes closed, as if she were clay.

The glazier with gray eyes shared tales of his travels and asked her to narrate the legends of her people, as if she were Scheherazade.

One by one, they pleasured the housekeeper, so she might reach that place where humans achieve the divine.

With their mouths, tongues, and fingers, Rosa's lovers came to please her and, to their surprise, like a starving orphan, her sexual appetite was not easily appeased – so much to discover, so much to feel.

When a gallerist who represented Mateo's work in San Francisco arrived for a weekend, which she did now and then, often at the last minute, she too visited Rosa and introduced her to flavored nipple cream and gadgets meant to amplify sensation, bringing Rosa to another level of ecstasy. When she returned a month later, she gifted Rosa with a vibrator, vigorous and quiet, a revelation she enjoyed for years, before parked in a drawer and forgotten.

From the first, Rosa set one rule: *No penetration, no procreation*, which they all respected for their safety as well, and because their intent was only to pleasure her and, by so doing, please Mateo.

In the throes of ecstasy, no matter the charm or the sexual prowess of her lover, Rosa never uttered a word, hardly a sound, swallowing that natural impulse to keep private her wicked secret life.

There may have been lovers who wanted more of her than moments in the dark, but they understood this was not an option. A few may have been in search of the whore to the Madonna. No matter. She studied sexuality as she studied language or the stroke of the paintbrush, never suspecting her patron had arranged for her erotic schooling with those he trusted to serve.

Sylvia, without knowing about Rosa's bedroom passions, continued to scold.

Mateo has been good to you, but you must have a man who will love you as you should be loved.

I am content. I am loved, Rosa protested.

Sylvia threw up her hands. *Buen amiga, we are who we are. Mateo will never be the man to a woman. And he is known to be reckless. Such lives have consequences – illness of body and spirit.*

They both made the sign of the cross and kissed their lips to the heavens in silent prayer.

You are a woman and an artist. Do not settle for less, Sylvia insisted. *There is more for you than Mateo.*

Time and again, Rosa replied, *I need no more.*

Sylvia failed to recognize the smile of a woman well-pleasured. Nevertheless, she gave up arguing.

The time came when Mateo retracted to a small circle of friends. Strangers were no longer welcome. When he ate less of his favorite foods and only sipped at fine wine, Rosa prayed to Pichana Gobeche, the god of healing. She counseled with her mother, but without access to indigenous ingredients, she could do little more than add herbs to foods and tonics to his tea.

When Mateo descended into chronic brooding, when he ceased taking partners into his bed, Rosa too rejected her lovers, denying her own pleasure as a sacrifice to his well-being.

She watched helplessly as his subject matter and painting style devolved to dark themes and, before long, disturbing images of injured birds of paradise in stormy settings.

At dinner one night, he spoke for the first time of illness, as if to accept and dismiss all at once.

Vincent wrote to his brother ... Mateo closed his eyes to remember the precise words. '*Today, I made an agreement with myself, which was to regard my illness, or rather what's left of it, as non-existent.*'

In spite of that citing, he listened less often to his favorite music and paced his room late at night. He took less and less pleasure in all that once brought him joy, except for Rosa's company and her kindness.

The weaker his body, the more contracted his life, and hers, bonded to his, the same.

Tuesday, February 25th, the Centers for Disease Control flagged COVID-19 a looming pandemic. Two of the three metrics had been met: a high mortality rate and broad infectivity. This coronavirus was airborne and, although not yet proven, might be sustained on surfaces. The disease had been detected beyond China and the only measure yet to meet was worldwide contagion.

Four days later, the governor of Washington reported the first official death in the U.S., although two earlier fatalities in California would be attributed to the virus. Muddled medical guidance and limited empirical data made early intervention improbable.

As if to mirror turbulent times, the temperature in Laguna Beach shot to the 80s, fifteen degrees higher than average, ushered in by dry desert winds. And, like the dissonance of short winter days with summer-like weather, everything seemed topsy-turvy, any sense of normalcy shattered.

When Sharon leaves the flat for her morning walk, she's greeted by a piquant aroma she hasn't yet noticed, and as she scans the garden, Red emerges at the top of the steps on his way back from his hike.

What's up? he asks.

Smell, she replies, sniffing the air like a dog. *I'm not sure what it is, or where it's coming from.*

Like a woman's perfume after she's left the room.

Sharon is not surprised by his remark. He may have limited vision, but his nose, as if compensation, is acute. Scent and touch are the senses he relies on, beyond a compass, ruler, or metrics.

As she makes her way to the café, she zooms in like a hummingbird on the fragrance: white flowers on a vine of dark leaves climbing a utility pole. Jasmine, as if sprung all at once. The fragrance is intoxicating. She stops to feed on its bouquet and then discovers bushes peppered with star-shaped blooms yielding the same scent, as if this plant is determined to sugarcoat the last of coastal winter. She snips a flower between thumb and forefinger to slip into her pocket, but later, when she presents the evidence to Red, nothing of the scent remains.

He left extra early this morning, when the air was cool, thinking he might have to lay low the next day or so. Although his calves ache more often these days and his breathing is more of a pant, his long legs go far. He likes being above the fray, above the marine layer, and he's adapted to the elevation. His breathing is halting and shallow, and he likes the feel of a sweat.

After a five-mile hike, after two protein bars and a jug of electrolyte water, and a long hot shower with a cold-water finish, he feels spent, in a good way. The way he used to feel after a competitive tennis match or when he was a younger man after a winning basketball game. A deep ache mid-back is more noticeable than usual, so he pops a cannabis gummy into his mouth and nestles onto the patio chaise to read. As a warm breeze flows over him, he inhales deeply, gathering air into his lungs like a squirrel storing nuts.

Sharon has been working longer hours in town the last week or so and returns later each day. She claims she's *in the zone*. He gets it, but he's unhappy about these longer absences. He's still hoping to take the delayed trip and thinking about how he might lure her to more companionable pursuits in the future.

He opens the biography of Alexander Hamilton he's been reading. Brady played the soundtrack to the musical play on the drive to Yosemite, and, although he appreciated its inventiveness and the adherence to history, he had trouble understanding revolutionaries rap. Each day, at this time, he gets through only a few pages before his eyelids grow heavy, and he surrenders to a satisfying short rest, which makes it possible to stay alert later into the evening.

He may have been in a deep sleep, for how long he cannot be sure, when he's awakened by footsteps on the staircase and looks up to see Elena descending. He never heard her arrive. As he rises to greet her, he slumps over, barely breaking the fall with his hands as he hits the ground.

Elena rushes to his side and wraps one arm around his back, cradling his neck as he rolls over. She cries out to Rosa for a damp cloth and an ice pack, and then peers into his eyes, one hand over his heart, assessing the damage. Red feels the gentle touch of her hand in contrast to the hard stone at his back, and he smiles, to prove his faculties are intact. She smiles in return as she places two fingers to his wrist to measure his pulse, before placing a damp cloth Rosa has tossed down to her across his forehead and a soft ice pack to his chin.

I think I stood up too fast. I was looking forward to seeing you again, he says, as gallantly as possible.

As he leans forward to sit up, to prove he can, she nudges him back, and he yields to her authority, taking this opportunity to study her more closely. Her hair today is loose – dark brown waves flow around her face, well past her shoulders. Instead of hospital garb, she wears a white T-shirt with jeans. A thick colorful weaving frames her neck.

Your heart is racing, although I do not know your normal rate. You clunked your jaw on the way down, there is a little bleeding. She turns his hands over to check for scrapes, but no damage. She speaks slowly, softly, trained in triage. *For the moment, it would be best for you to stay still. Let's elevate your knees to make sure blood pumps above your heart, until we are sure you're stable. We would not want you to fall again.*

Thank you, Red murmurs, pleased suddenly to be tended to. His heart is still pounding, pulsing in his ears. His legs feel weak, as if they might not hold his weight. He closes his eyes and breathes with intention.

Elena watches him, while waiting to see if his heart rate settles within a normal range.

Just a little dizzy, he croaks, opening his eyes, surprised at the feebleness in his voice. *Nice to have a nurse near, although you don't look like a nurse today.*

My day off, sir, Elena says.

Oh, I'm so sorry...

As he starts to rise, she again presses him back.

No worries. Glad I am here, she says.

Debo llamar a 911? a voice above calls out.

Creo que no, Elena calls back, her attention still trained on Red.

Red cranes his neck upward and his eyes meet dark oval eyes peering at him from a sympathetic face.

He is at last face to face with the landlord. She's transcendent, like an ancient statue in a church – not a Michelangelo or a Raphael, rather a Mesoamerican divinity. Caramel skin clings to full cheeks, melting to a rounded jawline. Her eyes are deeply set, lids nearly invisible, and her mouth is perfectly round, like the outline of lipstick on a cheek after a kiss.

So nice to finally meet you, Rosa, he squawks.

Rosa smiles and her expression seems to say, *whatever happened can be repaired.*

Elena chuckles at his decorum in the middle of a medical mishap. *Better*, she remarks, not to Red but to Rosa, as she releases her grip.

Let's sit you up, slowly, please, she cautions, wrapping one arm around his back.

Once safely seated on the chaise, she presses his torso forward, head to knees, to quell any lingering dizziness. Red complies, briefly, before sitting back up.

I think I'm all right, he says.

Has this happened before? Elena asks.

No, he answers, leaning against the chaise.

You should see a doctor, she instructs.

My wife is on me all the time to drink more water.

Yes, this can be dehydration, Elena replies.

So sorry to have frightened you, he says.

Not at all, I'm glad I was here.

Sorry to have bothered you too, Rosa, he calls.

Rosa stands silent and still, like an apparition.

I'm surrounded by nurses and angels, he adds.

Elena is a lucky charm, Mr. Mervyn, Rosa calls. Her voice, also caramel, drifts down the stairs to him, like her music. *I'll leave you in her capable hands.*

Please, call me Red, everyone does, he calls out.

In my country, we use the formal with clients.

Red nods. *Money has changed hands, yes, but I am living in your home, so maybe less formal, yes?*

Without responding, Rosa disappears, and Red is unhappy to lose sight of her, but then she returns holding a glass of water, which she extends to Elena, who trots up to grab it and bring to Red. He swallows all the water in one long gulp.

Slowly, Elena says. *You don't want to be chilled.*

Nice and cold, he calls to Rosa. *Thank you. I was looking forward to meeting you, but not like this.*

Rosa nods. *Elena is good medicine.*

She is, indeed, Red responds.

That moment, as if summoned, Tammy appears at the top of the stone stairs.

What's happening here? she asks. *A tea party? I would have baked scones.*

She makes a beeline to Red, nodding to Elena, who steps back. She peers into one eye, then the other. She studies his face to assess the color. She sits beside him and puts two fingertips to her lips to indicate he remain quiet, before placing them to the pulse point at his wrist to take a count.

Calmer now, Elena reports. *Racing earlier. 120. And a sweat. As he stood, he fell.*

Good job, she says, then looks up to see Rosa.

Rosa, my dear, so nice to see you, Tammy calls.

And you, querida amiga, Rosa says, as she slips back to her sanctuary.

I brought fabulous chocolate, Tammy calls out.

The door is open, Rosa calls back.

I stood too fast, Red says. *My pressure may have been too low, or too high, I guess. I took an extra-long walk this morning. Might be dehydrated some.*

These Santa Ana winds will knock you on your ass. Terribly dry. What meds are you on?

Oh, this and that, he answers.

You don't have to tell me, but you should know, you can tell me anything, Tammy says. *I'm like your physician. Or a lawyer. Strictly confidential, I promise.*

Red smiles. *I appreciate that.*

Better yet, talk to your doc!

I will call when I go inside, but for the moment, it's wonderful to be surrounded by lovely women.

Elena smiles. *I must go. Listen to Tammy, Sir.*

Call me Red, please. And thank you, Elena.

Mr. Red, listen to Tammy.

Elena kisses Tammy on the cheek and takes off.

You know, I'm a great fan of chocolate, he says.

And you shall have some, Tammy replies.

She reaches into her canvas tote to retrieve a small gold bag of dark chocolate.

Belgian? The best! he exclaims at the label.

Isn't it? Hard to find the real deal around here. Parse it out, please, although a little caffeine might do you good right now. And beware, it's addictive. She laughs. *Of course, I could live on chocolate. And wine.*

Sounds good to me, Red says.

If you feel any dizziness again, call 911 please.

Can I call you instead?

Call 911 first. And call your doctor! she insists.

I will, I will. Listen, why is Rosa so reclusive? She didn't even want to come too close to the stairs.

Tammy moves closer to Red, a gossip pose. She wears a tank top so tight her breasts push into a pillow where, right now, he would like to rest his head.

Do you know what agoraphobia is? she asks.

I've heard of it, but I wasn't sure it's a real thing. Like Munchausen's Syndrome, something you only see in bad movies.

Oh, that's real too. Terrible thing.

So Rosa won't go outside? Won't leave the flat?

Most people who suffer are afraid of crowds or conditions where they feel helpless or stifled. Rosa's not so much afraid of what's beyond the safety of her home, she doesn't believe she belongs anywhere else. That's my theory anyway. She's established a living crypt.

I assumed she was just painfully shy.

She is shy, but she wasn't hermitic until Mateo died. Three years ago now. She was his companion, his assistant, his nurse...

How did he die?

You might say he wore himself out. He inhaled life. Lived large. He was also a good man. Gave a lot back to the needy and made sure Rosa had a home.

There are worse ways to go, especially if a loving woman is at your side, Red says.

And I remind Dave of that every day, she replies.

I'm sure you do.

They giggle like teenagers and Red delights once again in her good cheer.

You know, long ago, Laguna was a safe house for homosexuals. Gay bars and clubs. Mateo, I'm told, was quite the player, she says.

And now?

Not so much need to hide, I guess. And then a migration to the Springs. Mateo would never have left. Laguna was home for him and home for Rosa now.

Is Rosa gay? he asks.

Can't say. I don't think so, but no one knows.

Does her family visit? he asks.

I thought they would have come when he died, or taken her home by now, but they're not people of means, and she won't leave on her own.

Red nods, processing the intel on Rosa.

Thanks for being here, Tammy. I feel better now, and Elena's a godsend.

You were in good hands. She'll be a physician someday, although we need nurses. Where's Sharon?

She's working at one of the cafes in town, until mid-afternoon, as a rule.

Yes, I've run into her at Zinc, although not lately. You shouldn't be alone so much of the day.

I'm fine. Visit me any time, he says, with a smile.

Fine? Tammy asks.

Fine enough, for now, thanks, he assures her.

As you wish, Tammy says. *I'm going to drop off chocolate to Rosa and cut flowers, and then I'm off.*

Red hands Tammy the empty glass and stands, still a little wobbly on his feet.

Tammy moves closer. *Need support? I'm short, but I'm mighty.*

I can see that. At another time, I would have leaned on you just for the pleasure of it, but I'm fine.

Call the doctor, Tammy repeats, as she climbs the stairs to Rosa.

Red heads into the house and sits on the couch for a time, monitoring his breathing until he's satisfied he's beyond whatever knocked him down. He stands, sturdy again on his feet, with a sigh of relief and pride in his capacity to rise above this thing that ails him. He doesn't call the doctor and he doesn't tell Sharon what happened, only that he finally got a glimpse of Rosa when Tammy delivered chocolate. He describes what Rosa looks like and what he's gleaned about her, which Sharon has already discovered, but she hasn't mentioned, because Red has no idea, nor does she plan to tell him, she has been spending a lot of time with Sam, beginning on the day he and the boys left for holiday, and most of every day since.

*N*o one knows for sure what their relationship was, Sam explained to Sharon that first day together. *He was flamboyant in his tastes and his nightlife, which must have been hard, you know. Catholic. Cuban family. He was true to himself, and he was also true to her, in his way. Very protective. They were deeply bonded. For Rosa, there was no one else. I mean, she had friends, a few, and a bit of a life, but she was completely devoted to Mateo.*

I have a good friend who bends in the wind, so to speak, so it is possible they were lovers, Sharon said.

Sam shook his head. *There was a real purity to their relationship. Like nothing I've ever seen. As if she were his spirit guide. I mean, Rosa could be a nun, not the punishing kind, rather the absolvitory smile with a gentle touch kind. Mateo was more like a doting uncle or a patron. And we...*

We? Sharon asked, surprised by the plural.

Contractors. Associates. We were all very fond of her. Reverential, in fact, Sam said, without elaboration.

Do you see her? she asked.

She sees no one.

Sharon imagined Rosa like a fictional character: not the protagonist, nor a heroine, rather a secondary character not expected to matter much, who turns out to be pivotal to the story.

I find it difficult to imagine a lifetime devoted to a man with whom she could never have a fully realized relationship, she pondered aloud. *After all, Rosa may be monastic at heart, but abstinence, all these years? Maybe she had a lover no one knows about.*

Well, could be, I suppose… Sam hedged. *Would certainly make a good story.*

If Gaskell or Eliot wrote that story, it would be all about self-denial. High drama, she said.

I would say low drama, if any, he replied.

How do you mean?

Rosa is the opposite of drama, not that she has no feelings. She just makes the most of very little. Like a great stew, and she is a terrific cook, by the way. Simple ingredients transformed into the divine.

Mary Shelley would have made much of this.

Or Conan Doyle. Another storyline is that despite his party lifestyle, Mateo was a loner, at heart. Friends said he was truly happy only in his studio. An artist I know claimed he was more Cezanne than Van Gogh, whom he idolized, because solitude was his métier, even if invigorated by a crowd. I guess that's how he resisted the inclination to retreat too deeply into himself.

Which is exactly what she has done, she said.

Right.

They were seated at the edge of Zinc Café patio. Tables dotting the sidewalk were framed by wide white umbrellas, like a copse of trees, heaters tucked into their branches. Tiny birds zoomed all around to snare crumbs, their chirping a soundtrack. Coffee drinkers crowded together at tables, debating loudly, laughing loudly, sipping steaming brew in oversized mugs. Their exuberant chatter echoed the birds.

Speaking of a crowd, she remarked. *I've seen many of these folks here before. Often, in fact, like a posse. Like this patio is their clubhouse.*

You might say, yes, he said. *Habitual, like the lifelong villagers in Europe. Supposedly the secret to longevity, I'm told. I bet you're not part of a gang.*

No, not me. I do miss pals I've left behind though.

In Berkeley? he asked.

Some, but mostly fellow moms and good friends in Chicago and Boston. And you? You have a gang?

You get to know a lot of people after thirty years. It's a friendly town and we tend to run into each other more than plan visitations, although there are plenty of neighborhood parties, as you now know, and an active bar scene.

The best part of a small-town, she said. *So, tell me more about Rosa. Mateo left her the house, that's it?*

I'm not sure he had much at the end, although his later work sold well. He lived above his means, and he was generous to people in need. For her, especially significant, I think, for a migrant to have a home.

Absolutely. And he made that happen before he died? No hassles, about her being Mexican?

There were hassles, but she was his wife.

They were married? she cried.

A year before he died, they wed on the patio. A hippie priest dressed all in white presided, and a small crowd was invited to witness. Rosa got a little drunk on champagne. She wasn't much of a drinker, not then.

Not then?

She drank through the first year of grief, but no more. Mateo remodeled the lower level to cover property taxes and stay afloat. Tenants like you, you're helping to ensure her sustenance.

How do you know all this? Sharon asked.

As I said, small town. Also, Mateo's lawyer is my lawyer, Sam answered.

What about confidentiality?

He shrugged. *Mateo was already gone. And they were a fascination. Rarely have we seen such devotion, as incongruous as it was. Enviable, for a lot of us.*

Sharon was thoughtfully silent, prompting Sam to ask, *what are you thinking?*

I often wonder what it means to be devoted. To a person, or a passion, for that matter. How many of us are? Devotion, loyalty, duty, they're not the same. The greater question is, how much is anyone willing to give without giving up too much?

Why does devotion require sacrifice? Why can't you be dedicated to someone, or something you want to do, without compromise? Sam asked.

In theory, we can. In practice, not so easy.

I cannot be sure, or provide proof, but I think lots of people are devoted to each other in a balanced way. Never worked for me, but not for lack of trying, I hope.

You're a romantic, she said, with a smile.

Or delusional! Devotion, by definition, requires a target. In effect, Rosa ceased to exist without Mateo.

Never seen since? she asked, incredulous.

She was reported lurking on the periphery at her friend Sylvia's funeral last year. Not like Mateo's. At his, roughly two hundred attended, mostly men. Also people in the community who benefitted from his largess. They all paraded from the house to the beach with a passel of strolling violins. Quite the scene.

You were there? Sharon asked.

Yes. A friend of Dave's organized the paddle out. It was October, the water was still pretty warm. Maybe a hundred people in the waves, on boards or swimming. The rest watched from the sand as they circled into a group whoop, then a few elegiac words were spoken, and then they returned to the beach to rock out to the drummers from the full moon drum circle. Ever been? Positively primitive. They carried on late into the night. Even the police looked the other way.

Rosa must have been there, Sharon said.

No one saw her if she was, and Tammy knocked at her door on the way, but no answer, he said.

Terribly sad. And his paintings?

Mateo had already sold the ones he wanted to sell, so Rosa kept the few landscapes she hung at the rental, where you are.

Fauvist, yes, she said.

Right, the early work. He switched gears before he died, more Magritte than Matisse. I'm not sure where those are. Spooky images. Strikingly different.

She never had her own life, did she? she mused.

Well, her life has been better than she might have had on her own, he said.

But everything was about Mateo, she argued.

She loved him. And he took care of her. She might still be cleaning hotel rooms otherwise, he countered.

Or, she might have been an artist.

He also subsidized her education, he said.

Why would he do that if he didn't want her to expand her horizons? she asked.

He wanted her to choose her pursuits, and she chose to stay with him. Something to be said for a woman totally satisfied with a man, even if oddly so.

A complex woman, Sharon murmured.

Sam laughed. *Sorry, I don't know one woman who isn't. Way more than we mortal men.*

Is that why you read women's literature? Trying to figure us out? she chided.

I guess. But what I've read, selflessness is rare. I wonder if that's why so many of us are fascinated with Rosa. Nearly holy in her self-abnegation.

You've never been married? Sharon asked, too curious not to inquire.

He shook his head. *For me, women don't stick, not the good ones.*

Sharon stared at him a moment, trying to figure out if he was self-pitying or proud.

A friend of mine says they stick if they're meant to stick, that's a quote, she said.

Your friend could be my friend. The thing is, I'm too easily disappointed. I expect too much, I guess, he confessed.

Let me make sure I've got this right: you expect too much, so no one is worthy, she parroted back.

Sounds awful when you say it. Or maybe I just never grabbed the gold ring.

Maybe you like your life your way, she said, and before he had a chance to respond, she added, *I mean, we all do, but compromises must be made, unless you prefer to be alone, like Rosa. Or learn to be alone.*

Being alone works for you? he asked.

Sam stared as if he might see into her heart or read her mind, and she squirmed under his gaze.

Red and I were together a long time. We made a life, we raised sons, we tried to be supportive to each other. In the end, having hit a wall too often, I thought, okay, enough. We're done. So I started over, by going back, so to speak, to get what got lost along the way.

We don't always know what we're signing up for until after we've signed up, right? he asked.

But we think we do, don't we? she answered.

Sam smiled, knowingly. *I'm guessing you prefer the slow reveal. Literary style.*

The curse of the bookworm, she acknowledged.

The trick for me is to get past the rush, he said. *When that's gone, I get pretty ornery. I get ornery when I'm thirsty too, want something?*

Sharon studied him as he waited in the café for tea, as if committing him to memory for a sketch. She would tell Hank he's not handsome, rather ruggedly attractive, like the older Jeff Bridges.

When Sam returned, he sat, leaning toward her to speak as if he'd rehearsed. *So, something I need to say. I find that most women, wait, the wrong way to start a sentence. The women I've known, I mean, the women I've cared about, all have one thing in common. They're quick to denounce or resent what they don't like or want, but rarely express what they do want.*

Sharon had never heard that said in that way and she was loathe to admit she fit that mold: quick to reject what disturbs, without voicing an alternative.

I hope I haven't offended, Sam said.

No, although of course, all women are not alike and we do not like being judged in a block, but there is some truth to what you say. Too many of us don't feel the right to make demands. Maybe Rosa never got more because she didn't ask for more. How could she? She must have been drowning in gratitude.

He took her in and made sure she was as happy as a woman could be. And she knew she could count on him, Sam said. *That's more than most of us get.*

She was a moon in his orbit, she argued. *His housekeeper, his helpmate. So what if he cared for her? So what if he saw to her education. Isn't that a little like teaching a slave to read?*

On the surface, sure, but their relationship was symbiotic. He had care and companionship, and she's safe, she's independent. She paints now, she lives in a beautiful place. I'd say that's a happy ending.

Still feels opportunistic to me, she said.

Transactional, I suppose, he acknowledged.

Or she chose a road more easily traveled, as so many of us do, she remarked, as if to herself.

Do you regret the way you got to this point in time or just that you didn't get here sooner? he asked.

I made choices I thought were best then. I had choices. What I regret, or resent, is that I made most of the most important decisions on behalf of the people I loved, not always in my best interest, she said.

What was it then? You didn't think you could do or be what you wanted without undue compromise? My mother used to say what's good for mom is good for all. Why didn't you believe your aspirations were worthy?

Women of my generation suffer an insidious form of self-doubt. Maybe still. Too many see doors ajar, not open, and we consider everyone else first. We have a heightened sense of duty to the people we love.

Maybe you were afraid you might fail, and then the means would have been too great. Is that self-doubt or is it martyrdom? he asked.

Sharon felt as if she had been smacked. She sat back and stared at Sam with obvious dismay.

I've offended, sorry, I am so sorry, he pleaded.

What gives you the right to judge? You don't know me. You don't know what my options were. You have no clue what I was dealing with, she argued.

No, right, you're right. I'm sorry. I'm just frank to the extreme. My sister calls me out on this all the time.

You do not have the right, Sharon repeated, disturbed not only by his superficial appraisal, but by the truth in it. She had leaned into the easier path, as noble as she might have thought it was at the time. She chose security. She chose a traditional lifestyle. She could have forfeited the safety net in favor of her goals, and she could have challenged Red to support her on her way. In truth, she was no more devoted to her own aspirations than to her marriage: a painfully sobering realization.

What does it really matter now? she muttered. *I'm getting what I wanted, just later than sooner.*

Sam leaned in seductively. *Earlier blooms, they open with color and scent, but later blooms are the more spectacular for taking their time. Maybe you've always been on the right path.*

He took Sharon's hand and pressed it between his for a moment before bringing one palm to his lips to kiss. A sharp electrical charge ran through her body.

I only express myself, as judgmental as I am, to people I respect, he said. *Never good to hold back, not words, affection, or intention. That's the road to regret.*

Every one of her senses were engaged and if they had not been at a café in full view of prying eyes, she would have kissed him, and she might have said, if she were a woman to speak up, what I want right now is to be with you.

Let's take a walk, shall we? he suggested.

They strolled past shops toward the towering Presbyterian Church and then to a sculpture garden behind a stone wall, where they sat on a bench facing a fountain, sheltered by statues reminiscent of Rodin. After a while, Sam took her hand again and they made their way toward the ocean and on to the boardwalk along the beach, uphill to a picturesque spot where the iconic finale in *Now, Voyager* was filmed.

Let's not ask for the moon, we have the stars, Sam recited, in a mock Bette Davis accent.

Sharon laughed, visualizing the famous actors fusing their cigarette smoke.

They continued through Heisler Park, a winding path above the rocky coast, and as the sun began to descend, they turned back toward town.

They walked slowly, trying to slow time, until they arrived at Sam's white pickup truck.

Would you like a ride? Or, well, would you like to come to my place? he stammered.

She imagined Mrs. Gaskell's spirit commanding restraint, yet she wavered. She would have liked to consummate the day, but she also felt an inclination to flee. Self-doubt reared its ugly head: fear of being seen naked at this age, fear of sexual clumsiness or inadequacy. Fear of ruining a second chance.

I think a ride home is best, she answered.

Is that what you want, Sharon? he asked.

She saw in his gaze what she most needed: she can tell this man anything. She can be herself. No need to hold back. Still, she hesitated.

As well as a late bloomer, I am not impulsive, she answered. *Take it or leave it.*

He laughed. *That's the ticket, speak your mind. I'll take it.*

When they arrived at the garage at the rental and Sharon opened the door to step out, Sam stepped out as well and came to her side. He pressed her gently against the truck, his body close and warm, waiting for a green light to kiss.

He wondered if she were the sort of woman who might stick. One thing he knew for certain: they were too old and too wary of past hurts to play games.

They kissed – a deep, ever-deepening kiss. A kiss so charged, Sharon regretted her hesitation.

When at last they parted. Sam escorted her up the stone stairs and after another kiss, took off.

Sharon listened to his footsteps, the car door open and close, and the thrum of the engine, watching as his headlights illuminated the street until dark again.

She felt painfully alone, the flat silent, vacant without Red or her sons, and now, without Sam. She hardly knew this man, but his absence filled her surroundings. She remembered the same feeling after her sons were born – moments before, a promise, and moments later, as if they had always been.

And then, Red invaded her thoughts. There was a time, long ago, she wanted him, needed what he had to give, she thought, and then, day after day, she let go, resenting what he could not give. Sometime soon, she will have to let go for good. What might he need from her between now and then, she wondered, and what will she be willing to give? Or give up.

Too stirred to sleep, she brewed chamomile tea, wrapped a blanket around her, and sat on a chaise on the patio late into the night, contemplating what is owed to another in the name of love. She shuddered at the prospect of romance and erotic pleasure, which she had been certain were no longer options, like much relinquished to age or uncertainty.

She is not monastic, like Rosa, yet she has lived in isolation too long. Denied herself a fuller life. She's old enough and free enough to throw caution to the wind. Why not? she pondered, with a surge of delight. Only a fool wastes a second chance.

In the 17th century, Dutch artists adopted a style of painting that became known as Vanitas. Before then, Memento Mori, meaning *remember, you must die*, was illustrated with images of skulls, clocks or smoldering candles. Classic specters of death.

Vanitas paintings evoked ephemerality in new ways, encouraging the letting go of self-indulgence – the vanities – that serve no purpose in life. Plantings or flowers might be in full bloom, but tainted by an ominous presence: a bone, a dry leaf fragment, the sand of an hourglass voiding slowly. Graceful flower petals would be frayed at the edges, implying fragility, and branches bowed to the ground in acquiescence.

Stop paying attention to blooming, these Vanitas painters argued. *It is not the blossom that matters, it is the substance.*

If Rosa had been more astute, or sophisticated, and less blinded by her love for Mateo, she might have been alarmed by his shift in subject matter and style. Instead of portraits of elegantly sculpted faces and flamboyant clothing, or hills speckled with colorful boxy houses, he began to create surreal clusters of birds of paradise. One after another, predatory and fearsome, their beaks pointed at each other in heated debate, as if descended into anarchy.

Bird of paradise, the plant, is recognized for its unique configuration of flower: three orange and three sapphire blue petals meld into one. The bird for which it's named, found mostly in New Guinea and Australia, is rivalled only by certain pheasants or hummingbirds for its vibrancy. In tropical climates, it is said to signify fidelity. An emblem of devotion.

If, as Mateo told Rosa, a bird in flight embodies hope, there was no doubt that his Vanitas versions symbolized despair.

Day after day, he painted birds of paradise – all startling and haunting in their exaltation of doom and a warning to release the hold of a material world.

Instead of sun-drenched or peacock blue, the petals of these were blood red, their beaks scorched or withered, muddied or permeated with mold or fungus. In the backgrounds, branches of palm and eucalyptus trees dangled or littered the ground, perhaps stricken by a storm, set against bleak skies or hillsides mottled with fire-blackened remains.

Portraits of paradise fouled, as if nightmarish bird-plants might repel the shadow of death, when, in truth, Mateo knew, they ushered death to his door.

Sharon left Red with a shopping list he decided to fill on his drive back from his appointment with the oncologist. He might have gone directly to a nearby Trader Joe's; instead, he took a scenic route through a tony neighborhood in Newport, along broad tree-lined streets spotted with oversized houses and bounded by stucco walls or manicured lawns.

He cruises along in Sharon's hybrid, which he thought might be too tight for his size, but he's found quite comfortable. He does not bother with the GPS, as the compass is in the landscape here: north and east to the mountains, west and south to the sea. Like sailing by the sun. He likes being able to center himself on the terrain.

He stops at a market he's heard has a good wine selection and where he's certain he'll find the staples on her list: olive oil and garlic, which deplete quickly with all the grilling and roasting; Dijon mustard for the vinaigrette dressings she favors; vegetables and salad stuff, bread and chips, and the like.

When married, Red stopped at the supermarket only when he received a call to pick up milk or eggs on his way home from work. His palate, as Sharon has more than once pointed out, is middling. Midwestern. His mother's meal planning was regimented. Monday, roast chicken. Tuesday, roast beef. Wednesday, pot roast. Thursday, stew. Friday, fish, which she breaded and fried, and Saturday soup, the remains of which she froze for blizzards or neighbors in need. Sundays, honeyed ham or, if affordable, leg of lamb, his favorite, with mint jelly.

As demanding as Sharon's schedule was, she carved out time most nights to cook a variety of what she believed to be nourishing meals, a repertoire of dishes to please and also meet the appetites of growing boys. Years later, she condemned her efforts for being too heavily laden with pasta dishes or rice casseroles. Too starchy, she said, although seemed right at the time. Their kitchen was filled with the aroma of hearty food, and leftovers in the fridge for late night snacks or when time was too tight for more than a rushed meal.

Today, Red feels a virgin, in effect, at an upscale market stocked for chefs or the food obsessed, and, because this place is new to him, he's unsure of the layout. With nowhere to be and no other errands, he starts at aisle one and meanders to the next, perusing well-stocked shelves and end-aisle displays, reversing one to another like switchbacks on a mountain road, with the same sense of disorientation.

The store is stocked with goods that have little to do with need and everything to do with want, and he stops frequently to gape at the profusion of brands and ingredients, all, to his mind, superfluous.

In this contentious political season, on the way to a presidential election, and the concurrent pervasive racial tensions, Red has become terribly conscious of the material abundance afforded only the well-heeled. Choice is a luxury, what most of his life he thought the definition of success: choices and luxuries. Even so, neither he nor Sharon were big spenders and they were devout savers. In this way, they managed to educate their sons and build a retirement nest, an achievement very few can claim. Now, living simply in retirement, and despite the frills of a retreat at the beach, he wonders, not for the first time, what it means to be successful. He has never taken the time for that sort of deliberation. He followed a linear path to what he believed was the good life and a solid foundation for his sons. It's a cliché to say time is the truer metric, he knows, especially when time is growing short, and he also knows ample quality time is a perk of affluence. Nevertheless, he's grateful for what he's earned and unabashedly pleased to reap the rewards.

In a rare show of impulsivity, he succumbs to the seductive merchandising. Why not see what money can buy? He takes jars of sundried tomatoes and sweet red peppers because a sign claims they taste great with fish. He picks up a red lentil pasta, which he thinks would infuriate an Italian but will please Sharon. He buys tortilla chips infused with sea salt and lime, and crackers with olives and figs. In the refrigerated case, he grabs beet hummus, because the pink color catches his eye, and guacamole Sharon will doctor with lime and cilantro. In the produce aisle, he chooses vine-ripened whole and cherry tomatoes, organic oranges, bright yellow lemons, large red grapes, basil, cilantro and parsley. At the cheese counter, a potent Pecorino and a cheddar, and a goat cheese log. The scent of cinnamon hazelnut coffee calls to him and prepared smoothies promise antioxidant benefits. As if a reward for a preponderance of healthy choices, he grabs two bags of chocolate chip cookies, one with macadamia nuts, the other with sea salt and streaks of caramel.

He takes his time choosing wine, filling a six-pack with cabernet and pinot noir, and another with dry whites. And then, the crowning glory: chocolate fudge, pistachio, and coffee-infused ice-cream. Why not enjoy dessert tastings as well as wine? he thinks.

At check-out, he unloads the cart and watches each item slide to the scanner. When it adds up, although he shouldn't be surprised, he's wowed by sticker shock, and makes a mental note to tell his sons about his shopping spree, hoping to delight them with his spontaneity and largess.

At the car, after he loads the trunk, he slumps into the driver's seat, not a moment too soon. The smallest exertion tires him lately. He breathes deeply until his heart settles to a steady pace. The scans, the doctor explained, indicate a slow creeping metastasis, beyond the lungs and the lymph nodes surrounding the chest cavity, but not yet to the major organs. Chemoradiation is the next step – a treatment Red has promised to schedule no later than April, and which he hopes to do locally.

Since he returned from holiday with the boys, he has decided to advocate to extend their stay. He's more intent on exploring surrounding towns and, he hopes, enjoy more time with Sharon, although she's been increasingly preoccupied. He suggested she work more often at the flat to take advantage of sea breezes and ocean view, but she said she prefers to study at a café and then relax at the rental.

He hasn't expressed his disappointment beyond a shrug or a sulk, which of course, she noticed, so, last night, she suggested they visit the meditation garden on the way to San Diego one day soon and, instead of streaming a film, they played backgammon on a board they discovered in the spare closet, a game they used to play on holidays, and the one board game Sharon enjoys. Tonight she has promised a sunset stroll at the Montage resort, where a path winds through formal landscaping above a breathtaking beach.

In fact, Red told Barry on a phone chat earlier, *Sharon seems more relaxed and in better spirits than she's been in some time. She seems happy to be here. We should have spent more time like this sooner.*

You didn't have much free time, my friend. You were busy building a business and then managing a business, and Sharon was busy too, Barry said.

Even long weekends would have been a good idea, Red said. *Women need that. Pay attention, pal.*

Oh, you cannot teach this old dog new tricks, but I hear you. Don't beat yourself up. You know what they say about hindsight.

2020. Ha. The right year for it, Red said.

Right. And, lest you've forgotten, Sharon wasn't happy, period, and she let it pile up like bricks into an unbreachable wall. That's the way she is.

Yes, but I must take some responsibility for that.

What's the point now? Barry asked.

Right, too little, too late, Red muttered.

Sharon's words. Sadly true. He has to face the fact there is as little chance of changing course in their relationship as defeating cancer. All the more reason to coax a bit more time with her while he can.

Back at the rental, he shelves the groceries, has a snack of tortilla chips with the pink hummus, which, to his surprise, tastes as good as it looks, drinks two bottles of water in rapid succession, and settles onto his chaise. He used to consider this down time, but here rest feels right. Just what the doctor ordered, although difficult for him not to fear he's wasting time. His father used to say, *idleness is the devil's workshop.*

As he looks out over the flower line to the waves, he hears the slider upstairs open. He sits up, listening for Elena, but no. Perhaps Rosa wanted a breath of fresh air. He waits for the music, but no sounds other than the hum of traffic below.

This may be the opportunity he's waited for. He has also purchased dark chocolates, recalling Rosa's fondness for the sweet. He goes back into the house to retrieve the box and climbs the stairs to place it by the door; however, fearing the chocolate will melt, he calls out to her.

I've brought a gift, Rosa. A thank you for rescuing me the other day. But it will melt in the sun if I leave it.

There's no response at first. *Or I can leave it at the front door,* he calls. and then, as he's about to head that way, Rosa comes to the sliding door, peeking out like a tiny bird wary of a hawk.

She smiles when she sees Red holding up the chocolate. *You are kind, Mr. Red, thank you,* she says.

Chocolate lovers must stick together, he says.

As he extends the box, she opens the door and grasps the edges with two fingers as if the touch of another person might be painful, and then turns back.

Red hurriedly calls out. *Sharon said you wove the rugs – do you sell them? My sons need something decorative for their apartments.*

Rosa stands inside, out of harm's way. *They are not for purchase.*

That's too bad. What about your paintings, do you sell those?

No, she states flatly.

Because they're incomplete?

The moment he speaks, he realizes he should not have seen her unfinished paintings and she will know he's been spying on her.

I don't sell them, she repeats.

But may I see them sometime? he asks, hoping she did not make the connection.

Thank you for your interest, she replies, a non-response, so Red tries a different tactic.

I like the paintings here by Mateo Perez. I've been reading about Fauvism, in that book on the shelf. Are there others of his I can see?

In the museums, she answers.

Right. Do you paint in a similar style? he asks.

Like his early work, yes.

Oh, he painted in periods, like Picasso?

No one is Picasso, she says.

Red notices a small smile on her face and he too smiles. *That's true. What did Perez paint later?*

Rosa doesn't reply, and as Red is about to pose an alternate question, she says, *he painted his end.*

Red is shaken by that thought, unwilling as yet to face the implications of the end of his own life.

Do you paint ends or beginnings? he asks.

There is another pause before Rosa answers. *Perhaps they are the same.*

Her words ring a bell. Something Sharon said once about a novel, something about beginnings and endings being merely entry or exit points. One of the literary comments she used to make to challenge him to think differently. Expand his mind to the abstract.

Maybe that's what all art is about. Like the books my wife studies – more about how it began and how it ended. What's between, the details, the logistics, we say in my business, that's what matters. I was an engineer. How it begins or ends, less important to the between, right? The means are how things evolve.

Red realizes he's rambling, and not sure why or how Rosa will interpret, but just as he hopes to revert to the subject of art, he is gripped by a coughing fit.

Rosa disappears and emerges a moment later with a glass of water. She watches him, waiting for the fit to end. When at last he catches his breath, panting, but not coughing, she reaches out the glass to him and he takes it with a grateful nod, sips, sips again, and then, certain the bout is over, gulps down the rest.

Thank you. Sorry for the bother, he says.

You are feeling better? she asks.

Yes. Comes out of nowhere sometimes. Takes a few minutes to pass. I'm fine now, he says.

Rosa smiles a smile of comfort. She knows what illness looks like. She knows what dying looks like. She turns back inside, but before she shuts herself in, she calls out, *thank you for the chocolate, Mr. Red.*

The volume on the music is turned up and Red is crestfallen, like a teenager who's spruced himself up for a party, hoping to dance with a girl he fancies, but she never shows up.

He describes the encounter to Sharon at dinner. They are sitting at the dining table enjoying the pasta she prepared with his ingredients. He has uncorked a fresh bottle of wine and pours a taste like a sommelier – first a sniff, then a swirl of the glass, and then, with a satisfied flourish, pours a glass full. Sharon chuckles and he smiles sheepishly at the pretense.

They share in that moment a sense of well-being in good food and wine, and a broad sky turning dusky blue. Red takes a deep breath, a satisfying breath, and without coughing. He feels better tonight, despite the medical report, which he hasn't mentioned, nor has Sharon inquired, because he never told her he was seeing the physician.

Does she look like a Zapotec? Native American? That's the image I have in mind, Sharon asks.

Well, she's short, squat, mocha brown, with thick hair, not long, kind of wraps her face like parentheses.

And small? Odd how large she looms, she says.

Small, but sturdy. Earthy. Hard to reconcile with self-imprisonment, he elaborates.

Agoraphobia is a delicate psychology, she says. *You don't want to frighten her.*

But she must be lonely, don't you think? She lived with him so long, and to live in his house after he's gone, must be hard, he says.

I imagine so, she says, touched by his empathy.

She sips the last of a South African white he's purchased, which also pleases, and pours another half glass. She eases into the relaxation of the wine, the scene, the simple pleasure of their lives at the moment.

However odd her life seems to us, she may be content, she muses.

Content or resigned? he asks.

Good point. Not the same, she says.

I was thinking today how fortunate we are to have had the choices we've had. I wonder if Rosa chose her way of life or got stuck with it? he says.

Sharon is reminded of her conversation with Sam about what we choose or what is chosen for us.

Choices can be so confined by limitations they're not choices at all, she responds. *What was Rosa to do? Young, migrant. Mateo must have seemed a savior, but gratitude may have compromised her ability to explore alternatives. Still so. She's trapped by the failure to see what's possible or how to get there.*

Were you trapped in our marriage? he asks.

Sharon is baffled, and moved, by the question. Irrelevant now, but strikes a nerve. She swipes at tears on her cheeks.

Why now? she asks. *That's the sort of question you should have asked a long time ago.*

I was busy building a business. Making a life for us. Not a good excuse, I know. I should have asked. I should have done a lot of things differently. I wasn't there, but I'm here now.

He stares at her, eyes pleading for forgiveness, and to her silence, murmurs, *I know, too little too late.*

Sharon wipes away the last tear and places a palm over his hand.

We had a good long run, and we have terrific sons. We're in this lovely place, we're getting on fine. More than fine. We're blessed. More than most divorced couples, for sure. More than most, period. I didn't mean to go south on us. And I'm sorry I've been preoccupied. This retreat is a wonderful gift. You might say we have the moon, why ask for the stars? she adds, recalling Sam's impression from the film.

Red is confused by the quote, but he nods as if he gets it, assuming a poetry reference.

Right, good, thanks, he stammers. *No more post-game analysis. No existential angst. Promise.*

Ah, but I thrive on the existential, she says.

They laugh together and clink wine glasses to toast the moment, savoring amiability.

Sharon thinks off season may be more than a breather. Off season may be restorative after all, and in the vibrant winter sunset painting the sky tonight, the promise of spring.

Sharon and Sam have taken off after the morning traffic hour for Long Beach, where his company is installing glass for a building downtown and he's been asked to be another pair of eyes on the finish.

Like Red, he has been pleading for more of her time, and an overnight, so she planned their escape by telling Red she's meeting with a colleague in Los Angeles. When he offered to drive her and wander while she's busy, she declined, insisting she will need all afternoon, likely dinner as well, and, she hastened to add, she might spend the night.

Disappointed, but with no reason to suspect an indiscretion, Red asked her to check in by nightfall, so he won't be concerned, and his response exacerbated her guilt, although not for long.

Sam drove, and while ambling north along PCH, he described the distinction of each town they passed, echoing the bookstore clerk's lecture. They shared a laugh at the geological schematic and debated the true meaning of place – the sense of aligning to a landscape or a community – and Sharon felt the distinct pleasure of dialogue with a man interested in deeper meaning. More to the point, a man who wants to hear what she has to say.

Once past Huntington Beach, Sam drove into a section of Long Beach where canals flow like Venice, and then near the busy container port to wave at the Queen Mary anchored there, before dropping her at a hip coffee shop in the arts district to work a while.

She's people watching instead, and why not? she thinks. She's taken a respite from academia, as tickled as a student playing hooky. Nothing like a change of scene to lift the spirits, not to mention spending time with a man who only weeks ago was a stranger, and now seems a permanent fixture.

The café is populated with an eclectic mix of patrons: elders in conversation or reading, the younger holding hands while pretending to study. Sometimes they sneak a kiss and Sharon smiles, recalling her first days and nights with Sam, while Red and the boys were at Yosemite.

Having failed to share contact information the day they shared their stories and walked around town, they showed up the next morning at Zinc to find each other. They laughed when they arrived at nearly the same moment. After small talk and seductive glances, Sam stood and, without a word, Sharon followed him to his truck. They drove up the hill past the retreat house, higher still, revealing ocean and hillside views more breathtaking as they made the climb. He turned at last onto a narrow road and then parked in front of a garage partially obscured by bougainvillea with blooms as pink as a baby's cheek. Lining the driveway, lavender fronds swayed in the breeze, their scent as intoxicating as the portent of coupling, and as she stepped from the truck, he took her hand to lead her up a path sheltered by tall trees with long pine needles sprouting from their barks to a large wooden deck.

His house, as expected, was wrapped by glass, with an entry door so thick that, once closed, silence filled the interior like a cloister. The space had a comfy lived-in look, not as cluttered as contented: a fringed blanket tossed across the arm of a reading chair; gardening shoes and gloves by the door; piles of books on a large round ottoman in front of a long brown leather couch with mismatched pillows strewn about.

Sharon scanned oversized framed architectural photographs on the walls, all of urban environs.

Your photographs? she asked.

No, but photographers I know and appreciate.

Have you been to all these cities?.

Not all. I hope to.

These sorts of photographs are more powerful in black and white, she commented.

He nodded. *I gravitate to the monochrome. Feels nostalgic, even if not my lens, and even if I've never been there.*

Sharon nodded. *Like pining for another era.*

The good ole days that maybe weren't so good? Or never existed at all? Sam chuckled. *Did you know there's a word for that? Anemoia. I stumbled on it just the other day.*

Never heard that word, she said.

He smiled, self-consciously, as if Sharon might have inspired his search for such a word. As if she has provoked a longing for what might have been, and that, like the sexual static between them, sent shivers from her head to her toes.

There's a site online where all sorts of invented words perfectly capture an emotion. There's a book too. Voila! Anemoia. Nostalgia for something we've never known, or experienced, he explained.

Nostalgia for an unknown, Sharon said, mulling the word. *Wharton was especially good at evoking that emotion.*

He smiled. *If we're talking Wharton, we ought to have tea. I have a few varieties.*

I think I'm fully loaded with coffee, she replied.

An awkward silence landed between them like a rockslide, Sam's typical charm and confidence buried in the rubble, as she caved briefly to uncertainty.

He gestured to her to join him on the living room couch. He sat at one end. She kicked off her shoes and sat near, not adjacent, legs bent with her arms folded around her knees, facing him as she might have once sat on someone's bed in a college dormitory. In that pose, she felt younger and freer than she'd felt in years, and she relaxed again into the moment, waiting him out. Sam, as it turns out, was waiting her out, so they filled the air between them with idle conversation, comparing notes about his house and her cottage in Oakland, until the suspense was more than she could stand. She smiled, and leaned forward flirtatiously, so he could not misinterpret, and then leaned in to a kiss, a kiss as tender and as sexually charged as the first.

Unwilling to concede again to caution, she stood and removed first one earring, then the other, and then she took his hand, her desire unmistakable.

They stayed in the entire weekend, except for a hike at the top of the world, meals concocted out of whatever was in the fridge or a quick trip to pick up pizza. They listened to music, his favorites and hers, and they shared more of their histories.

They spent more time in his bed than anywhere else, making love both nights and both mornings as well. They showered together and soaked in his hot tub together. And, every time he touched her, inch by inch, he whispered, *tell me what you want.*

Sharon was tentative, as she's prone to be with men. She has never been sexually aggressive and not one to make demands. She prefers the chase. With Sam, she had no choice. Top to bottom, bottom to top, as his fingertips scanned her body, he insisted she tell him what she wanted, or not, arousing passion until she could barely breathe.

Until she too pleaded, breathlessly, *tell me what you want.*

When Sam answered, *surprise me*, she did, and she surprised herself as well. Repeatedly.

By their last morning, they laughed at how sore they were. Spent, in the best possible way, they agreed.

She's recalling that weekend when Sam returns from the glass inspection and she stands to kiss him, like one of the students. He smiles with delight. They walk a ways, holding hands, and Sharon feels like a fictional character who has discovered love when least expected. Or, as she would tell Hank, found romance and rediscovered lust.

After lunch at a busy gastropub, they drive south to the Museum of Latin American Art to track down Mateo's painting in the permanent collection. At the front desk, a young brown man with purple tinted hair searches the database in response to their inquiry and points them to a gallery down the hall.

Dead center, he says, with a satisfied smile.

The gallery is empty and as still as a chapel. Pin lights point toward paintings like stars. All the art in this room are portraits and although they are on a mission, they skim the walls, observing each painting, one by one, until Sam suddenly stops in his tracks.

My God, he cries. *It's Rosa.*

Sharon is shocked by what she sees.

Rosa? But this woman is nothing like the Rosa described to me, she counters.

Oh, it's Rosa. He's painted her as she might have been, I guess, or could have been, without him, maybe.

The sign on the wall reads Fauvist, Mateo Perez, Cuban. Sharon stares back at the portrait of a woman without any indication of the holiness or earthiness ascribed to the landlord. This woman seems a woman of the night. A tango dancer or a gypsy. Her mocha skin is heavy with make-up. Wide almond-shaped eyes are exaggerated by thick dark lashes, like a doll or a puppet. Eyebrows are pointedly arched, the nose wide at the tip. Pursed lips are tinted wine-red. The one adornment: long dangling silver earrings.

Wavy hair the color of freshly tilled soil frames her face and crests at shapely, bare shoulders, where the portrait ends – above the breast line, as if Rosa is naked. A woman meant to please or to be pleased. As vulnerable as vulgar. The sort of female memorialized by Cervantes and Dickens.

The painting's title: Viajeva Cansada.

The Weary Traveler.

Disturbing, Sam murmurs.

Sharon nods, troubled by the image.

Makes you wonder about their relationship, she whispers. *This woman is...*

Furtive, Sam interjects.

A woman to use, Sharon observes.

She stares at the painting, hoping to grasp its full meaning and, while transfixed, Sam turns to the adjacent portrait and gasps.

Mateo! he cries. *I thought just the one here.*

Painted in the same bold color, the same sharp angles and thick strokes, and the same carnality, this portrait features a swarthy seductive male.

The label reads, Unnamed Self-Portrait.

As if they were meant to be a pair, she murmurs.

As if he had no definition beyond the paint, he comments. *Sharon, meet Mateo,* Sam says, with a bow.

The Mateo in this portrait has thick dark hair and a tightly trimmed beard and mustache, known in Cuba as candado, meaning padlock. Bushy eyebrows reveal wide jade-green eyes, as Sam described. And, like Rosa's portrait, only his head and shoulders are visible, but he wears a T-shirt as golden as a full moon.

The great surprise is his face, split down the middle: the left painted in vibrant blue, with blood red at the edges, like an inferno, and the right, buttery yellow, as if a gentler nature. The duality screams for recognition.

That blue is like the blue in Van Gogh's starry sky, Sharon says.

Prussian Blue, Sam replies. *The first modern pigment, although it was an accident.*

How so? she asks, still staring at the portrait.

An alchemist, Johann Dippel…

Wait, he was the inspiration for Frankenstein!

Really? He was working with a pigment maker to synthesize red dye made from the cochineal, the insect, and they made an error that resulted in this blue.

Maybe that's why Mateo used it – a nod to Rosa.

He nods. *Likely. Or to Van Gogh.*

She gazes again at Rosa and back to Mateo.

You're right, I would have fallen for him. And, oddly, they seem meant to be together, she remarks.

How so? he asks.

It's almost as if he wanted to share his strength with her. I mean, his color and bravado. And she shares her innocence. Crazy? she asks.

As good an explanation as any, he responds, troubled by the memory of his carnal nights with Rosa.

They stare at the paintings a few minutes longer before leaving the gallery. After glancing at a sampling of other works, they drive back to Sam's for a night of lovemaking.

In the middle of the night, Sharon awakened in the dark, disoriented. Although curled against Sam's warm body, comforted by his gentle steady breathing, she thought for a moment it was Red. As if she were back in time and they had never separated. As if he was not dying of cancer and they were merely on holiday. As her eyes adjusted to the dim light, she realized with relief where she was.

Do we always feel this melancholy, then to now? The ambivalence of the maybe? she wondered.

She slept fitfully until birds chirped loudly from a pepper tree and morning light slipped into the room.

At breakfast, they again discuss the portraits.

I'm bothered by Mateo's depiction of her, Sharon says. *I know it's an abstraction, of sorts, but brooding. I cannot imagine what Rosa made of this, picturing her as seductive as submissive.*

If she ever saw it, he says.

Good point. He may have kept it from her.

I'm still not sure what to make of it.

Ambivalence, she murmurs. *Do you think this is his view of who she was, or what he thought she could be, or should be? Terribly confusing.*

What of his own self-portrait? he replies. *Façade split in two – two minds, maybe two hearts.*

Two minds, two hearts, she murmured.

Are we all a divided between who and what we want or what we need? Sharon will frequently wonder what was at the core of Rosa and Mateo's enigmatic relationship. There was no question they were bonded by love and loyalty, even if not a traditional bonding. Aren't there all sorts of relationships? And, if they were exemplary, devotion might be defined as nourishing in one another what is most essential. Protecting one another from an unforgiving world.

Love without intention or judgment, or reward. The more she thinks about it, the more precious it seems.

March 1st, thirty-two countries had reported cases of COVID-19, and in the U.S., eighty-nine had been confirmed. Within days, eight more deaths were tallied and one hundred twenty-six cases, the count too small to proclaim a crisis, rather a looming threat.

Tammy set about sounding the alarm. Dressed in her tight-fitting uniform, her straw gardening hat looped behind her shoulders, she alighted at the top of the stone steps like a gladiator ready for battle.

Red waved as he stood from his chaise and she smiled, holding up one finger to indicate he wait while she climbed the stairs to Rosa's balcony. There, she pounded on the glass door, calling to Rosa to come out.

To Red's surprise, Rosa obeyed, heeding the urgency in Tammy's call; however, she hovered at the doorway, so Red climbed half-way and situated himself on a step, in view of her, while Tammy eased onto a higher step between them, like a mediator.

This is how it begins, she said. *Plague is not on the other side of the world now. Viruses, even the most benign, like the common cold, which, you likely know, is a coronavirus, are vigilant. Hard to treat. They require only a warm host to thrive, and they seek out hosts as if their lives depend on it, which they do, then they grow bolder and mutate and spread farther.*

What's to be done? Red asked. *We can't avoid flu, not even with vaccination, and all of us catch a virus now and then. Lousy, but not deadly.*

This is way worse. Better immune systems might survive with little damage. Others must avoid exposure.

Rosa had no reaction, as if to suggest she avoids exposure as a way of life, and Tammy called her out.

You think you're safe, Rosa, but Elena floats in and out of here like the breeze, and who knows what she will bring with her from the hospital.

Rosa somberly nodded consent.

I would be happy to shop for you, Red said.

Tammy smiled. *Dear man, you absolutely need to be extra careful yourself. Let Sharon do the shopping.*

I'm the designated shopper here, he declared.

She sighed. *If you insist, go less often. Stock up. Avoid contact with shoppers or workers. But I urge you to order for delivery as often as you can.*

I don't interact much with people, he said.

I would beg to differ, Tammy replied. *Seriously, keep a distance. And leave the groceries outside a few hours or wipe them down with antiseptic.*

You have got to be kidding! Red exclaimed.

We don't know yet if this virus survives on hard surfaces. The keyword is caution. I brought you masks.

Masks? Like the Asians? he asked, incredulous.

Right, they understand the threat of the crowd. Not professional grade, hospitals need those, but good enough. Wear it when you go near anyone. Cover your nose and mouth. In the supermarket, double up.

Red shook his head in dismay, and amazement, as Tammy handed each of them a couple of masks.

Keep them at hand, please, she instructed.

Yes, mam, Red answered, with a salute, and then called to Rosa, *I will shop again in a day or so.*

Thank you, Rosa said. *Thank you, Tammy.*

Text me a list, Red called out, as Rosa retreated. *And let me know anytime you need provisions.*

Rosa turned to him with a smile, her face lit up as if complimented. *Sí, Señor Red. Las provisiones.*

And there it was: with a shared word and an act of generosity, Red befriended Rosa.

Two days later, Rosa texted a shopping list and left her credit card in an envelope on the balcony, weighted down by a potted cactus. When Red delivered the groceries, he knocked, to indicate the bags had arrived, and they chatted on opposite sides of the screen. Four days later, he texted to let her know he was planning to shop again, and she texted back a short list, but this time, when he climbed the stairs with the bags, she invited him in, and when he offered to help put the groceries away, she reminded him to leave them outside. He chuckled and she smiled, and they agreed how easily people fear the unknown.

I took a journey, long ago, when I came to this country, she said. *Faith conquers the unknown.*

I hope you're right, he answered. *But what shall we have faith in? The potential to combat an invisible, stealthy enemy? A civilization compromised by human frailty? The unknown may have the greater power.*

Rosa contemplated his words.

And you, do you have faith, Mr. Red, she asked.

You might say, for me, faith is based on problem solving. I believe we find the tools to surmount whatever may seem formidable.

What Rosa did not say was how much she appreciated his certainty in the throes of uncertainty.

What Red did not say was how grateful he was for conversation. Sharon has been gone later each day and he feels less alone in this moment with Rosa.

Elena continued to stop by often, keeping her distance, and briefly chatting with Red before climbing the stairs to the balcony to check on Rosa.

What's happening at the hospital? I hear they're war zones, he asked the other day.

Changes are in the air, she answered, *but what exactly will change, this remains to be seen.*

Red has been impressed with how circumspect she is, like Rosa. Is it their culture, he wonders, or the necessity of staying below the radar? The more often he visits with her, the more he realizes he would have enjoyed having a daughter and, to his surprise, he despairs of never knowing a grandchild.

Sharon used to tell the boys you cannot lose what you never had, a saying passed down by her father, perhaps a salve to his own regrets. What Red feels of late is not so much loss or what might have been, rather nostalgia for what cannot be had.

Nothing has changed, not that he can explain, but Sharon seems to be slipping further away from him instead of closer, as he had hoped.

COVID-19 spread rapidly. Italy was already on lockdown. The U.S. recorded its first thousand cases and subsequent deaths. Advocates for the elderly and homeless warned of deadly boiling pots. A cruise ship stranded off the coast with twenty-one confirmed cases sailed into Oakland, greeted by healthcare workers in protective gear who marshaled a quarantine.

Everyone, including children, were advised to wear masks in public and maintain *social distance.*

I'm thinking you should leave sooner than later, Barry advised Red.

Back to Chicago? Why?

No, come here. We've got room.

Thanks, but why? I'm quite comfortable here.

They're going to limit flight travel, domestically too. You wouldn't want to get stuck there, Barry said.

But I would, Red replied. *Perfect place to ride this out. Easy to stay out of the fray. How long can it last anyway, before they get on top of it.*

Who knows? But it doesn't look good. If you pay attention to what's going on in other countries…

I do, and I see that China and Italy, where people live on top of each other, have the greater contagion. Chicago or Austin, neither seem better options, Red interjected.

Well, that's a fair point, although we live in the hills, as you know. Sequestered by nature. And your landlord will toss you by June, if not sooner, right?

We're friends now, so maybe I can negotiate for June. By then, hopefully things will improve, Red said.

Friends? Barry asked. Since when? And what do you mean by friends?

Friendly may be the better description. She's like a hermit crab – stretches out her pincers now and then, otherwise hides in her shell. I'm shopping for her now, so I've been approved for entry.

What's it like up there in the inner sanctum?

A painter's studio, not much more. Really, hardly

*anything more. Three canvases going, all landscapes,
all roads or paths going nowhere,* Red answered.

What's that about?

*Not sure. When I asked, she wasn't forthcoming.
She said the brush would go where it was meant to go,*
Red quoted.

A little obtuse, if you ask me, Barry said.

*She says road art is as common as road stories.
She cited Derain, Braques, among others. Well known.*

So now you're an art student? Barry asked.

Never too late to be educated, Red replied.

When Red asked Rosa why there are no people
on her paths, no journeymen, in effect, Rosa paused
before she answered, a thoughtful pause like a rest in
music.

*There is no one because it is my path alone, the
destination yet to be revealed,* she said.

Well, what would be the optimum end point, Red
asked.

That is the quest, she replied.

Few people are comfortable without clarity, Red
knows. He's a perfect example. Rosa, however, to his
mind, seems to embrace the unknown like no one he's
ever known, and in this, unexpectedly, he feels more
comfortable with her than anyone ever before in his
long life. Her willingness to exist without a destination
in mind, or to reside within the conceptual, makes him
better able to conceive of his own life at this time with
acceptance, rather than resistance. Like knowing the
marine layer will eventually burn off, and return.

Probability versus possibility.

She may be taking steps to find her way past the uncertainty to, well, maybe, meaning, Sharon posited at dinner that night. *On the other hand, she seems to savor the puzzle. The open-endedness. That's rare.*

Rosa is a person of faith, Sam said when Sharon told him what Red described of the art in the upstairs studio. *Real faith, not religion, per se. She embraces destiny, which is by way of embracing the unknown.*

I know what she's doing, Hank pronounced when Sharon updated her on Rosa's story.

Do tell, Sharon asked.

Hank ignored the sarcasm because Hank had a different interpretation of the mystery of Rosa. A very dear friend had once suffered from agoraphobia after her second child was born – a rare form of post-partum depression. Hank also has encountered students who come to college filled with enthusiasm for freedom long denied, but shrink into dorm rooms to hide, unable to step into the brink without a safety net.

Rosa is painting her way out of her self-imposed seclusion. She's in a profound state of grief and she's using the canvas to inch her way from the confinement that protects her to a life she cannot yet define. Using art to plot her escape. Impressive.

Makes perfect sense, Red replied, when Sharon shared Hank's commentary. *Although, I don't believe Rosa is conscious of that. She's just, well, in transition.*

They had just concluded comida, empty plates and glasses scattered on the table, like a still life.

Another thing. There's no artwork on the walls upstairs, Red said.

None? Sharon asked.

Only a framed print over the dining table, Van Gogh's Starry Night Over the Rhone, I think, he said.

I'm impressed you recognized it, she said.

I remember a few, he answered, proudly.

Did you know that painting was drawn from a scene in Dickens? From Hard Times. A secondary hero, Stephen Blackpool, gazes at a star as he contemplates his imminent death.

I didn't know that, of course, but Rosa mentioned Dickens as well, he answered.

Mateo was an avid reader I've heard, she said.

Who told you that? Red asked.

Sharon stammered. *Tammy, I guess. She seems to know Rosa better than she lets on.*

Red nodded. *Rosa is quite fond of Tammy.*

Isn't everyone, Sharon said, with a smile.

Red too smiled. *Rosa's hungry for conversation. She was quite chatty today.*

What did you talk about?

When I asked about the Van Gogh, she said, now let me get this right... she said the painting shares the diffused light and soft, no, she said subtle shading of Doré's painting, Houses of Parliament at Night. That painting apparently impressed Van Gogh when he lived in London when he was young. And, she said, while he lived there, he was captivated by Dickens.

That man shows up everywhere! Sharon cried. *He had a huge influence on writers and artists. I'd write about him if there was anything left to write, although he was also a bit of an ogre, you know.*

Red sipped his wine and sighed with pleasure: Rosa's company, good food and conversation with his wife, and a golden moon against a clear night sky.

Rosa has read all of Dickens, maybe because of the connection with Van Gogh, with Fauvism, I mean, he remarked. *She has one of those leather-bound sets. She told me Fauvism was the first art movement of the 20th century. The bridge, the passage, you might say, from post-impressionism to cubism. Interesting, right?*

Listen to you! Sharon exclaimed, filing a note in her mental cabinet that Fauvists, like Victorians, were the transition to modernism.

I've been paging through that book on Fauvism, he continued. *If someone like Rosa had been my art history teacher, I might have paid closer attention. Her face lights up when she talks about art. It's contagious.*

Sharon smiled, his enthusiasm also contagious. At the same time, she felt surprisingly deflated. She had the uncomfortable sensation she's been replaced. No longer the favored companion.

She should be relieved. Friendship between Red and Rosa will take some pressure off her. He'll be less alone. She'll feel less guilty about her absences with Sam and maybe less awful about her deception. Rosa seems to be good for Red and he for her. Sharon knew she should be pleased. The best possible scenario right now, all around. Still, she had to shake off the tug of possession.

Vincent van Gogh traveled to London in 1873, just twenty years old. A fledgling art dealer, he walked every morning to the gallery in Covent Garden across Westminster Bridge and strolled back on long evening walks. Entranced by the glimmer of stars on the River Thames, he admired Gustave Doré's painting, *The Houses of Parliament at Night*, which he said perfectly captured the grandness of the great city. Fifteen years later, he reimagined that majesty in his homage to his own star-filled nighttime riverscape.

London was becoming then the world capital for graphic arts, known as black and whites. Painters too trained their eyes on the everyday: men and women waiting at end of day for a pub to open; weary street cleaners pushing carts; inmates marching in a circle in a prison yard. Van Gogh was entranced by the art form and amassed during his lifetime two thousand prints and engravings. He said these draftsmen had the same effect on paper as Dickens with words.

Impressed as he was by emerging modernity, he was disturbed by the dark side of industrialization, not only what he observed, but what was revealed of the gritty street life at the center of Dickens' stories, one of several writers who inspired him at the time.

Later in life, when his mental health suffered, even as his art achieved new heights, London returned to his consciousness. In a letter to his sister, written from the asylum where he resided for a time, he said of his painting, *The Bedroom*, modeled on his room in Arles, *I wanted to arrive at the effect of simplicity as described by Felix Holt.*

He referred to George Eliot's working-class hero in *The Radical*, published in 1866, a novel that also inspired his drive to be an artist of the people. Despite opportunities to rise in status, Holt chose an existence of material simplicity and moral rigor, as Van Gogh would aspire to all his days.

Mateo too thought of himself as an artist of the people, and from a very young age studied Van Gogh's paintings in scrupulous detail. On his first trip to New York City, he sought out every work on display, and he hoped to visit the museum in Amsterdam, although he never got there. His earliest drawings were modeled on the Dutchman's later work, the catalyst for Fauvism.

In *Starry Night over the Rhone,* streetlamps served as a metaphor for the dissonance between the classes Van Gogh witnessed, and Dickens exposed. Rosa too loved that print and held on to it all her life.

In their many discussions about art, Mateo often returned to Van Gogh as his muse. *Look at the line of this or that*, he rhapsodized. *The exquisite play of light. The passion in his texture.*

He recited to her from biographies and museum catalogs he had collected, and together they read aloud Irving Stone's biographical novel, *The Agony and the Ecstasy.* In his immersion in Van Gogh folklore, he also became enamored of Dickens; however, with roots in communist Cuba, he rejected the construct of a communal society, instead devoted to individualism.

The day came when Mateo lost his passion even for debate. When his theories of the supremacy of the creative life felt hollow to his ears.

Awakening mornings in pain and struggling through the day to make the simplest effort, he called his lawyer to the house to update his will to safeguard Rosa's future. He was painfully aware his dependency on her, and an exalted ego, repressed a nobler instinct to nudge her into the world. He had held her back for his gain, he confessed to the lawyer. As an expression of gratitude, he re-imagined the lower level to provide her with an income and to ensure she would never be alone. He designed plans and engaged a contractor. Sam was hired to reinforce the glass wall and install the sliding entry door.

On a bright September afternoon, warm breezes blowing from the sea, friends gathered on the patio to witness Mateo and Rosa's marriage.

She wore a white cotton peasant dress Sylvia embroidered at the trim with sprays of lavender. He wore a white silk shirt open at the neck over a pair of loose-leg linen pants. At Rosa's insistence, they each carried two birds of paradise stalks, clipped from their garden, to consecrate their union and signify devotion.

Mateo was more deeply touched than he ever imagined. He had difficulty holding back his tears as a young priest performed the ceremony and, at his direction, a cellist played Saint-Saens' *Le Cigne – The Swan* – a classical wedding song.

Afterward, they dined on food lovingly prepared by Sylvia and church friends and drank champagne gifted by Mateo's favorite saloon.

At the end of the day, in a haze of drink and joy, Rosa stood at a mirror and whispered, *Senora Perez.*

There was no honeymoon, and their lives were no different than before.

Mateo painted every day, although fewer hours. He rested late afternoons on the patio chaise where Red would recline years later. In inclement weather, he relaxed on the living room couch while Rosa read aloud from their complete collection of Dickens, acquired from a rare books dealer.

Like the grandfather in *The Old Curiosity Shop*, Mateo took long walks after dark. He wore a tan felt hat and an espresso brown flannel jacket, gifted by a fashionable friend, which, he told Rosa, made him feel elegant in a Dickensian way.

At first, she watched for him from their patio. When his steps grew faltering, she wrapped a shawl around her shoulders and walked with him, arm-in-arm, often silently, or commenting now and then on a sweet fragrance or a plaintive branch lit by moonlight.

When they nodded to passing neighbors, their neighbors smiled, charmed by the enchanting artist and his lovely wife, arms linked, footsteps in sync, enjoying their evening stroll.

Their mutual devotion a consolation in a world splintered by conflict and confusion.

March 11th, the World Health Organization declared a pandemic.

We have rung the alarm bell loud and clear, the Director General announced.

Hospitals were scrambling, ill-equipped for an onslaught of the sick or the challenges of treatment. Supermarket shelves were emptied as quickly as they were stocked. Paper goods were in high demand and hoarded, sterilizers and home sanitizers as precious as gold, and face masks the new fashion. Air travel and the hospitality industry came to a screeching halt as borders closed, political fingers pointing angrily across the globe. There was talk of shutdowns and curfews, as in Europe, and college students were sent home early for spring break, without a timetable for return.

Reporters juggled speculation, misinformation and misunderstanding. Stock market indices bounced up and down like an EKG. Social media exploded with conspiracy theories.

Watching CNN that morning, not yet despairing but disconcerted, Red discussed the latest with Barry, who again urged him to relocate to Austin, where he would have company and, when needed, care.

Soon, he pressed. *This will last way longer than we think. The Spanish Flu a century ago, lasted years!*

I have comfortable space here, and company, not to mention better weather, Red argued. *And don't buy the bull this is another Spanish Flu!*

Weather should not be a factor, Barry replied, ignoring Red's dismissal. *We have lots of room. We can hole up here indefinitely.*

His argument fell on deaf ears. Red would not be persuaded to leave. He was settled at the flat, had established hiking routes, favorite places for coffee and baked goods, and a friend upstairs. He enjoyed living with Sharon, despite occasional friction, and hoped she might agree to stay longer.

His brothers called to offer shelter as well and he was grateful, but stalwart.

I'm sure this will pass before long. The best medical minds are on it, he argued, and believed.

Therefore, he was shaken, and alarmed, when son Brady called to postpone their next visit.

Sorry, Dad. I know we planned these trips in advance, but my old roommate, Louis, remember him? His wife's an epidemiologist, at Hopkins, and she said this virus is seriously contagious. Assaults the immune system. We can handle it, but we don't want to make you sick. No way.

Red had the sudden, hopefully irrational fear he might never see his sons again.

Dad, you do understand, right? We don't see any alternative, not now, Brady pleaded to Red's silence.

Of course, of course. Most sensible, yes. I'm sure they'll find an antidote before long. We can wait it out.

We'll be there by your birthday, come hell or high water, we've agreed, Brady insisted, and Jamie echoed when he called later in the day.

Red turns seventy on June 2nd. The date seems as distant as incomprehensible, and he had hoped to soften the blow by celebrating with Sharon and the boys in Los Angeles, which now seems unlikely.

I'll miss you guys, but I applaud your caution, he conceded. *Yes, you're young, but my neighbor, a nurse, says wash your hands and wear a mask.*

We're on it, Dad. See you on-screen, Jamie said.

Red, prone on the couch, his head propped on a pillow, digests the news while staring through the glass to a vast blue sky. No clouds today, yet he senses an encroaching storm, like when he was a boy at summer camp, sun high, rushing to bring canoes and paddles to shore before thunder assaulted the sky.

Sharon was already gone this morning before he returned from his hike, even though he cut it short when his calf muscles cramped severely, crying for a break. He'd like to discuss all this with her. Consider next steps, best options, together.

He decides to walk to town to stretch his legs also pick up magnesium, which is said to curb the cramping. It's nearly Noon. They could have lunch. He has never interrupted her work schedule before, but he has cause. They should review the decision the boys have made, and consider how to help them stay safe.

He is determined now to extend their retreat as long as possible, to wait out the worst of it. He will also suggest they fly the boys to California and park them in a rental nearby. Panic will produce vacancies. Better the boys get away from the cities, where density breeds incubation.

He's reasoned it all out in a matter of minutes and expects to persuade them all with his logic.

He will also mention the WHO was resolute, with prompt action, cases can be curtailed, although acknowledging a pandemic has never in history been controlled. The key, the Director said in his statement, is containment. Red looked up the most recent graphs of case projections, rising alarmingly, then dropping toward the axis and back up again, like sound waves. Correlations are difficult to ascertain and simulations unreliable without more data. An information abyss.

On his way to town, he stops at Heidelberg Café, where Sharon stops occasionally to pick up muffins. He watches the town greeter, Michael is his name, spin on a top like a whirling dervish, waving to passers-by without a care in the world. He's seen this guy before, the latest in a legacy of greeters here, and he's been impressed with his ebullience, despite the repetitive motion. An engineer could never be so ritualistic.

Sharon isn't there. Down the street, he stops at Laguna Coffee, unable to resist the scent of roasting, for a coffee. Once in the heart of town, he glances into a café near the post office, but she's not there. She's not at Zinc either, where chatter, loud and animated, is all about the pandemic. He detects resignation but not panic, and realizes these folks are always awaiting the big earthquake, another fire or mudslide, so they are decidedly more judicious.

He walks down the street to Anastasia's, where she sometimes takes brunch, but no luck there, and then toward Main Beach, where he stops to watch runners along the water line. Their footprints follow, then disappear in the surf. He has the thought Rosa might paint this like a road, if she ventured out, although how might she capture ebb and flow on canvas? He trudges up the hill to Urth Café, where there's a line waiting to order and tables on the patio are filled, but she's not there either, so he reverses the route, stopping again at Zinc to pick up a scone to go.

He only now realizes it would have made sense to call her first.

As he pulls his phone from his jacket pocket, he sees her step down from a white pickup truck across the street. The driver too steps out: Tammy's friend, Sam. She's smiling at him the way a woman smiles at an intimate and they walk down the street seamed at the shoulders.

He feels a hard blow to the gut, as if he's been in a street fight, as he realizes his wife has another life here. Correction, he thinks, his ex-wife, which doesn't make him feel any better. He wonders now if some of the hours she claims to be working or exercising, she might be somewhere else. On the other hand, maybe he's jumped to conclusion. Maybe she hitched a ride. Maybe he said something amusing.

Then again, their chemistry is conspicuous. Impossible to ignore.

Perhaps, he thinks now, she stayed with Sam, not a colleague, on that overnight to Los Angeles.

He knows he's often oblivious to much beyond his orbit, but he's no fool. With the realization Sharon is involved with another man, an ache penetrates his body like a deadly virus might, deep into his bones and into his heart.

There have been only a handful of moments in his long life when something hit him this hard.

He can hardly breathe. The same feeling when his mother, sixty-five years old, dropped dead from an aneurism. The way he felt on 9/11, when he knew the country was penetrable. When a junior associate in his firm, stoically suffering from depression, took his life. Moments of no return. However, these were the result of human frailty, deeply rooted anger or despair. What he feels right now is the agony of personal betrayal.

In all their years, Red never deceived Sharon about anything. Whatever his shortcomings – an often-infuriating reserve, insensitivity, and self-absorption – he would plead guilty to these, and that he took her happiness for granted, guilty again, but he was never dishonest. He would never have been disloyal, and he expected the same.

He trails them down the street like a detective in a B-movie. They walk through a passage by the post office to an area shaded by umbrella-topped tables and circled by shops. They sit side-by-side, knees grazing.

Red crouches behind a bush. He would laugh at himself were he not so agitated. When he calls, Sharon glances at her phone and lets it go to voicemail, then reconsiders and listens, before sharing with Sam.

The pandemic is official, Red reported. *I figured you were consumed with work and wouldn't have heard. The President will declare a health emergency. The boys have cancelled their next trip. We should talk about how best to proceed. When will you be back?*

She texts Red she will return soon, and he texts back a thumbs up, before slipping from his hiding place to retrace his steps. He stays out of sight, making his way on a street parallel to PCH. He walks slowly, not ambling, rather trudging along. He doesn't notice the scent of jasmine. He doesn't glance to his right to appreciate the ribbon of blue. He sees only detritus at his feet: shredded napkins, crumpled flower petals, rotted lemon peels.

When he arrives at the flat, the music is playing upstairs. He shouldn't intrude, however he climbs the stairs to the balcony and knocks.

Rosa comes to the screen and peers out at him quizzically, detecting in the slump of his shoulders and downcast expression he's burdened by a great sorrow. When she opens the door, although he says he wants to fill her in on the latest news about the pandemic, she knows there is more on his mind.

When Sharon returns, Red is not at the flat. She peeks into his room and calls out to him in case he's in the bathroom, but no sound. She checks her phone to be sure she hasn't missed another message, then she calls, but no answer.

She's instantly alarmed. Every day they have been on retreat, except the holiday with the boys, he's been at the flat when she returned from town.

Where could he be at this time of day? she frets. He hiked early this morning and he's already shopped this week. He sometimes stops at the patisserie, but that never takes long. She told him nearly an hour ago she'd be back soon, so where is he?

She berates herself now for not recording phone numbers for the nearby hospitals. He may have fallen or collapsed somewhere. She should have taken better precautions, because he thinks he'll sail through these months without incident. In truth, she has embraced the same optimism.

She googles the local hospital and calls. When she gets to a human voice and explains, she's advised to call the police, as they can track down if he's been attended by emergency services. Just as she's dialing that number, she hears footsteps on the balcony stairs and looks out to see Red descending with a sprightly step, as if not a care in the world. As he lands on the patio, he stops to watch the sun making its way to the western sky, before he turns to the sliding door.

Sorry, I'm behind schedule, he says as he enters.

Sharon nearly collapses in tears with relief.

Where were you? she cries. *I was worried sick.*

No cause, he responds.

No cause? Maybe you should let me know where you are if you won't be home, she scolds.

You don't let me know where you are, he says.

I don't have to. I don't have cancer!

Sharon immediately regrets her response. *I was frightened, that's all. I'm sorry. Out of order.*

I get it. I was upstairs, he says.

With Rosa? she asks.

He nods as he heads toward the kitchen. *Shall I open the wine?*

I thought you've shopped this week? she asks.

I have. We had a visit. A good chat, he replies.

Sharon realizes Red has no more wish to share details of his time with Rosa than she will of Sam. She has no clue what sort of relationship they have, or is evolving, but she cannot imagine they will be lovers. From all accounts, Rosa is too conventional. A woman of high ideals is not one to have a tryst with a tenant. Not to mention the age difference. On the other hand, there was that hint of carnality in her in her portrait.

We need to talk about next steps, Red says.

His tone of voice is perfunctory. Business-like. He used to speak to her this way at the end of the day when he was unable to shake off engineering mode, and she wonders if he's had some bad news, or if he's in greater pain. He tends to go formal when he's hiding what he considers weakness.

What Sharon could not imagine is his injury is emotional and she the source. If she knew, she would argue it's not infidelity or disloyalty, albeit duplicitous.

Red has already reasoned this out for himself. He has no claim on his ex-wife, whatever illusion he may have had about retreat. And Rosa may be better company anyway. She's kind and compassionate, they have no history, and she requires nothing from him.

There are a few things to discuss, but it can wait until tomorrow. I'm a bit tired, he says.

He doesn't tell her he will stay on, indefinitely, with or without her. He will hike hills and absorb the winter sun into his thinning bones. He plans to have delivered what he needs and pass the afternoons with Rosa. He'll be happy if his sons join him, but will understand if they don't. No crystal ball, no way of knowing what's next, but he will not go to Chicago, he will not burden Barry, or his brothers. Nor will he inconvenience Sharon, or his sons. He's resolved.

I guess it's time to start dinner, he says, opening a bottle of wine to breathe. *I never got to the market, but we've got leftover roasted veggies, maybe pasta?*

Sharon stares at him perplexed. He's impossible to read right now, but she has no wish to argue. She's had a lovely day. She'd prefer to hold on to the uplifting feeling she has. They'll deal with the rest in due course.

I'll take care of it, she answers, heading to the kitchen, where she pours their wine and opens the fridge to take stock of options.

Red takes his glass with him to the living room and eases comfortably onto the sofa. With the first sip, he makes a mental note to order more cannabis for the pain and call Dave to set up a surf lesson.

Tell me something good, preferably sexy, and not to do with viral earthquakes, Hank says the following morning, when Sharon calls.

Are the catastrophizers in charge? Sharon asks.

Nero has been fiddling. Now, we burn. MERS, SARS, Ebola and Swine flu, merely smoldering. We are in for it.

Sharon is sobered – Hank is not an alarmist.

I should be paying closer attention to this. Red is, but until yesterday, neither of us was overly anxious.

What happened? Hank asks.

The boys canceled their trip and Red announced this morning he plans to stay here until June, or longer.

Will you stay as well? Hank asks.

He would like me to, Sharon says.

And wouldn't you want to, because of Sam?

I don't see how that will work.

Where there's a will, there's a way, Hank says.

I'm struggling with the deception. And I have to get back sometime, Sharon replies.

Why? You've got all you need. Your defense will be postponed or virtual. We're taking everything online. No campus life at all for an indefinite time.

That's the punchline? Go online? Sharon asks.

That has a ring to it, Hank answers. *By the way, do you know the derivation of that term, punchline?*

I forget, Sharon answers, distracted by a sense of pending disaster.

From the old Punch and Judy puppet shows, Hank says.

Sharon laughs. *Of course.*

Punch, who by the way looks an awful lot like Dickens' Fagan, beats his wife to death, Hank says.

Ugh! Sharon groans.

Also kills a child and a policeman, among others, and he's wickedly self-satisfied, Hank says.

That's certainly one way to end a relationship, Sharon mutters.

Are you looking for a way out of retreat or out of the tryst? Hank asks.

Inextricably intertwined, for now. I don't see how to stay or go without making a mess. Until the science fiction movie we're living in rips a hole in the universe to reveal a parallel path, I'm damned if I do and damned if not, Sharon exclaims.

So how do you feel about Sam? I mean, how do you really feel about him? Hank probes.

Hard to say, Sharon answers.

Oh, come on, you can tell me, Hank says.

I guess the word is smitten, Sharon confesses.

Smitten for the fun of it or for the longer term?

Too soon to tell, but I do love being with him. He makes me feel, I don't know, young, or at least younger. Sexier. He brings out the best in me.

Nice. Sounds like something that might last.

Wait a minute, aren't you the woman who says commitment is over-rated? Sharon asks.

Yes, but you're the Victorian!

Sharon laughs. *Listen, Victorians were not at all dispassionate and hardly asexual. They just prioritized responsibility – to each other and to society. Duty, above all else. Imagine that?*

Which is a model for commitment, Hank says.

Commitment, not devotion. Not the same.

Oh my, you've gone Rousseau! Hank chides.

Yep, the rationalist, that's me, Sharon agrees.

Commitment is fine, while it works, Hank says.

Right. Commitment in stages, so to speak, which is of course antithetical, Sharon counters.

But some of us don't have the devotion gene.

Sharon detects remorse in Hank's voice, despite her dogged opinion.

Is it possible to love unconditionally? she asks. *Aren't relationships by definition transactional? And, I wonder, is the opposite of devotion self-preservation? Are we all at heart self-serving?* Sharon ponders aloud.

Human beings are by nature self-serving, Hank says. *Like other animals, we get what we need, one way or another, beyond food and shelter. We delude ourselves we're rational. We romanticize altruism. We are self-serving in the truest sense of the word, meaning self-preservation and self-satisfaction. If I allowed my life to be beholden to anyone else's destiny, I'd be lost. Besides, romance has too short a shelf life.*

You should package that lecture, Sharon says. *Speaks volumes right now. And admirable, truly, just difficult to reconcile with our upbringing,* Sharon says.

Perpetuated by fiction, my friend. Selfish women must be punished! Tossed under the train.

Sharon chuckles. *Too true.*

You know I'm devoted, in my own way, to many things. Education. Equity. Friends, family, and yes, to emotional and physical satisfaction, Hank states.

'*You cannot find peace by avoiding life,*' Sharon murmurs.

Nice. Did I say that? Hank responds.

Virginia Woolf.

Of course. She drowned herself, didn't she?

Hank! Sharon cries.

Talk about self-preservation, Hank says. *Listen, let's face it, you're a romantic, and last time I looked, the Brontë's, Eliot, even Gaskell, the prude, were high on love. And Virginia? With all her gloom and doom, she believed in romance.*

Leonard was the devoted one, Sharon says.

As you are to your sons, your friends, and you're living with your ex-husband for god's sake!

That's not devotion. That's kindness. Here's the real question: can a woman be unfaithful to her ex-husband while living with him? Shame on me.

Will Sam keep the secret? Does he want more?

I don't know. He's been a loner all his life, but I have a feeling, hard to explain, he was waiting for me.

Hank laughs. *And here I thought he's another player, like me.*

Maybe he's tired of playing, Sharon posits.

Maybe the threat of death from pandemic makes a man want more before he dies, Hank says.

Maybe he's waited for the real deal!

They both descend into laughter, until Hank says, *I repeat. You're a romantic.*

You don't think this virus will last past summer, do you? Sharon asks, sobered again.

Might be year-end before we figure it all out.

Yikes. Red has made his decision, but the boys have yet to weigh in, Sharon says.

Sharon, what do you really want?

I might be better off in my own space, but if I leave Red, and especially if, rather when he gets worse, the boys will want to care for him. What I don't want.

That's their decision to make, and your Karma to face, Hank says.

Hell, I feel like there's a bug burrowing under my skin, poisoning me, slowly, Sharon says.

Welcome to our new world, Hank responds.

Why don't you take a breather? Sharon says. *Come to Laguna this weekend. Red will be glad to meet you and you can check out Sam for yourself. I miss you.*

Oh, how I would love to get a closer look at this: bonded to one, hot for the other. But I've got one meeting after another and we've been advised not to travel, even locally. Nothing to be done but deal.

Madness, Sharon mutters.

I urge you to forego decisions based on what's best for Red, or your sons, or Sam. You cannot please all the people all the time, Hank says.

Not all, but three lives intersect with me.

Four, if you include Sam.

Great, quadruple guilt, Sharon says.

Suffering is optional, Hank advises.

For most of us mere mortals, that's easier said than done, Sharon replies.

Two days later, Sharon and Sam dawdle in bed, clinging to time together until decisions have to be made. She has not yet mentioned that Rosa has received her first cancellation, and expects more, so Red believes they can remain on retreat indefinitely, if they choose.

With the specter of pandemic hovering like the specter of death, they discuss how this might impact the way of life people have come to believe in.

You have to wonder what might change. I mean, what we might choose to change, in our way of life, our values. The direction we're headed, he says.

We do tend to look back before we look forward.

At a time like this, for sure. And we regret choices that seemed right at the time, he says.

The paths taken versus not, she says, nodding.

On the other hand, I doubt Rosa would change a thing, he remarks.

Nothing? Hard to imagine, she counters.

She was at peace with Mateo, I believe.

He seems to have made her happy, until he was gone. And now, nothing, she says, saddened, again, for the reclusive landlord.

Sam is looking at her longingly.

What else is on your mind? she asks.

I'm thinking about what I've missed, like meeting you sooner, he whispers, his lips grazing her neck.

Better late than never, right? she says, reaching for him.

That afternoon, when she arrives at the rental, there's no sign of Red. She's just as irritated as the last time, but now she supposes he's with Rosa, although he has not alerted her.

In the hollow of the empty flat, she frets, again, the day might come when he's absent because he's in medical distress. She won't know where he is or what to do. He may need caretaking before long and how will that play out in the shadow of a deadly virus?

When they were married, Sharon was usually home before Red, and she always knew where he was. When he went out of town, meeting with colleagues or dining with clients, she had no reason to worry. She never questioned whether there were other women – he wasn't that sort of man. She's the one who cannot be trusted these days, and this one-two punch of uncertainty and pandemic feels like a sinkhole in-wait.

Twenty minutes later, Red strolls in.

You could have let me know where you were, she says, before he can say a word, outraged by his blatant disregard for her feelings.

He nods without apology and sits on the couch, nestling back against the pillows as if he hadn't a care in the world. Sharon sits on the arm of a chair facing him, leaning forward with her hands on her knees like a parent about to lecture a child who's behaved badly.

Red, recognizing the stance, speaks before she has a chance. *I wish you would think positive, Sharon. Get a handle on your nerves. If something happens to me, you will know, I assure you. I am sorry I'm late. I lost track of time. Rosa and I were talking about air.*

Air? Sharon repeats. *Deep in conversation about air, so you lost track of time.*

Red ignores her sarcasm. *That's right. We were talking about why air changes temperature at different elevations and why it smells differently from place to place, season to season. She told me farmers in Mexico take their cue from changes in the scent of the air, and the soil, also the barometric pressure. They know when to plant. No calendar, no Farmer's Almanac. They pick up the scent. They know when the rains will come, and then, the precise time to harvest. I was telling her how I always knew snow was on its way because I smelled that iciness that precedes the snow. Remember? Rosa, who has never seen snow, was enchanted by that premonition.*

Sharon stares at him, bewildered. She does not begrudge him this friendship, she's confused by it.

I've had a lovely afternoon and I hope your day was good, he remarks. *And I'm hungry. I could go for a burrito. I'll pick up. Won't take long. Fish or veggie?*

Sharon takes a moment to recalibrate. Choose your battles returns to mind; however his safety, and her sanity, is ground worth battling.

Sure, sounds good, but Red, listen, anything can happen, any time, and I...

I'm fine. You mustn't worry so, he insists.

You cannot expect me to live here with you and not worry. Maybe you could just let me know where you are if you're not here, please, Sharon pleads.

Are you planning to let me know where you are when you're not here? he says.

Sharon hears the severity in his voice, but she doesn't understand why.

You always know where I am. I'm in town, at a café or at Pilates class. Maybe a walk. I never go far. I'm on foot every day and I always have my cell phone.

Right, he mutters, with a sigh of exasperation.

Sharon hears the disappointment in his sigh and sees the sadness in his eyes. What is he not telling her? She will have to coax it out of him, she thinks, but Red interrupts her thoughts.

Strange circumstances, I know. So, from now on, if I'm not here, I mean, after hiking, and if there's no music upstairs, you can assume I'm up there. I think Rosa appreciates the company. I do. Oddly, we're sort of kindred spirits. And, if anything happens, I will make every effort to get a message to you. If not, you can panic and call the cops. Deal?

Humor me, please. Leave the slider ajar and I'll know you're on the grounds. Will you do that? she asks.

I'll try to remember, he agrees.

It's getting warmer now, we can leave it open. Bring the outside in. Okay?

I said yes, he retorts.

Okay then, yes, deal, she agrees.

She offers him her hand to shake, as if a detente has been reached, and when he takes hers, he holds it tightly, holding on to her, in effect, wishing he were in a position to coax her back to him, but then he lets go, asking, as if the moment never happened, *taco or burrito? Fish or veggie?*

The next day, when Sharon returns, the slider is open to the screen. She's comforted, also grateful for a bit of time to decompress before the evening meal.

Her days are more compartmentalized now, a deeply etched divide from morning to night, present to past, Sam to Red. She's been anxious about whether she will be able to complete her PhD on schedule. Her advisor echoed Hank's comment on all things being up in the air, including her defense.

At dinner that night, they avoid discussion of politics or pandemic. Instead, Red goes into a lengthy description of climate change on the southern coast, which he's been studying. He cites rising sea levels, coastal erosion, and the degradation of the marine ecosystem. He launches a meteorological explanation of the coming May Gray leading to the June Gloom. He's nearly giddy with his findings, always fascinated with microsystems.

After they sip the last of the wine and clean-up, she tells him any film tonight is fine, but Red surprises her by saying he'd rather read, and then settles into a chair by the fireplace with a hardbound copy of Dickens' *Old Curiosity Shop*.

Nothing Red has said or done of late shocks her more than reading Dickens, especially this early work, less often read.

Rosa lent it to me, he replies to her quizzical expression.

I wonder if Rosa, or Mateo, gravitated to Dickens because he writes so often about orphans, also the underclass, she remarks.

Red looks up. *Hadn't thought about it that way. She reveres Dickens, particularly this one. She likes the girl, Nell, she said.*

Sharon nods. *A lovely character. The upside of Dickens' people is the victory over oppression. Well, some of them. I do wonder if leaving her family behind, even over time, even protected by Mateo, I mean, maybe all immigrants feel orphaned, in effect, even if it was their choice to spread their wings.*

She speaks of her family as if, well, as if they are here with her. Not like an orphan, or a migrant, he says.

Red returns to reading. He's the one to interrupt her, as a rule, and now she realizes she's trying to get his attention, stung by his dismissal of her concerns. He's decidedly detached, as if she's no longer relevant.

She has the sudden sinking sensation he knows about Sam, although she cannot imagine how.

When he peers toward the sea, as if to reassure himself of something, she too glances in that direction, where a half-moon glows on the surface of the water, its simplicity a stark contrast to chaos all around.

She's had her full of Gaskell of late, so she goes into her room and pulls her worn copy of *Frankenstein.* She never tires of reading it or teaching it.

Subtitled *The Modern Prometheus,* the mythical Titan who bestowed fire on mortals, fire confers heat and light, but is also deadly: the great paradox of want and resistance. Her students debate the dichotomy. They equate dissonance with ambivalence.

What are we all so afraid of? Sharon murmurs.

Pardon? Red says.

Sharon chuckles. *Sorry, didn't realize I'd said that out loud.*

She holds up the book to show the cover.

Oh, the monster, he says. *How many times have you read that book?*

Maybe too many, she answers.

I guess I just never got it, he says.

The existential dilemma, she says.

Sorry?

I mean the novel. Also the demon of desire.

Hmmm, he says, and then returns to Dickens.

I may have told you before, but Shelley started the novel when she was a teenager. Still amazing to me.

He pauses. *I wonder if Rosa has read it.*

Surely a story Mateo would have appreciated. At heart, it's the duality of the beast within us all, until catapulted outward, and feared.

The good, the bad and the ugly? Red asks.

Sharon smiles. *Also the essence of creativity.*

Red makes a mental note to tell Rosa.

In 1816, nearly two-hundred years ago, and a hundred years before the Spanish Flu pandemic, in what became known as the year without summer, an eruption at Mount Tambora, Indonesia, ushered in anomalous climate conditions across the globe.

Shelley, then Mary Godwin, and her soon to be husband, with friends, including the poet Lord Byron, were trapped for three days by prolonged cold and fog at a mansion in Geneva, Switzerland. To pass the time, Percy Shelley challenged them to write ghost stories, and *Frankenstein* was born, setting the stage for gothic fiction, although the novel was not completed until after Shelley lost her firstborn child, intensifying her preoccupation with the meaning of human existence.

On that same weekend, Lord Byron's physician, John Polidori, wrote a tale called *The Vampyre*, the first of that genre as well, which remains as much a fascination in the 21st century.

Twenty-five years later, Dickens would publish *A Christmas Carol*, the first of his quest to examine the supernatural realm.

Are we all haunted by incongruities? Sharon wonders. Weather phenomena or global health crises? At best, they portend the inauguration of new literary forms, and at worst, the end of lives as we live them.

She glances at Red. They could be miles apart. Under very different circumstances, retreat might have been the realization of a romantic ideal: a marriage of mind and body. Tonight, the rift between them seems more intentional than in the past and she is deeply saddened, as if their marriage has only just collapsed. Grief renewed.

Red is engrossed in Dickens' dense descriptive language – not as formidable as he recalls from youth, and the panorama of characters amusing – although hardly mystery page-turners or biographies he prefers.

Despite his disappointment at what's come of their retreat, he feels oddly at peace tonight, which he attributes to Rosa's calming influence. She's a balm to what ails him. He can tell her anything. He will soon disclose the cancer and his hope he will outlive the prognosis. He might confess he fears dying alone.

Dickens said of March, '*it was the season when summer was in the light and winter in the shade.*'

The duality of the transitional season..

ave does not appear on the morning Red has scheduled a surf lesson, and he waits nearly an hour before checking his phone, which he's left in the car, to listen to an apologetic message that Dave's helping Tammy with a project and then heading north to visit his sister. He promised to make contact on return, with no indication when that might be.

Red again leaves the phone in the car and sits on the sand. The sun is just showing its face above the trees and surfers on boards dot the water like seabirds, floating and bobbing, waiting for the moment to rise.

A young man, maybe twenty – lean and tanned – passes by with a board under his arm, like a surfing poster-boy, and asks if Red needs assistance.

Red explains he was to meet his neighbor Dave for his first lesson and the boy smiles.

Dave's a pillar on the water. Not like him to miss the dawn patrol, he says.

Maybe I got the date wrong, Red answers.

Must be super important, like, rad, for Dave not to show. You can ride with me. Feel the board, he offers.

Kind of you, but I wouldn't want to interfere with your surf time, Red replies.

A small south swell today, perfect for a beginner, the boy says, urging Red to take the plunge.

Well, if you're sure, I was sort of stoked.

The boy laughs at the antiquated expression. *Hold on,* he says, and runs to his car for a wetsuit.

Better wear this, he instructs.

The wetsuit requires considerable tugging and by the time it's on, Red's courage starts to fade.

If it's my time, it's my time, he assures himself, and with a thumbs up, he trails the boy into the water.

My eyes were bigger than my stomach, so to speak, Red explains to Rosa when he returns later that morning. *I was exhausted just getting ready, and then, trying to stand, my balance is not what it was, nor my strength. I should have known better.*

Rosa listens without comment. She knows now to wait Red out unless a response is required.

The young man was kind to give up precious time in the water. We paddled out, I sat a bit, he gave me a few pointers, and then we waited, not long. He had the radar. I would have tried sooner, but he was patient, and when he said, finally, let's go, I lay on the board, and he stood. It was fantastic! A rush, as my sons say. However, when I tried to stand up, I failed. Repeatedly. The boy, Kevin was his name, was very kind. Rode me in a few more times. Wish I'd tried long ago, but I cannot push this envelope. Too old now to learn new tricks like these, sadly.

Red doesn't mention the strain in his calves, the shortness of breath, despite never going the distance, nor the chill in his bones: cold water tinged with terror.

I think you were brave, Rosa says, her kindness mitigating his disappointment. *I myself would never challenge the sea.*

Nice way to put it, Red responds. *The sea won.*

The sea will always win, she says.

Kids like this one, and old pros like Dave, they stay in the saddle, he replies, sadly.

They must feel like gods when they do.

Mythic gods for sure. Not for mere mortals.
Would you like some tea, Mr. Red?
That would be lovely, Miss Rosa.

Rosa laughs. Although she smiles frequently, a charming half-smile that reveals little of what she's thinking, she seldom laughs. Smooth and melodic, her laughter is a counterpoint to the roar of the waves earlier and the roar of reproach in his head.

She gestures to him to sit at the round table, under the Van Gogh print, and sets the kettle on, busying herself at the kitchen counter.

Red gazes out at a sun now high in the sky, thinking of surfers who set their body clocks to waves the way sailors follow the stars and Mexican farmers scent the air. He'd rather not give up so easily, but he has to respect his limitations. Engineering, contrary to the general impression, is not about invention, rather reconfiguring what is for optimum utility. An engineer adapts to constraints, and these days, he considers his options within the context of age, illness, and now, global disorder. He's far from family and friends, and the woman he had hoped would share his final days is on a different path. He's lost her again, and despite profound disappointment, he feels, with Rosa, like a winter sun: bright and essential.

Rosa serves the tea in a porcelain pot. She puts matching mugs and cloth napkins on the table, with a platter of small domed cookies smothered in powdered sugar. Red pops one into his mouth, delighting in its sweetness, then wipes a bit of powder off his shirt with a grateful smile.

He looks over to the three paintings of different paths. Although they have advanced some since the last visit, they are still incomplete. Flower boxes now adorn the houses on one road, but still, no windows. No signs of life anywhere. In the most complete, she's added thicker brush strokes to a dark leafy forest, more foreboding than the others.

He finds it hard to reconcile her simple comforts with the anguish in her art. Is it longing embedded in endless roads or helplessness? The manifestations of an orphan or something else he cannot grasp?

If you had one wish, Rosa, just one thing you would like to have or do, what would it be? Red asks.

I have what I need, she answers.

But there must be something? Even if not a thing, a hope? A wish? We all have dreams, he insists.

What is it you want, Mr. Red? she counters.

Yesterday I would have said I want to surf. He chuckles. *Today, I'm not sure.*

Maybe you want to drop out of a plane?

I suppose I could be a cliché. Surf. Bungee jump. Zipline. Not me. Not keen on death-defying adventures.

Red blanches at his words. He is defying death. He has elected to refuse additional treatment and stay here, on retreat, rather than accept the care of friends or family. He too has what he needs, for now.

So, what is it you wish? Rosa asks, in the voice of a child asking an elder to explain the meaning of life.

Nothing dramatic. Maybe the opposite.

Rosa waits for him to clarify and he has to think about what it is he wants to express, or if he can.

I think, well, I think I want to belong, he says, with a shrug and a sheepish grin.

You mean you don't know where you belong?

Not so much where, but to whom, or what. My sons believe no one belongs to anyone, very Zen, but I'm not talking about attachment. Something like purpose. Direction. Without work or family, or passion, like yours for art, for example, what is there? I suppose I'm just a typical retired workaholic.

We all have purpose, Rosa says. *We are witness, participant, or catalyst,* she recites, recalling Mateo's words. *Which are you, Mr. Red?*

Put that way, I'm a catalyst. In my work, my life, I made things possible for others. I solved problems. That's what good engineering can do.

There, you have purpose, she says with a nod.

But I'm not able to facilitate anything anymore. And you've evaded my question, Rosa. Only a monk wants for nothing.

She smiles. *Perhaps I am a monk. La monje.*

Sharon will tell you I am monkish. I enjoy the company of friends and family, I do, I just hate bustle. Too many distractions. Does that make any sense?

Por supuesto. Of course. I am the same.

But there must be one thing you wish to make your life more complete? he insists.

Rosa nods, a contemplative nod. She stands to refill the teapot, but stops at the counter, staring into space as if wondering what she might reveal. When she returns to the table, she sits, without expression, and so silently, Red fears he has offended her.

She's trembling. One reluctant tear drifts down her cheek.

Not wanting to say anything that might cause her further harm, Red stays silent, wondering what it is she wants. What she needs. What can he do for her?

Just as he's racking his brain to find something supportive to say, she stands again, facing him head on, and when their eyes meet, he sees her profound sadness. Without a word, he takes her hand the way a father might comfort a daughter, or as a brother might hope to protect a beloved sister, and Rosa allows her hand to rest in his as the trembling slowly dissipates.

At last, as if with tremendous effort, she speaks in a voice as tentative as a Dickens' urchin, and so muffled, Red isn't sure he has heard her correctly, but he thinks she has said, *I want to go home.*

SPRINGTIME

But the cloud never comes in that quarter
of the horizon from which we watch for it.
Elizabeth Gaskell

March 19th, the governor of California issues a statewide shelter-in-place decree, one day before the same directive by his counterpart in New York. The CDC urges Americans to keep six feet apart and stay home. Health emergencies have been declared in several American cities, and New York City, what will become known as the epicenter, has already shut down to non-residents.

This is one of those moments, Sharon tells Hank, *when what you know, what you've come to expect or rely on, day-to-day, year after year, turns a one-eighty. Work, school, personal life, any sense of well-being goes topsy-turvy, right? Mind and life altering.*

And if you're paying attention, it will play back for years, again and again, Hank responds.

Right. Kennedys. King. 9/11.

Bush v Gore, haunts me. Now, Breonna Taylor. Hard to process, Hank says.

Heinous, is all Sharon can say, the shooting by law enforcement only days old and incomprehensible.

Hard to equate assassinations or terrorism, and police misconduct, with a deadly virus, but this might define this generation, Hank says.

We can only hope, sooner than later, we will all be referring to the time before covid, Sharon says. *BC.*

BC, Hank echoes. *And, if there was any doubt we are one human race, at least on this planet, it's debunked now, because although every human will be hit, the poor and the needy will be hit the worst.*

Sadly so, Sharon acknowledges.

On top of all that, Mercury is in Retrograde! Hank remarks, with a laugh.

Sharon is stunned by the sudden shift in tone, but she knows Hank well enough to know she seeks humor, and an upside, as an antidote to despair.

Which is the only thing that might explain the chaos I'm watching right now, Sharon says.

She's standing next to her car in the parking lot at Gelson's, a popular upscale market. Roughly fifty shoppers are lined up at the entrance, clamoring like children at recess. Many wear masks, making them seem a parade of bank robbers. Some talk on phones or stare at phones, as if an essential truth will appear to save the day. Others commiserate. Anxiety hovers over them like fog.

A beleaguered manager at the front of the line is taking heat for staggering entry. He's trying to save the store from being overrun or his staff overwhelmed. Voices rise in anger. The buyers who have made the cut navigate the parking lot with carts overflowing with paper goods, milk, cheeses and coffee, meats and fish, frozen foods, bottled waters, wine and beer. A couple parked nearby debates what they might have missed, even as they struggle to load their SUV.

It's Armageddon. Unbelievable, Sharon says.

Remember when we said this was a science fiction movie? We spoke too soon. It's the apocalypse.

Dystopian, Sharon mutters.

I was at the Bowl last night, huge crowd, and we're socialists, we share, but someone might have killed me for the last batch of berries, Hank says.

Sharon is still reeling from an argument with Red this morning over his plans to stay put. She had hoped to use Hank as a sounding board, but Hank has been called to another meeting online, she says, with her apologies. A harbinger of things to come.

I'm with you in spirit, my friend, Hank says, as the line goes dead.

Sharon is waiting for Sam, whom she called on her way, hoping to see him sooner than later. Whatever the duration of quarantine, what a radio commentator she listened to on the drive here called *house arrest,* she cannot fathom how they will spend time together beyond a clandestine meeting like this. She already feels the noose tightening. People will be expected to cloister at home, although someone must shop now and then, and shopping will be her responsibility now, as Red has agreed, reluctantly, to limited exposure. He insisted he intends to continue hiking, while she hopes to continue her in-town or beach walks.

A regular change of scene will be imperative, otherwise people might behave like rats in a maze.

She told Red she prefers her sons stay put, and when she suggested Red move in with one of his brothers, he dug a deeper trench in his sand.

Stay or go, Sharon, whatever you like, but I urge you to consider staying here. Exercise good judgement.

Maybe your judgement is not right for all of us…

So, go back north, fine, although if the boys are here, we can all be together. Think about it that way.

Sharon was flummoxed by his intransigence. The impotence he must feel about all this has made him unusually grouchy, although, to his mind, the problem is already solved.

What pains her even more than the reality of a pandemic, and the certainty that many will be sick or die, lose jobs or will have no choice but to work, risking their health and the health of their families, more than any of this is the realization Red will grow sicker over time. That's a given. Tammy's words haunt her: he's more vulnerable to the virus. Even if he escapes that, his condition will worsen. He shouldn't be alone. If he won't agree to hospice care, if she can even get him in on short notice, she will have to do exactly what she hoped she would never have to do, if only to protect her sons.

When she agreed to retreat, she imagined a short exit ramp from the final phase of her studies and now cannot see where the road goes.

And now, her dissertation defense is postponed indefinitely. She's broken-hearted. Having moved half-way across country and studied for five years, a global event over which she has no control will deny her reward. She didn't tell Red, she couldn't bear to talk about it, and she had nowhere to go to suffer her sadness alone. A glimpse of close-quarter quarantine.

I won't press you any further, Red concluded. *I've made my decision and now it's up to the boys. I guess when they decide, you'll decide.*

Afterward, Sharon slunk back to her room like a surly adolescent, and then, pummeled by a searingly hot shower, screamed until she was depleted. Red was consumed with TV talking heads debating draconian end-of-the-world-as-we-know-it scenarios and he only nodded when she emerged, dressed, hair still damp.

When she announced she was going to shop for what they may need in the next week or so, Red texted Rosa to ask what she needed as well.

Make sure to pack the groceries separately, he instructed, as he handed Sharon the list.

Of course, she answered, and fled.

Sam has been circling the lot and when he finds her, he parks and jumps out of the truck. Sharon falls into his embrace, and he holds her so close, she feels the pounding of his heart and his warm breath on her neck. She would like to stay in his arms until the madness ends.

When they pull apart, he swipes the mist from her hair on his cheeks and they chuckle.

What the hell is going on? he says, noticing the chaos at the market entrance.

They're storming the shelves, she says.

Sam shakes his head in dismay. *This is crazy.*

I'm still trying to figure out what a stay-at-home order is. The so-called shelter-in-place, she says.

Can acronyms be far behind?

She nods, but cannot see the humor right now.

What else has happened? he asks, aware of her pained expression and the body language of defeat.

Classes have been suspended and my defense is on hold, she answers.

Oh Sharon, what a disappointment, he says.

Sharon struggles to hold back her tears.

My advisor said I will have to be ready at a moment's notice, but I'm not sure how to focus while all this is going on.

Hard to focus on anything, he answers, and then hugs her again to commiserate.

The numbers in Europe are staggering. And I'm worried about my boys. They're both in an urban petri dish. Although China got on top of it quickly, I think.

Maybe. They divulge so little their data cannot be trusted, he comments. *What will your sons do?*

Red wants to bring them out here. If he weren't so committed to Rosa, he might have looked for a larger place, but for now he's on the hunt for a flat for the boys.

Sure, but will they want to be out here, without their people? Without any social life? he asks.

I suppose they will hang out there with friends, from a distance. They shouldn't fly anyway, she says.

Or they could drive. Load up the car with food, drive through Starbucks or McDonald's for filler, if those places stay open. Sleep in the car. Maybe five days. Wherever there's Wi-Fi, they can work, right?

Sharon sighs. *Knowing them, that's what they will want to do. The pretense of family togetherness will be tantalizing. How can I say no?*

I think you have the right... Sam starts to say.

I do not want them to have to tend to Red, when he gets worse, and if this goes on much longer, they will. They have no clue what that sort of caretaking is like.

No one does until you go through it, he says.

Sharon ignores the comment. She doesn't want to hear it and she doesn't want to debate.

And, while Red and I have done well, a retreat is not total isolation. He's increasingly disgruntled.

With what? Being stuck in Laguna? he asks.

Oh no, he's thrilled to be here. With me, I think. He must have had an expectation for retreat and he's not happy with the result.

Sam nods. *He was aiming for a reconciliation.*

I never, never played into that notion, she says.

Even so, he must have harbored hope.

He's dying. What was to be gained now?

Last chance to patch what needs to be patched?

Red used to say a good engineer leaves no loose ends, Sharon says, with a loud sigh.

Your retreat, and now a chance to stay longer, is exactly the opportunity for him to do that. And you, with your compassion for him, will feed right into it.

Sharon shakes her head forcefully. *No.*

You guys are not on the same wavelength.

We've never been, she says.

Never? he questions.

Okay, that's not fair. Rarely.

Maybe you should ask. Pin him down, he says.

What's the point? He's resolved. Why be holed-up in Chicago, he said, when he can hike the hills and nap on the patio. Watch sunset with a glass of wine.

Sounds like he's hunkered in. And he's right, it is a good place to be stuck in place.

For how long, that's the question, she grumbles.

Sam grasps her hands. *At the risk of sounding equally selfish, why don't you lock down with me? We might hate each other in the end, or we might have a wonderful time. Would surely make a great story – how our love affair survived a pandemic.*

Sharon is as flummoxed as she is flattered. At the same time, she's inclined to take flight from both men who want more from her than she may want to give. Then again, why should she forfeit what could be great? Why should she weather this storm alone?

Impulsive, I know, he says, *but, if ever there was a moment to seize, this is it. Think of my home as a bed and breakfast with benefits! Or we can rent a boat and sail away, like Love in the Time of Cholera. This is the chance of a lifetime, literally.*

Sam laughs, but his eyes betray his longing. *Teach me to cook. We can read to each other, dance all day. Anything we want any time we want.*

Sharon is certain any woman in her right mind would jump at his offer. Madness not to take the leap.

I'm not one to throw caution to the wind, as you know by now, although you're right, if ever there was a time, this is it, she says. *But I don't see how I can...*

Sharon, there is only one question to answer: do you want to be with me? he demands.

Yes, I do. But...

No buts. We go from there, he insists.

Sounds so easy, but how can I abandon Red?

You gave him nearly three months. You kept your promise. He's got Rosa for company and Tammy will surely watch out for him, he argues.

Speaking of Tammy, have you seen her?

No, why?

Dave was supposed to give Red a surf lesson the other day and he didn't show. He left a cryptic message he was helping Tammy with something and visiting his sister, and we haven't heard from either of them since. Red walked over there yesterday, no one was around.

It's not like Dave to blow anyone off, or not to be in the water if he's in town. I'll check in on them.

He pulls her closer. *Back to my proposition, and I mean that in the best possible way.* He chuckles. *Get what you want. What we both want. Red will have all that he needs, and you'll be nearby, in case. I am not heartless, but he's not your responsibility anymore.*

You make perfect sense and I'm usually a better decision maker, but I'm overwhelmed, she whimpers.

This is not a moment for pragmatism. This is the moment to trust your instincts. He grips her shoulders, as if he might shake her into submission. *The moment to decide what you want, not what you don't want,* he instructs, like a headmaster.

You're not making this any easier, she counters.

Sorry, but I prefer to look forward. You're stuck in the past, I'm afraid. He takes her hands in his again. *I don't want to be a sidebar. I don't want to see you now and then when you have spare time. When you're not with your family. I'm no good being parenthetical. All or nothing for me.*

So, here's the summary from my perspective, she says. *You want me to want what you want, Red wants me to want what he wants, I'm concerned about my kids and we're about to fall into a black hole.*

Sam steps back and sighs, dropping her hands.

When you put it that way, seems an impasse. The men in your life know what we want, so decide what's best for you. Something has to give. Or someone, in this case. I'll wait you out, for now, he says, and then kisses her, before climbing back into his truck.

Sharon watches him drive away. She has yet to feel the full fear of this virus, but she dreads losing a chance at a relationship that may never again present. Nevertheless, she cannot fathom telling Red and her sons she plans to move in with someone they know nothing about. She hates to disappoint Sam, but sees no happy ending for anyone.

When Sharon left for the market, Red climbed the stairs to Rosa. The music was on, so he hesitated, but she was the one person he could talk to. He also wanted to make her aware of the new restrictions. She avoids the news, shielding herself from evil spirits, she says. For this reason, among others, he feels especially protective toward her, although no one is better suited to riding the pandemic wave. She could be a prototype for lockdown: an isolate satisfied with music, painting, and literature, and nourished by memory.

His motives are far from pure, he knows this. Spending time with Rosa is his salvation; less so, hers.

When he lands at the balcony and knocks, she peeks out and welcomes him, as if awaiting him.

Two hours later, when Sharon returns, Red is on his way down the stairs. He was listening for her. As he makes his way across the patio, she emerges at the top of the stone stairs laden with shopping bags.

He grabs two. *Anything left at the store?* he asks.

When she answers, *not much,* they laugh.

She heads back to the car to retrieve the rest, while Red delivers Rosa's to her balcony, and then he returns to help Sharon wipe boxes and bags. When she asks if there is anything new to know, he answers no.

They are all treading water, and until there is better intel, or clear solutions, they will talk around each other until they're blue. Looks like we're in for the worst and unprepared for any of it.

As perturbed as he is, he's not argumentative, for which she's grateful. She cannot bear harsh words or cross purposes right now.

As she washes up at the sink, she also wonders if he has increased his cannabis intake or changed the mix. He's unusually relaxed. No matter, she thinks, as she prepares the comida, seeking distraction from her own thoughts. She seasons salmon and salts broccoli. Red retrieves half a baguette from the freezer to warm. While describing the madness at the market, she piles mats, napkins and silverware, and hands them to him, and after he sets the patio table, he returns for the food. Once the meal is cooked, she pours the wine. The food smells good and with wine in hand, they toast the moment with gratitude.

Although they got a later start than usual, the days are growing longer. Daylight lingers.

Nonetheless, before they even have a chance to notice, the sky has grown dark, and a day that will be marked in history ends.

They carry plates and accoutrement back to the kitchen. Red washes while Sharon wipes the table and makes sure to put everything back in its place, ready for another day.

Music or movie? she asks.

I'm a bit tired, I think I'll turn in, Red replies, but he stands in place, as if awaiting instruction.

She sees resignation in his eyes and weariness in his stance. She hates to see him forlorn. This turn of events is a sad disruption to their retreat. Whatever hidden agenda he might have had, the finale should have been better than this.

On an impulse, she steps forward and wraps her arms around him. Red leans in to her, gratefully, eliminating all distance between them. They embrace with solidarity – the bonds of longstanding affection – without desire or regret.

Sharon is reminded of their dinner last fall, when their early lives flashed before her eyes. When she saw only the difficulties of the past. What they feel now, what many people will feel in the pandemic era, is nostalgia for loved ones they failed to appreciate, as well as a future without limitations and without fear.

When they separate, they have tears in their eyes, yet they smile: a brief gratifying connection.

Sharon wishes she could sleep tonight with Red or with Sam. Hold on to a loved one as a way of holding on to life, more precarious than ever.

Instead, she sleeps alone, tossing and turning with anxiety.

Shortly after midnight, as she's finally falling asleep, Red goes into a coughing spasm. His bark is sharp and deep. She reaches for a sweatshirt to throw on, but as suddenly as it started, the coughing slows down. She tiptoes to his door to listen, waiting for the coughing to subside and then for his steady breathing. She has an awful image in her mind now of what it must be like when breathing will not sustain life: to die for lack of oxygen, whether COVID-19 or lung cancer.

Hank was prophetic when she asked how she will be able to leave. She left Red years ago. She cannot leave him again. He needs her now. His body will be nourished with sunlight and clean air. They are on an even keel. Despite their rocky past and the challenges ahead, the moment may be fortuitous. Red is where he should be and, perhaps, so is she.

osa and Mateo's wedding day was the last day Mateo was his convivial self and, that night, he slept deeply, not with exhaustion, although he was after the long day, rather satisfaction.

He had secured a future for Rosa and, perhaps, he might find forgiveness for his sins in the next life.

Rosa's belongings were moved into the spare room. She reset her altar on the chest, on her precious rug. She slipped into her new bed, purchased for her new space, with fresh sweet-smelling sheets. She kept her door ajar, listening to Mateo breathe in his room across the hall, enjoying the novelty of proximity.

Beyond remodeling the lower level, which was both a disruption and a pleasure for Mateo, their days remained the same, for a while. Rosa rose with the sun to tend to chores, he later, and after his double dose of espresso with sweet bread and fruit, he painted at an easel set up in the living area facing the sea, and then rested in the afternoons to restore his strength.

Before long, unable to stand at the easel more than an hour or so, his shoulders increasingly sore, his neck heavy on his head, he perched on a stool commandeered from a friend's bar, leaning in to apply paint, and, when asked, Rosa assisted.

Like the Maestro, Mateo remarked, referring to Matisse, whose helpers served as his brush when his vision dimmed.

Mateo was taken by surprise, and impressed, with Rosa's command of his technique, having no idea she had studied his painting all their years together and had mastered his style.

It was at this time he began sketching decaying birds of paradise. At first, they had a hint of sunlight on the leaves or translucency in the beaks, which made them seem more majestic than decaying. Before long, however, he shifted to images of chaos, more and more disturbing. He directed Rosa to apply strokes thicker or thinner, or where a background needed darker paint. Although troubled by this new thematic, she followed his lead, becoming his eyes and hands, also his voice to admirers no longer welcome to visit, because Mateo refused to be seen in a weakened state.

One afternoon, late in March, after the equinox had arrived, although winter chill persisted, and as the sun descended through low clouds, Mateo closed the sliding door and sagged into his chair at the dining table. His eyes were rimmed with shadowy crescents and his cheekbones sunken, like a charcoal sketch of himself.

Rosa wrapped a blanket around his shoulders. She put on a recording of a Beethoven piano sonata. He listened with his eyes closed, thoughts returning to his youth, his parents and sister, so long gone, with a profound sense he would soon see them again.

Rosa smiled at the sight of his tranquility, while she finished a beef stew with healing herbs and spices. When she served the steaming fragrant bowl, Mateo inhaled the scent with pleasure and nodded gratitude, although he took only a few spoonful's and ignored the open bottle of a favorite Chilean wine.

Perhaps a cup of your special tea, in my room, he requested, his voice so raspy, she hardly heard.

He rose slowly, no longer trusting his senses, and made his way down the hall as Rosa boiled water until bubbling. She added to the infuser chamomile leaves and passionflower to calm, ginger for health, and flax seeds to soothe the lungs. She let it brew longer than usual to ensure its curative benefits, and then served the tea on a carved tray, a wedding gift from a ceramicist, with Mateo's favorite mug.

His bedroom was darkened by thick branches of a Tecate cypress he had planted when the house was framed, now nearly twenty feet tall. He awakened mornings to leaves licking the glass and soft light inviting him to inhabit the day. At night, branches rustled like a sonata to soothe his sleep.

He reclined on a king-sized bed, set against a tall wood headboard, layered with dense pillows and quilted blankets.

Please stay, he instructed, when Rosa delivered the tea, pointing to the large chair where he sat when dressing or undressing. Flipflops and mules lay below, waiting their turn, and Rosa noticed the soles were spotted with paint, as if a new art form.

After a few moments, eyes at half-mast, Mateo murmured, *here, sit here.*

He patted the bed by his side and Rosa sat. As he bent forward to sip tea, she plumped a pillow and layered another to cradle his neck, before he leaned back with his eyes closed.

After a while, when she rose to let him sleep, he called to her. *Forget whatever should be done. I need your warmth.*

Rosa curled up next to him, on top of a blanket and placed a hand on his. She listened to his breathing slowly settle into a resting rhythm, before she too slept, willing herself to teleport sweet dreams to her patron.

As weeks passed and his strength steadily faded, a new routine was established: she delivered tea soon after dinner and, as he slept, she coiled against his body to keep him warm, breathing his breaths as if her own, so that, should they stop, she would know. She had previously called the neighbor Tammy to ask what to do should Mateo cease breathing in the night and the kindly nurse told her to call any time.

While he slept, she reached one arm across his chest, her fingertips pressing gently at pulse points at his neck to calm his weary spirit. She massaged his temples with lavender and eucalyptus oils and inhaled his scent with joy, night after night, until he descended into the stank of the dying.

Mornings, she watched as he stirred, hoping for signs of recovery and, at the same time, praying to her gods for a peaceful passing.

In his final days, Mateo regaled Rosa with tales of the tortured lives of the artists he most admired, as if preparing to meet them in the afterlife. In addition to his beloved Van Gogh and Matisse, he cited, much to her surprise, Edvard Munch, the Norwegian artist best known for painting *The Scream.*

He's famous for that painting, Mateo said, *but there were nearly 2000 others. He, like Vincent, lived long in seclusion, and he too was institutionalized for a time. I cannot believe any being can stand before The*

Scream, which I would have liked to see in Oslo, without assimilating his despair for the human condition.

Rosa stared at the painting, and what she saw in that anguished face was less despair than a desire to repel fear. To banish what torments us. Munch, she would have said, illustrated a longing for courage in a universe beset by hopelessness.

When Mateo was too tired for talk, Rosa read aloud from Van Gogh's letters. These were filled with a hope historians discount. At his urging, she also read from Munch's journals, surprisingly poetic.

'We are flames which pour out of the earth.'

Mateo smiled. *Yes, we are,* he murmured. *And we all return to ashes. Van Gogh buried his demons in brush strokes. He cherished starlight on water, bright blue sky after rain. He illuminated suffering to implore mankind to pay attention. We are better than we know, he might have said. Dickens too, and Munch, would say we can do better. We can always do better, yes?*

Rosa considered his words. *Artists who light up a flat surface or define the world with words or music, these inspire faith. They see only the road ahead.*

Mateo smiled, satisfied his devoted companion had fulfilled her promise and that he had fulfilled his.

On the last day of his life, Rosa read aloud from *The Old Curiosity Shop,* and, in one particular passage, held a mirror to both their lives.

'Fearful of taking shelter beneath a tree or hedge, the old man and the child hurried along the highroad, hoping to find some house to which they could seek a refuge from the storm...'

As she read, Mateo's breathing slowed, until, at last, with a deep sigh, nothing more. Not a sound.

She held his hands and wept, until she forced herself from his side to call for assistance.

Her beloved was gone. After his memorial, after the music stopped and the last few mourners left her alone, she drowned her sorrows in the last of the wine and she slept in his bed for weeks, until the gods called to her. She turned to painting for solace and to keep faith with her destiny. She waited for a sign from the universe to move forward.

The day she met Red, she knew her journey was about to take a turn.

Sharon wakes to stillness. She's slept later than usual. A coffee aroma wafts from the kitchen to her room, so she knows Red is up and he's likely already hiking. The call of birds and the gentle woosh of sea breezes that usually rest gently on her shoulders like silk, today seem a dead weight. She cannot shake a sense of doom as she slips tentatively out of bed, as if she might encounter a predator.

This is how days will begin sheltering here. She can picture how it will play out. Red will take off early to hike, and in the afternoons he will nap and then visit with Rosa. She will be cooped up in the flat or on the patio. The dissertation defense will remain on the back burner; instead, she will review reading lists to ready for classes whenever they resume. She will have to attend faculty meetings online, and will visit with colleagues and friends on-screen, but they will all be asteroids drifting through dark matter.

With so much time on her hands, she thinks now she will research material to construct a syllabus around the modernist movements spawned by the painters and writers of the mid-to-late 1800s, which might also form the basis of a book. Publish or perish in academia is real.

She will have lots of reading time, so she makes a mental note to download a stack of books, but even she cannot read all day, and there's just so much to stream. She might walk now and then with Red, more often on her own. She needs exercise. Forward motion.

The sameness of days, which troubled them early on, will surely be suffocating.

When she calls Sam, the call goes to voicemail. He may be hiking as well. She has imagined he and Red crossing paths one day, hardly noticing each other, as if on parallel paths, which is where they all seem to be now: before and after without juncture.

She drags herself out of bed, fills a mug with coffee and adds a splash of milk, then steps out to the patio, wrapping a throw blanket around her shoulders. Technically it is spring, although not like a spring that comes after true winter, when trees and bushes shake off frost and stretch out to the warm. A marine layer here hugs the terrain and rarely burns off until late morning – a lingering gray famous for shrouding the southern California coast in the months before the summer solstice.

A particularly fitting landscape: all living things trapped in transition. No clarity, no destination, no sense of an ending.

She picks up the phone to call Red, to make sure he's not in need of anything. In truth, she needs to hear a human voice. She already feels disconnected. Hank is so often consumed by meetings these days, she proposed they text more than talk. Sharon misses her voice, but better than nothing.

Just about to get out of range, Red says when he picks up the call. *What's up?*

I guess hiking is an approved pastime she says.

I hope so. I don't plan to give it up, he replies.

All good? she asks.

Sure. I'll be back the usual time. And then I have a video appointment with my doctor, he adds.

You do? Why? she asks.

A follow-up, but they're not seeing patients in person unless it's urgent, which it's not, he answers.

Follow-up on what?

Some tests I took. Reviewing the meds and such.

When did you take tests? she asks.

A couple of weeks ago, he answers.

You never mentioned that, she says, bothered she has not been kept in the loop.

You didn't ask, he says, matter-of-factly.

Sharon is startled by his truculence, especially after their renewed affection. Before she can gather her thoughts to reply, Red says, *cancer was not part of our arrangement, so I haven't mentioned it. Just routine. Do we need anything on my way back?*

We're very well stocked, she says, and chuckles, hoping to defuse the tension. *Just hike and come home.*

Red pauses. He might have responded they are not at home. They are in limbo in a furnished rental, pretending they have a relationship beyond past tense, and while she consorts with another man.

He says, instead, *right, later,* followed by silence.

Sharon grips the cell phone in her hand as if he might call back with an explanation for being abrupt, but when the phone vibrates in her hand, she startles. Nerves on edge.

I was in the shower... Sam says.

I'd like to see you, she nearly whimpers.

Come for breakfast, I've got plenty.

Red has the car.

I'll pick you up.

Give me half an hour, she says, and rushes into the shower to ready.

Sam parks in front of the garage and texts her he's waiting. At the bottom of the steps, she finds him leaning against the truck like a teenager. He smiles with delight, as if she's a prom date, and, as he opens the car door for her, he leans in for a welcoming kiss.

He smells fresh. His hair is rumpled and damp. He hasn't shaved. She tastes a residue of toothpaste and for some reason this makes her smile.

I'm starving, she says, and climbs in.

At your service, he answers, as he backs the truck into the road and then heads up the hill.

Sharon relaxes for the first time in days, as if she's dodged a bullet, although she knows Sam awaits her decision, another hard conversation to be had.

At his house, on the kitchen counter, a wooden bowl contains chopped onion, sliced mushrooms, and halved cherry tomatoes. A handful of spinach leaves are wrapped in a paper towel, dampened by the drying. Eggs are waiting in a bowl and bread sliced for toasting on a cutting board.

He pours her a mug of coffee, refills his own, cracks the eggs and scrambles them, and then drizzles olive oil and a touch of butter into a skillet.

I told you I'm good with omelets. We will never lack for protein, but all bets are off on other nutrients.

Sharon sits on a stool at the island watching him prepare breakfast – a glimpse of what days might be like sheltering together. Mornings in this kitchen, nights lovemaking in his bed. She smiles at the image.

What are you so smiley about? he asks.

I was picturing living here, she replies.

Sam swivels toward her, a wooden spoon in his hand and a childlike smile on his face. He sighs with relief and leans in to kiss her.

Without meaning to, she's led him to believe a decision in his favor has been made. She should speak up at once, but cannot bring herself to ruin his delight.

How she wishes she were the type of woman to grab what she wants, whatever the consequences. She knows she will have to let him down, just not yet. Not at this sweet moment. As foolish as it is, she still hopes a better option might appear.

Letting go of Sam will be the hardest decision she's had to make since the divorce, and now, like then, she feels stuck between the proverbial rock and hard place. Only a romantic takes the untrammeled path. She's not that woman. She's not the woman she'd like to be. She will enjoy breakfast this morning and another rendezvous. That's all there is. Perhaps more than she's entitled to.

Tammy was asked to return to nursing service and she was proud to step up. Hospitals were calling on retired practitioners, teachers, also students, to augment hours and depth to an already overburdened staff. However, because of her age, she was denied intensive care service and reassigned to the operating room, where procedures were restricted to emergencies.

She had no hesitation. She ordered overnight delivery of two pairs of white leather sneakers with thick soles. She laundered uniforms and scrubs, and stayed up late researching protocols during contagion. Her only concern was Dave. What might she bring home to him? They talked it over and decided to keep him out of harm's way by staying with his sister's family in Huntington Beach, not too far to visit when conditions improved, and a good place to ride the waves.

All the masks, gloves and sanitation on earth will not prevent a virus from sticking where it wants to stick, she told friends and neighbors in an email. *Hospitals are war zones. Stay safe, stay at home.*

No one, despite warnings and media coverage, could conceive of the devastation of the pandemic, or the duration; otherwise, Tammy and Dave might have reconsidered. They have never in forty-two years been apart for more than a few days. Neither looked forward to the separation.

Dave also sent a message, and copied Red. *No visitors to the house, please. Arrangements have been made for groceries and essentials to be delivered. The*

Two weeks later, Dave developed a nasty cough. His head ached and his temperature soared. He lost appetite and even his sister's delicious baked goods tasted like cardboard. Within 24-hours, he felt like bricks had been piled on his chest and, struggling to breathe, he was admitted to the hospital and the ICU.

Dave had been away too long to have infected Tammy, but his sister, her husband, and a nephew, would all come down with the virus before the week was out.

Tammy left her post in Newport to go to him. She marched into the hospital wearing scrubs, with her passcode around her neck as if she had credentials there. At any other time, she would not have been stopped, but times had changed. Despite turning on her considerable charm and pleading for professional courtesy, she was denied access to the ICU. She would not give up – hammering residents and begging fellow nurses, to no avail. Finally, she convinced one of her surgeons to intervene and she was permitted to be on the floor where Dave was being treated, but restricted to the nurse's desk.

She could not tend to her beloved husband and she couldn't even hold his hand, but she was present. She recorded messages on her phone, which the ICU nurse played for him, although she was uncertain if he heard her voice. She could only hope, even attached to a ventilator and in a coma for four days, Dave would know she would move mountains to be by his side.

When he became less responsive and his oxygen levels dipped dangerously low, a sympathetic night nurse looked the other way when Tammy slipped into his room, and where, in a hazmat suit and mask, she sang their favorite songs and spoke words of love, until his last breath.

Although no one was permitted to see the dying or the dead, much less sit at their side, she managed to say good-bye.

Death moves in a surprisingly steady stream, as a rule, but mortuaries and crematoriums were flooded. Memorial services or funerals were not an option – a stake in an already broken heart. She waited a week to claim the plain brown box containing her husband's ashes, and then sat holding it all night, as if Dave were with her. She poured them both a glass of wine and drank first hers, then his, while regaling him with the latest news.

At dawn, she walked down the hill into town and up the hill, through the park, to Diver's Cove.

Although not a surf beach, it was here Tammy and Dave, young and in love, declared their intention. On a warm summer night, after dark, no one in sight, they disrobed and slipped into the water, where they promised to be true. In the years since, they returned to this cove to marvel at their good fortune and waded into tidepools there with their children.

She sat on a rock outcropping, toes dipped into the froth, dropping handfuls of ashes into the water. Little by little, she released the love of her life to the sea, leaving the last of him for her daughters.

She sat, heart and body so heavy she was not sure she could move. At last, she inched her way to a boulder in the water, its hard surface a sign of times to come, and sat there, all day, hardly moving, hardly breathing, watching the roiling of the sea, as if Dave might yet emerge from the waves.

The few walkers or runners on the cliffs above might have imagined her a statue – a mythological creature of the sea finding it hard to breathe on land.

She remained there until the last sliver of light slid behind Catalina Island, until all color fled the sky, and until she could barely see the horizon. Stars never broke through the clouds, as if grieving with her.

At last, with great effort, she stood, stretching her tired body in preparation for the walk home and to facing the rest of her life without her beloved husband.

A few days later, she was back at the hospital on ten-hour shifts and insisted on serving in the ICU.

One way to mourn is to make every effort to save another life, she told friends. *At the very least, comfort the sick. No one should die alone.*

The following days played out as imagined. Red took off early each morning for the trails and Sharon hiked with him on alternate days. He led the way, proudly pointing out curious rock formations or an elegant bend in the view. He also cautioned when too close to thick brush or thorny branches. As they walked, she admired unusual foliage or a fragrance in the air. Sometimes, she inquired about an offshoot of the trail or a steeper stretch toward town.

They avoided proximity to other hikers and bikers, masks hanging on their wrists like bracelets – an accessory they never could have predicted.

They returned a couple of hours later to the flat, having nowhere else to go, to showers and snacks, and while he napped, she perused educational materials, and in the afternoons, when Rosa's music ended, Red climbed the stairs to visit with her, returning a couple of hours later for their comida, after which they video chatted with the boys or old friends, or watched a film.

The new routine set in as quickly as when they first arrived: safe, amiable, fraught with uncertainty.

Rosa suggested to Red he invite Sharon to join them for afternoon tea. *She must be lonely,* she said. *No more human energy at the café. No more preparation for her defense or plans for her future.*

Red agreed, however reluctantly. In truth, he would rather have kept Rosa to himself, like a child who hides a rock collection under the bed.

She seems to be doing fine, he said. *She walks, she reads, she loves to read, and I suppose she meets up with Sam when she can.*

He had told Rosa about Sharon's other life, and as Sam is a common name, Rosa had no reason to suspect he was the glazier who once pleased her in the night; yet, intuitively, she knew. She remembered him as thoughtful and passionate, with longings yet to be expressed, burrowing into her body gently, snug and seamless as his glass walls. He sends flowers each year on the Day of the Dead – a kindness she appreciates, although she's never acknowledged.

Facing fear of the pandemic, and loneliness, Rosa imagined Sam wanted a companion; perhaps he hoped to find a long-lasting partner, at long last.

Sharon accepted the invitation, anxious to meet the mysterious paragon of devotion. That morning, however, she felt unexpectedly hesitant, as if a spell might be broken. Red too seemed anxious, skipping his nap, busying himself with a creaky door hinge that refused to be tamed.

When the music stopped, they both climbed the stairs, and when Rosa opened the sliding door, she offered her small warm hand to Sharon, not to shake but to hold, guiding her into her sanctuary.

Sharon noticed at once the three large canvases filling the room like marble pillars in a church, but she kept her gaze on Rosa, who glided through the flat with the serenity and composure of a sylph, just as Sam had described. Nothing like the weary traveler of the night in the portrait at the museum.

They chatted affably, commiserating over the state of the world, commenting on the prolonged chill and the persistent gray. They sipped mint tea between bites of sugar cookies. Sharon expressed her gratitude to be able to shelter at the flat, seizing an opportunity to express her admiration for the comfy furnishings, the lovely rugs, and Mateo's original artwork.

While chatting, Sharon looked up at the Van Gogh print as if she had encountered an old friend, and when she asked to see a photograph of Mateo, Rosa blanched.

Oh, I meant no disrespect, Sharon cried.

Not at all, Rosa replied. *I thank you. No one asks about Mateo. No one except Mr. Red. In this country, the dead are gone, but for me, the spirits remain among us. Mateo is here with us.*

She smiled and stood, leading Sharon and Red to the front bedroom, where an altar, *la ofrenda,* Rosa translated, was displayed on an old chest. Surrounded by traditional mourning paraphernalia – orange flower petals, flickering tealight candles in glass containers, bits of shredded paper, two dried birds of paradise and one tiny sandcastle – were two photographs: one of Mateo as a strapping young man on the beach, the later with Rosa on their wedding day.

The elder Mateo was starkly differentiated from the younger by the shadows outlining his eyes and the hollowed cheekbones, nearly cadaverous.

Sharon saw nothing in either photograph of the divided persona in his self-portrait; however tears filled her eyes, as if she'd known him.

Rosa wrapped an arm around Sharon as if she were the one in need of comfort, and they stood close, sharing the sadness of loved ones lost.

That was the first and last time Sharon met with Rosa. When she extended a reciprocal invitation to join them at comida, Rosa declined, unwilling to descend the stairs.

Sharon would have liked to see Sam or talk to him, but he was awaiting her decision, texting daily. *Are you packed yet? Say the word and I'm on my way. Inquiring minds want to know.*

When she could no longer stall the inevitable, she mustered the courage to meet, and left a note for Red saying she was taking a walk.

She made her way downhill toward PCH, then crossed to a passage near a viewpoint at a secluded cove. As she walked, a new and powerful scent greeted her, faintly reminiscent, and she stopped to scope out the culprit: honeysuckle. As sweet as its namesake, although different from its cousin on the New England shore, with frills on the edge of its fabric, not shaped like the tiny trumpets she remembers.

The scent recalled childhood summers on Cape Cod, where honeysuckle sugarcoats the beaches. Her family spent many vacations in the town of Truro, in a modest cottage they rented every season from an older woman claiming six generations in residence. When she passed, a granddaughter moved in year-round and her father was outraged, as if a personal affront.

Summers are short enough. Why live in extended acquiescence, as if year-round off season? he argued.

For him, as for Red, familiarity meant comfort. Summer holidays were their reward after cold winters and rainy springs, and a tenuous year of academia.

For her mother, summer holiday marked another year of life, another season to cherish.

When Sharon arrived at the sculpture garden, Sam was waiting, and he smiled with delight to see her again. How much she will miss his smile, she thought, as they embraced.

The gates were locked, so they strolled hand-in-hand toward town through typically populous streets, as eerily quiet and bleak as Pompei buried in volcanic ash. They stopped at the church rose garden, buds readying to bloom, dictated by a cycle impervious to man-made disasters.

With little preamble, distraught but resigned, her voice quivering, regretful, she told him she will not shelter with him.

I wish things were different, I do, but I feel I must remain at the rental until the worst has passed.

Sam stared at her with obvious disappointment, scanning her eyes in search of a side door.

Your boys are coming? he asked, as if to justify her rejection.

No. Jamie has moved in with Brady and his girl, Delia. They have more room, they'll all be together. Just me and Red, and Rosa, here, for now, she said.

Strange times make strange bedfellows, he said. *I guess I misunderstood at breakfast that day.*

Please forgive me, she pleaded. *I was so happy to be there with you that morning. Enchanted, in fact. Under any other circumstances, I'd be all in.*

That's bull, you know, he grumbled. *It's not about circumstances. It's about being true.*

Sam, I did not mean to lead you on. I was unsure, even then, and I cannot commit to full time, but we can find time, now and then, like this. Better than nothing, right? Until a better time...

No, he said, emphatically.

Just until the nightmare ends, she beseeched.

I told you, I won't be a sidebar, he insisted.

You are not a sidebar. This was only our first act. An intermission. We'll get back on track when it's over. Rekindle the flame as soon as we can.

This flame has been extinguished by a lack of will, he retorted.

Now you're being harsh. I must think of my sons.

What you mean is you must protect yourself from what they think of you. Maybe you should give them more credit. Let them show you what they're made of.

My boys will soon be down a parent. They need to be sure they can count on me. They need to trust that my intentions are always in their best interests.

I think they need to learn from you to lead with their hearts. Life is not always rational, certainly not predictable, which is the message in all this.

I admire your idealism, but so much easier said than done, she quipped.

Only requires the will. Remember when I told you I resist people, women I said, who do not express, or act, on what they want? So, one more time. What do you want, Sharon, he demanded.

I want to do the right thing, she answered.

For whom? he asked.

For the people I love.

Okay. There it is. You will get what you want.

Sam... she cried, desperate to plead her case.

Listen, I drew a line in the sand. We're together or not. We're headed into unchartered waters, and I would have liked someone by my side. I thought that someone was you, but I won't share.

He smiled, but weakly. *I understand, I do. I'm disappointed, in you and for us, but I get it. I'll make peace with all this. I'm used to a solitary existence. Not my choice, but there it is. I'm sorry too, but that's the way I'm built.*

With one last embrace, they parted, and Sharon slowly made her way back to the flat. Her heart ached. By the time she got there, she was as exhausted as if she had climbed a mountain. At the top of the stone stairs, she stopped to stare at a swarm of birds of paradise, which seemed in that moment condemning and absurdly sanguine, all at once.

Red watched her from the living room. She seemed so downtrodden he was sad for her. At another time, he would have been glad to see her suffer the consequences of her decision, but not today. She had chosen in his favor. No surprise. Sharon would always choose duty over desire. Need over want. He's not sure he would have done the same and he hopes he can find a way to express his gratitude. On the other hand, he realized, he's too much like Mateo – he should have nudged her out the door for her own good.

The beaches were officially closed – no squatting, no towels, no toys or blankets or chairs. Only shuffling on the sand allowed, at least six feet from other walkers. Sharon followed the rules in order to feel the sand beneath her feet and smell the sea. At higher tides, she watched her footprints vanish and, when low, she pressed her toes against the froth, as if to prove she still exists.

In the sky, a war raged between spring gray and summer blue, paralleling the battle between politics and science being waged in the media. Laguna's City Manager came down with COVID-19, bringing the threat closer to home. Daily case counts, published online, indicated growing numbers of hospitalizations followed by increased fatalities: a biblical shadow of death darkening all their doors.

Sharon had trouble adjusting to long days without deadlines. She slept late, watching glimmers of first light from her bed. She lingered over coffee and could not resist doomscrolling or staring at TV news reports like roadkill. She downloaded digital samples of novels she's missed, scanning the first few pages to decide what to read, but her mind drifted. She hunted for recipes online and ordered spices to suit. She threw herself into meal preparation while Red was upstairs with Rosa, listening attentively to podcasts at the same time as if eavesdropping on dinner party conversation.

Days passed. They had no further discussion on where to be or for how long, although Red believed they would last the many months predicted for lockdown, which only weeks ago seemed unfathomable.

Rosa told Red all of her bookings were canceled and they were welcome to stay indefinitely, and when he conveyed her message, he breathed a sigh of relief, as if a stay of execution.

Sam's words and her obduracy haunted her, but she took solace in having done the right thing.

Mid-May, two months into their shelter-in-place order, and nearly five months since the start of retreat, Sharon returned from a beach walk later than usual. A thick marine layer shrouding in-town streets trailed after her as she climbed the hill, then suddenly cleared as she reached the stairs. She turned to gaze down the hill into the mist, and then back to the clearing, as if an omen, like a light at the end of a tunnel.

She could not have been more mistaken.

The slider was closed, but not locked, and the flat empty. She took a shower and made herself some hot tea and waited, wondering where Red might be. An hour passed. He never returned so late from a hike. She gazed out to the patio as if she might see him materialize out of the haze, but saw nothing but mist having climbed back up the hill, obscuring any sort of view. She waited a little longer before calling his phone. When there was no answer, panic reared its ugly head.

Hearing no music from Rosa's flat, she climbed the stairs to see if Red had returned and decided to visit earlier. She would have to intrude on their privacy to be certain. Rosa will understand, she hoped. At the balcony, the drapes were closed, so she could not see in. She knocked, then knocked again, answered by silence. She tried the handle of the sliding door, but it was locked. She walked up the side path to the front door and rang the bell. No answer there either. No light from inside, no sound. She was frightened now for Rosa as well. What might have happened?

She returned to the flat to call the police, but when she reached an automated menu, she hung up, too agitated to press buttons, and then called Mission Hospital, greeted by a message advising where to go or numbers to call having to do with COVID-19, as if all other emergencies were on hold. As if no needs other than the ravages of a rampant virus.

The door to Red's room was ajar and when she peeked in, she noticed the bed had been stripped and the sheets tossed on the mattress. The closet door was open – all but two hangers were empty and on the floor, a pair of dress shoes he'd not had an occasion to wear.

In the bathroom, most of his toiletries and all medications were gone. Half-empty bottles of shampoo and soap were still on the shower shelf and an electric toothbrush on the sink. Damp towels were piled on the floor. Nothing more.

Red had curated his essentials, but why? She had the immediate supposition he had taken some sort of adventure with Rosa, but where would they go? There is no place to go. No adventures to be had. And why wouldn't he have let her know he would be gone, and for how long?

She stood there, her heart pounding, trying to make sense of what had happened, and as she stepped back into the living room, she noticed a folded notecard on the coffee table.

My dear Sharon. The flat is paid through June but you can stay longer if you wish. Annie, the property manager, will make contact. I'll be in touch with the boys. I will always be grateful for our retreat, and for all the years. Take care of yourself. With love, R

Stunned, flattened, as if she'd been pummeled, she stepped out to the patio and sank onto the lounge chair where Red usually rested.

The mist had withdrawn, and the street below, typically thrumming with a steady stream of cars, was empty. The ebb and flow of the highway down the hill, stifled. No walkers as far as the eye could see. She heard the loud shrill cry of seagulls, their soundtrack freed from daily competition with machinery, and, in the distance, waves lapped the shore.

Like the calm before a storm, or after.

Shocked, and frightened, her heart ached – the penetrating type of ache when something or someone crucial slips away, suddenly and permanently, with no chance to reclaim.

Red had kept the promise he made all those years ago: he had disappeared. And not alone. He had engineered the optimal path to the best place to hide until he dies, and he made it possible for Rosa to exit her prolonged personal lockdown. They both got what they wanted and, it seems, Sharon too got what she thought she wanted: spared another painful journey to the death of a loved one. On the other hand, the tether to her past is gone. Impossible to let go without the chance to say good-bye.

*H*e *what?* Hank cries, when Sharon calls to tell her Red has disappeared.

Vanished. Took all his stuff. Rosa's gone too. That's all I know, Sharon answers.

He's taken off with the landlord? I did not see that coming, Hank says.

I'm not sure he's taken off with her, not the way you mean, as much as they've gone somewhere she would like to be and where he can live out his time, at least that's my hypothesis.

You are so naïve sometimes, Hank insists.

Maybe, but I know Red. He's found someone to lean on, it's that simple. Someone he can help in return. He does that, he needs to do that. What he would call a win-win.

Well, you thought you knew him, Hank retorts.

Why do you sound so angry? Sharon asks.

I am angry. The real question is, why aren't you? Your ex lured you on retreat to keep him company, maybe he meant to get you back, who knows, and then, without a word, he disappears with the woman with whom he's whiled away his afternoons. You should be outraged!

I was the one having an affair, so I'm not sure I have a right to outrage, Sharon protests.

Seriously? You're no longer married. And you gave Sam up to do the right thing for your ex-husband, Hank argues.

The right thing for my sons. My choice. And I think Sam gave me up, actually, Sharon says.

Under duress, Hank says.

There's an awkward pause between them, until Sharon asks, *were you ever in a situation like this, Hank? Is this personal for you?*

It's personal because you are my friend and you've made enough sacrifices for your men. You don't deserve this. And no, I've never been in a situation quite like it, who has? The whole thing has been crazy from the start. It was always for Red's benefit, very little accrued to you, Hank insists.

That's not quite true. I had an all-expense paid winter holiday at the beach. We had time together as a family we would never have had otherwise. And Red and I, well, we sort of rediscovered each other in a better light. Not reconciliation, no, maybe restitution? Appeasement? That's what I'll hold on to. And then, there was Sam. A reward for good behavior, although too good to be true turns out to be too good to be true.

Aint that the truth. Listen, make no mistake. You were there with Red because you are a compassionate person, so, okay, some good came from it, some good comes from most everything if we pay attention, but this does not change the outcome. You should be outraged!

Hank, I am forever grateful for your solidarity. You're the world's greatest devil's advocate. I'm just not good at outrage. I simmer, as you know, so your outrage for me is appreciated. Nevertheless, keep in mind, Red only did what he promised to do, years ago.

So that's the synopsis? Hank asks. *Red told you he would disappear to die, and he has? Maybe he should have done that before he took advantage of you and left you flat in the middle of a pandemic!*

That thought also crossed my mind last night. So I guess I do feel a little outrage after all.

Good. Moreover, he had the audacity to convince you to stay with him in lockdown while he was plotting his exit, which screwed your future with Sam. Or is it too late? Hank asks.

That ship has sailed. If Sam had genuine desire to be with me, he would have been more sympathetic.

Yes, but who knows what might have been…

It's pointless to second-guess any of this, Sharon interjects. *I made a choice for myself and for my sons, so I have to take responsibility for the outcome.*

How noble you are. No wonder you're a Gaskell scholar, Hank says.

Ha! I spend too much time with Mrs. Gaskell. It's all north or south to her, no middle ground. No off season, oh no, only spring or fall, hot or cold, damp or dry. I fear I'm as unyielding as she is, Sharon says.

You're being too hard on yourself, Hank replies. *And what about Rosa? The agoraphobic angel devoted to her patron found another patron, right?*

She got what she needs. I don't begrudge her a bit. So did Red. Why shouldn't they? You said yourself, stay on track, don't look back, right?

Okay, okay, Hank relents.

Listen, she's out the door, back in the real world, and Red has someone in his corner. When push came to shove, he knew dying alone was not optimal. Sounds good, in theory, and in defense of a wife determined to avoid that ending, but alone is alone. Pandemic sure brings that home, don't you think? You cannot fault him for forging another path. If I were outraged at anything, it's that he always gets what he wants, well, mostly, although, I got what I wanted. I do not have to be his caretaker and my sons won't have to watch him die. He'll live on for them just as he was here. Tan and vigorous. Hiking and wine tasting! That's a good thing.

But Sharon, we both know you would have taken care of him, that's the paradox, Hank says.

Tears flood Sharon's eyes. Only a good friend would recognize that truth, which she considered late last night as well. She would have taken care of him, and she hopes he knew that. She argued otherwise, but truth hides within protest.

She would have held his hand and spooned his soup. She would have read Dickens aloud. She would have played endless games of Backgammon and watched the movies she would never otherwise have watched. To care for him would have been a fitting end to their history. Yes, she thinks, and she will remind her sons sometime, it's less about getting what you think you want than what matters.

SUMMER SOLSTICE

A wonderful fact to reflect upon,
that every human creature is constituted to be
that profound secret and mystery to every other.
Charles Dickens

Red watches the sun set from the plaza. Today is the solstice, the longest day of the year, the symbolic birth and death of this star. The days will shorten now, on the clock and on his own path.

He watches from this same table every day. Not a western vista, like the retreat flat, rather deflected southward, the sun fading before the day ends behind a cluster of verdant hills. A painted sky refracts color, rather than reveals, as if an echo, which is how he feels about most things of late. Weeks ago, he was on retreat and contented, now he's here, largely content, and, before long, will be gone for good.

As he has no Wi-Fi at his rental, he logs in at a café in the plaza, then he orders a drink and a plate of food, to watch the descent of night. By the time the sky is dark, he is sated and sedated, and ready for rest.

He spends only enough time on the internet to get a sense of what he should know. Sometimes he chats with travelers who find their way to the cafe in search of information or connection – a place where loners find fellowship. He gets that now.

Sunset, of course, has the caché, romanticized by poetry and dramatic films. However, these days, he believes sunrise has the greater appeal. Most of his life, he gave it short shrift, ironically, because he rose at dawn, almost every day. He hardly noticed. Too busy readying for the day. Sharon would have assumed he was neither interested nor entranced by the splendor of the morning sky, but he was merely preoccupied.

Preoccupied might be the word to define his life. Often lost in thought when he was a schoolboy or at sport in secondary school. As a striving apprentice and during the many years of demanding projects, not to mention attending to the logistics of life – husband, father, good neighbor. Is it no wonder everything else fell into his peripheral vision?

She accused him of being an absentee husband, which he was. Now, he is simply absent, preoccupied only with the rise and set of the sun, and the rugged elegance of a mountainous landscape.

If he's learned nothing, he's learned there is no point looking back, unless what can be learned can be applied. Otherwise, what is, is. What's done is done. Regret is wasted energy. Second chances, rare.

Sunrise is its own reward – the birth of a new day. The great reward of sunset is the revelation of the night sky: billions of stars glimmer above. The best part of this ritual. A shooting star zooms through the night sky. Mythological constellations emerge like a blueprint stamped against a dark dome. The bright north star will light his way back to his bungalow.

He sleeps well here, awakening to the spectacle of sunrise and the privilege of another day. He takes walks along a creek bed, cool and grounding.

Tomorrow morning, he will ponder, as he does every day, whether or not he made the right decision. He has had to hold back from making contact with Sharon and his boys. He misses their voices. On the other hand, what must his sons think of his abrupt departure? Better to leave well enough alone.

Besides, if he wasn't here, where would he go? The pandemic has changed everything. He has no wish to be dependent, end up in a hospital or hospice, only to suffer the isolation of the aged and infirm. And die an even more horrid death.

He's better off here and they're better off where they are. He hopes they escape the virus and he hopes he has not lost their respect or affection. He would like to be remembered well.

Disappearing is an act of love, he told Sharon, long ago. He kept his word. He knows she would have tended to him if he stayed, largely out of compassion, and a sense of obligation. He would have hated for that to be their finale. He has spared her, and his sons, the burden of a slow death, which is the least he can do, in return for all they have given him.

He may have been preoccupied most of his life, but he tried to do right for the people he loved. One makes choices within a context of what is known and what is feasible. That's all there is. He will die far from home, but not alone. And he has liberated Rosa from her prolonged hermitage. Problems solved.

SUMMER/FALL

...for not only have I always had trouble distinguishing between what happened and what merely might have happened, but I remain unconvinced that the distinction, for my purposes, matters.
Joan Didion

Summer in Berkeley isn't really summer as we think of summer – the sun not high in the sky, the nights not balmy. The fog that shelters San Francisco Bay year-round is a summer singularity on the eastern shore, making days more like spring and nights like fall. Warm weather lands on the calendar early autumn, when sunlight burns through the mist, temperatures rise and, as a rule, students return and city life bubbles up like champagne.

Sharon drove home at the end of May, the day protests over George Floyd's murder circled the globe. She listened on the radio to raging and grieving voices, and to reflections on the unrelenting plague of racism. Since then, global despair over the pandemic, as well as divisive politics, worsen by the day and, since home, she feels like she was convicted of a crime, sentenced to solitary confinement. Even those who prefer solitude feel profoundly alone and there is little consolation in knowing everyone is the same.

This city too has been effectively boarded up – no campus life, no crowds, no gatherings.

She orders dinner now and then from one of the local bistros, if only to help keep them in business. Otherwise, with no one to cook for, she scrambles eggs for dinner or heats canned soup. No comida. No sea breezes or sunsets over Catalina Island. No beach walks. No conversation. She stays in most of the day and then prowls the neighborhood after dusk, like a mole or a bat, shielded by evening shadows.

The streets are empty at all hours other than dog walkers or essential workers en route to jobs that keep the economy going and save lives. Screens flicker sunup to past midnight. UPS and Prime trucks own the roads. Even the homeless have taken shelter, no one to notice or provide, while the birds have founded an urban aviary, darting from curb to branch in search of scarce detritus for nests and crumbs for hatchlings.

Her dissertation defense was again deferred, for the best, because she cannot concentrate, and she's terrified to fail after all this time. She's in a time warp, like college students forced to go home to childhood bedrooms and the restrictions they had escaped.

Elders die in record numbers and kids struggle to study online, facing an even greater threat to their mental health. Isolation is traumatic. Making matters worse, social media more than ever anchors ideology and TikTok has emerged as the new theater.

Every aspect of modern life seems to have been altered, exaggerated, or fantasized.

She mailed an e-birthday card to Red early June and was advised he read it, but no reply. Knowing he got her message, or someone did, was small comfort.

A group of protestors surrounded a statue of George Eliot, in England, fearing it might be removed in response to destruction of confederate monuments in the U.S. Sharon was appalled by the misinformation perpetuated by the internet, although impressed by their intent.

Summer was crushingly quiet without classes or structure, and terribly lonely. She loses track of time, sleeping in spurts, teaching sporadically, and then wandering the cottage in the dead of night as if she has lost something that cannot be found.

Sharon, Hank, and Isabella, the mathematics professor, meet Fridays late in the day for happy hour. What has been dubbed a pod, they set up lawn chairs, properly distanced, on one or another's driveway. They drink wine, nibble finger foods, and pretend life has not changed drastically. They vent, sometimes argue, and laugh at all that is ludicrous. Other days, they hibernate, tucked into pandemic prisons, battling the demons of the modern era as Victorians struggled with modernity two centuries ago.

To keep from going mad, she loaded watchlists with films and series she's only recently discovered by scrolling endlessly through streaming search engines. She signed on to an art history class, which she finds hard to follow online, but which makes her feel more connected to her own students. She looks forward to video visits with the boys and they regularly text about the news of the day, which varies by the second. They too take classes online, to beef up resumes or pursue odd interests, on furlough from their jobs.

As if to verify an apocalypse, fire season roared into California early, burning thousands of acres and forcing families from their homes. By year end, record acreage will be destroyed, and, in the east bay, smoke was so thick, lockdown took on new meaning: hard to breathe wherever they were.

Brady's birthday in May passed, hers in August, Jamie's September – celebrated with little fanfare on-screen. Thanksgiving and Christmas will be the same.

So-called summer ended with persistent fears and threats of anarchy in response to the presidential election. No one trusts anyone to keep them safe or to protect their loved ones or assets. Nor does anyone believes anyone has their best interests at heart, all waiting on bated breath for a vaccine or miracle cure, in order to awaken from the nightmare.

Sometimes she pauses on a walk in the hills to admire a birdcall or inhale the scent of a flower, and when she turns back toward the horizon, she cannot see where she started or, looking forward, an endpoint. The difference is, on a trail, there is pleasure in the passage. Rosa's roads to nowhere seem prophetic now.

Most afternoons, she sits on the couch facing the front door, as if Red might suddenly appear. Late July, a loud knock made her jump up, as if she had manifested his return, but when she opened the door, a UPS driver was waving good-bye from his truck and four boxes were piled on the doormat. She knew at once by the size and heft they were filled with books. Labeled by number, in box one was a note from Elena confirming that Red and Rosa had fled to Mexico.

In the village, he is tended by Nayeli and Rosa's sister, Dora, she wrote. *He rents a casita on the grounds of family friends. Local plants, spiced tea, essences and tonics keep him well, and herbal anti-virals keep him safe. He is content. I hope you are well,* she wrote.

Sharon slumped to the floor, note in hand, and wept, relieved to verify at last where he was and that he was in good hands. She called the boys and they too cried with relief, and shared their hope, still, they might see Red again, although she had already shared with them his long-ago declaration to disappear at his end, the most heart-wrenching conversation she ever had with her sons.

In the boxes were the full collection of Dickens, an illustrated compendium of Van Gogh's letters and one of Munch's journals, a Matisse retrospective and oversized collections of other Fauvist artists. She has been bequeathed a lesson on creativity and will use the material as a foundation for the curriculum she has been researching for when pandemic madness ends. Something to look forward to.

Late October arrived, the scent of mustard seeping down from the hills on smoke from smoldering fires. Winegrowers scrambled to save what was left of their crops. Goblins, witches, and tricksters, however, were nowhere in sight.

On the Friday morning before clocks were to be set back, the days to be shorter and darker, she turned on her computer and noticed an email from Barry.

She knew at once what the message would be – there was only one reason he would make contact.

Red passed away peacefully last night. I'll be in touch with the boys and execute his wishes as soon as possible. Rosa's family will see to his burial. Be well.

There would be no funeral, no one to ease their grief. Jamie and Brady will mourn on their own, as Sharon will do, until they can embrace again.

Now, and for the foreseeable future, she spends sleepless nights pondering the meaning of devotion, and, by extension, how we choose to inhabit our days. If, as she believes, life is a matter of tradeoffs, how do we decide what matters and what can be discarded or made to wait, like a plant in dormancy until the new growing season. She thinks often of her mother as well, who cherished every season of remission, each a welcome reprieve, like a retreat.

In this artificially induced, prolonged off season, she wishes now she had escaped with Red to a village where every day would be about living, not dying, and not longing for something to change beyond a shifting panorama of stars. A place where the sunrise would be more precious than sunset.

She will never see Red again. And not a word from Sam. Love lost, love denied. She will wonder for years to come how she could have walked away in one lifetime from two good men who cared for her and, in the wake of that, remain perpetually trapped between what was and what might have been.

The first chapter of OFF SEASON
is adapted from a short story, "The Divorcée"
in the collection
RATIONAL WOMEN [2020]
produced first as a play at the
San Miguel de Allende, MX
Short Play Festival [2013]

ABOUT THE AUTHOR

Randy Kraft has published two novels, a story
collection, and several stories in literary magazines.
A retired journalist, she is a book reviewer/blogger:
randykraft.substack.com
She holds a Master's in Writing [1999]
Born and raised in NYC, she resides happily
in Southern California.

COLORS OF THE WHEEL [2014]
tackled the challenges of mixed-race relationships.
SIGNS OF LIFE [2016]
explored the impact of traumatic loss on friendship.
RATIONAL WOMEN [2020]
shed light on how women approach relationships in a
supposedly liberated era.

www.randykraftwriter.com

ACKNOWLEDGMENTS

Dedicated to Rusty
with love and gratitude for his legacy:
Dana, Julie, Spenser, Aslan, Christopher & Thomas.

Thanks to the Readers
Chris, Deborah, Jacques, Kevin,
Marrie, Roberta & Susan.

Thanks to the Cheerleaders
Robyn, CQ, Laura, Carol, Paul, Leslie, Andrew,
Amy, Vince, Andrea, Byron, Edie, Joy, Darcie, Sandy,
Deana, Valerie, Marianna, Linda, Leah, Lin & Betsy.

Special Thanks
Tracey Moscaritolo, for her story and her art
Dana Kraft, Naturopath/Curandera
Laguna Beach, Berkeley, Oakland & Oaxaca.

Inspiration & Reference
James Baldwin, André Derain, Charles Dickens,
Joan Didion, Gustave Doré, George Eliot,
Elizabeth Gaskell, John Keats, Henri Matisse,
Edvard Munch, Christina Rossetti, Mary Shelley,
Vincent van Gogh & Virginia Woolf.
Fauvism, by Sarah Whitfield
The Dictionary of Obscure Sorrows, John Koenig